THE ALCHEMY OF SORROW

A FANTASY & SCI-FI ANTHOLOGY OF GRIEF & HOPE

SONYA M. BLACK, ANGELA BOORD, LEVI JACOBS,
INTISAR KHANANI, KRYSTLE MATAR, VIRGINIA MCCLAIN,
QUENBY OLSON, CAROL A. PARK, MADOLYN ROGERS,
RACHEL EMMA SHAW, CLAYTON SNYDER,
K.S. VILLOSO & M.L. WANG

EDITED BY SARAH CHORN
ORGANIZED BY VIRGINIA MCCLAIN

Published by Crimson Fox Publishing
Turner, Oregon - USA

Cover art illustration by Zoe Badini ©2022
Cover design by V.M. Designs ©2022
Map of Grief & Hope by Diana Sousa ©2022
Interior Illustrations by Kerstin Espinosa Rosero © 2022

Hardcover ISBN: 978-1-952667-93-0
Paperback ISBN: 978-1-952667-94-7
Audiobook ISBN: 978-1-952667-95-4
eBook ISBN: 978-1-952667-92-3

THE ALCHEMY OF SORROW

A Fantasy & Sci-Fi Anthology of Grief & Hope

M.L. Wang, K.S. Villoso, Intisar Khanani

Sonya M. Black, Angela Boord, Levi Jacobs, Krystle Matar,
Virginia McClain, Quenby Olson, Carol A. Park,
Madolyn Rogers, Rachel Emma Shaw & Clayton Snyder

Edited by Sarah Chorn & Virginia McClain

Table of Contents

Content Warnings

THICKER THAN WATER - CAROL A. PARK
bullying, torture, forced captivity, serious injury, violence, weapons

DEATH IN THE UNCANNY VALLEY - M.L. WANG
death/dying, hospitalization, terminal illness

SUMMER SOULS - CLAYTON SNYDER
death/dying, drinking (recreational), weapons

RELIQUARY OF THE DAMNED - RACHEL EMMA SHAW
bullying, classism

THE QUIET - MADOLYN ROGERS
battlefield violence (weapons, gore, death, corpses), pregnancy loss/infertility, depression/suicidal thoughts, child abandonment/sacrifice

THE PAPERWEIGHT WATCH - KRYSTLE MATAR
mentions of alcoholism and/or binge drinking, bodies/corpses, bones/skull (animal), bones (human), classism, death/dying, mentions of murder, swearing, terminal illness, violence

EDITOR'S NOTE

SARAH CHORN

A few years ago, I went to my doctor for a routine cancer screening. I'd just been through treatment, and we were sure it was gone. The doctor, however, felt another lump in my neck and my bloodwork was loaded with tumor markers. I remember sitting in the chair and shattering in a way I never knew I was capable of. I have felt pain before, but this was something beyond even that. A realm all its own. A feeling so powerful no words would ever do it justice. I felt both too hollow and too full at the same time.

How do you breathe when you have no air?

I was drowning on dry land.

Suffocating on sorrow.

The whole world was closing in on me and all I could think was, *Not again. Not again. Not again.*

Someone was screaming. I'm pretty sure it was me.

The doctor and I talked next steps. When the appointment ended and my surgeon had been contacted and things were underway, he stopped and told me something that has stuck with me all these years: I might not know what you are feeling, but I know grief.

I think about that phrase a lot. There is a devious simplicity and graceful surrender to it that I find both enchanting and powerful.

You and I might feel things differently, but I know what it is to ache.

The simple acknowledgment of those complex emotions, of that pain, gave me permission to feel it.

It was okay to not be okay.

Recently, the pandemic has wreaked havoc across the world. Many people have been hospitalized and there has been a lot of death. For the first time in history, we've been able to watch the death toll climb in real-time.

Each number added to the total is a ripple in the ocean of life, touching everyone connected to that person: friends, family, coworkers, and more. Each number represents dreams and hopes and tomorrows. We've watched it happen because what else could we do? And those miracle workers, angels of nature, on the front lines are waging wars I cannot begin to fathom.

I might not know what you are feeling.

But I know grief.

When Virginia approached me about this anthology, the first thing I thought about was the pandemic, all the pain, the impacted lives, and the forever-changed families. Literature, art as a whole, has always been a way for people to explore, test boundaries, protest, but mostly, to connect. I felt like, perhaps, what the world needed was someone to say what my doctor said to me:

I might not know what you are feeling.

But I know grief.

Here, we have thirteen stories told by some of the best writers in science fiction and fantasy, each addressing grief and hope in their own unique ways. In a science driven by the heart, they mix their emotional elements to create something truly wonderful.

Perhaps reading these stories won't exactly be easy, but the journey will be worth it. You'll explore fae lands and other dimensions, possible futures, and kingdoms on the brink. Here be dragons and warriors and watchmakers and tinkers writ beautifully. Here is pain, and you will feel it. Both the loss and the wound it leaves behind, the frayed edges marking a hole where something used to be.

I promise, however, that you will also see the light at the end of the tunnel. The healing. The end which is all the sweeter for the depths we travel to get there. Here, you'll find catharsis and understanding. The human story as told through the eyes of thirteen brilliant authors. Acknowledgment of pain and a burden shared, made all the more powerful for its raw honesty.

Perhaps what you need right now is someone to say:

I might not know what you are feeling.

But I know grief.

And this anthology does just that.

Sarah Chorn
May 27, 2022

Anthologist's Note

Virginia McClain

Organizing an SFF anthology of any kind was never really something I expected to do. Organizing one centered on the themes of grief and hope, even less so. Indeed, "organized" is not usually the first word my friends would choose to describe me. But the universe has an odd sense of humor, I guess, so here we are.

In June of 2020 both of my parents died on the same day. Their deaths were completely unrelated events, and they'd been divorced for over 20 years, making the coincidence even more surreal. Due to covid travel restrictions, I couldn't visit either of my parents before they passed away, and I also couldn't go hug my siblings and grieve with them in person. As you might imagine, that only compounded my feelings of loss and sorrow.

About a month after that horrible day, I found myself—as I so often do—turning to writing in order to process my emotions. The resulting fantasy story, *Thief*, is a raw expression of some of the struggles I went through when my mom died.

But fantasy stories dealing expressly with grief are few and far between, especially those that lean into themes around healing and hope. As such, I struggled to find a place to share *Thief* with readers. Eventually, I reached out to editor Sarah Chorn to see if she wanted to help me bring to life an anthology on grief and healing—to make a space not just for my story, but for others like it. She said yes, and from there we both started inviting authors to join the project. In fairly short order, we gathered together the 13 incredibly talented authors whose stories you'll read in these pages.

As with any project of this size, the reality of things is often a bit different than what we have in our heads at the start. When I first thought of creating this anthology, I pictured a collection of great stories wrapped up in a pretty cover, selling well because of all the awesome people involved. That may yet be part of our story, but more than soaring sales and a pretty book, this project has created a beautiful community. First, amongst all 13 authors—who I now consider my dear friends—and then amongst our 605 Kickstarter backers, all of whom have shown us so much love and support through both backing our project and through comments and connection in our backer communities on Kickstarter and Discord. So many people have shared their own stories of grief with us, and already, before a single one of these stories reached our readers, we were receiving messages of gratitude, inspiration, and rekindled hope.

When we first came up with the title *The Alchemy of Sorrow*, we considered ourselves clever because our stories were all about the hope and good that can be found even through our darkest hours. Belatedly, we realized that this project itself is an act of alchemy. We have taken our individual sorrows, and turned them not only into stories, but into friendships, kinship… and a wondrous sense of hope, love, and even joy.

It is my dearest wish, as the organizer of this collection, that you, dear reader, are able to find some portion of the hope and love we have discovered through *The Alchemy of Sorrow*.

SEA OF SORROW
ISLAND OF ISOLATION
BRIDGE OF BELONGING
VALLEY OF DESPAIR
VILLAGE OF COMPASSION
CHASM OF DOUBT
QUICKSANDS OF TRAUMA
RIVER OF REFUSAL
GUILT RIFT
BAY OF BARGAINING
SWAMP OF STAGNATION
WOODS OF ENTREATY

BRIDGE OF TIME
OASIS OF RENEWAL
MOUNTAINS OF ACCEPTANCE
DESERTS OF DEPRESSION
LAKE OF SERENITY
GARDEN OF HEALING
BRIDGE OF HOPE
RUINS OF RAGE
MEADOW OF MEMORY
THE MAP OF
Grief and Hope

LULLABY

K.S. VILLOSO

Lullaby

K.S. Villoso

Your hands left me that second day.

I cannot say for certain when it happened. I cannot count. I don't even really know what a day is. I know the pattern—I know your heartbeat, how it speeds up when you are frightened, how it flutters when you hear the man's low, rumbly voice. How it rolls when you sleep, like the waves in the oceans I've never seen, lulling me to join you in dreams. And ah, such beautiful dreams we shared. In my mind's eye, I can still see your raven hair, your dark skin, your sparkling eyes. I can smell the warmth of your neck as you hold me in your arms, dance with me in circles until the air spins above us like fireflies on a dark night. I hear the laughter in your voice as you tell me that you love me and ask me if I know exactly how much. As much as the world, you answer for me, as much as the moon and the clouds and the sky. The universe, you tell me, cannot possibly contain your love.

I know little of the things you speak of. But I know you. And so, I know when your hands left me. I don't know why they did. Was it because the man left? After you and he raised your voices at each other—him, muffled against this hollow chamber of mine, you, shrill and strong, like lightning—something shattered inside of you. Even if I cannot count, I sensed your ache. I heard your tears and longed to kiss them away. But you wouldn't let me. You were closed to your dreams that night; the darkness, a locked door keeping me from comforting you. I tapped and called for you, but you couldn't hear. Wouldn't.

And now, even while awake you ignore me. I'm leaning against you, searching for the warmth I had grown accustomed to in the short time I have come to know you. I feel only the cold caress of emptiness. Surely you could feel it; surely you knew I was still here. Yet your hands remained at your sides. The voice that had once been so bright and full of cheer now sounds dreary, murky water instead of a rolling sea. You don't tell me how happy you are that you're going to meet me soon. You don't even sing to me anymore.

Later, we went on a journey.

We used to go on long walks, back when I could still feel the warmth I'd grown accustomed to. In those moments, the rhythm of the ocean changed, resembling the flow of a river—gliding, softly gliding. And you would speak to me, one hand on my back, and tell me stories of your childhood. How your mother called you Nuthatch, for the birds that used to roost outside your bedroom window, and how you would wake up early just to hear them sing. How your father made pottery, and how he tried to teach you to make things using clay, setting you on one side of his workshop with a bowl of water and a bag of fresh earth. You had no patience for the pots, but you loved to fashion figures of living things…horses, goats, birds. The figures grew over time, turned into statues; the villagers praised you for the lifelike quality of your work. Your parents were ecstatic.

They were less amused when you made them move on their own.

"What has no life may never live," your father told you. "Listen to me, Nuthatch." When your eyes wander to the dead rabbit on the side of the road, he slaps you hard enough to get your attention. The temptation of turning dead things alive is evidently too much. Then he takes away the bowl and the bag of earth, forbids you to ever touch clay again.

But of course, you do not learn your lesson.

Witchcraft, they said. Your child is practicing witchcraft. Others called you monster and threatened to throw you down the well, to burn you alive. Whatever you did frightened the villagers, told them you would bring the wrath of the Holy King's army upon that forgotten corner of the world. Your father's rage was not enough. Your mother's pleas fell on unhearing ears. They called the priests to take you away. If they had come, you would have been turned into a warrior for the king, an unfeeling weapon of destruction like others before you. They would have taken what power you had and stripped it for their own needs.

But they didn't. Like a long-awaited typhoon that decided to drift away, you heard nothing but silence on the day they were supposed to be in the village. You remember holding your breath, feeling it turn cold in your mouth. You had been almost looking forward to them. That was the first day you found a dead bird, a nuthatch like your namesake, and made it fly across the rooftops. It reached as far as the second house before tumbling over the eaves, straight into the gutters. Because of course, it would. What is dead can never be alive again.

It was your mother who saved you, in the end. Your mother, who found a man in town who knew a way to smuggle you north where he said the gifted are given power instead of becoming slaves. You don't know what she had to do to convince him you were worth his time. You don't want to. The morning that changed your life, he arrived on a horse-drawn wagon, more beautiful than anything you had ever seen in your few years of life. You could see the villagers peering through the windows as you climbed aboard, gazing back at your family. Brothers—you have forgotten how many. Your father, too ashamed to look you in the face. And then your mother, who looked because the pain was worth drinking in another moment of your existence, who loved you the way I dream you could love me, too. You didn't see what they saw: you, so young and unafraid, walking away from the only world you had known and into a new one. You, with no concept of time or distance, thought that tomorrow was as close as yesterday and that surely you would be back soon. You had no idea that soon could feel like a lifetime.

Along the road, you saw an overturned cart and what looked like a priest's bloodied robes in a ditch. The man told you to avert your eyes and gave you a doll to distract yourself with. It was a delicately carved wooden thing with real hair and a dress of blue and green. For the remainder of the trip, you made her dance on your lap. The man caught you at it once and chose to look away. He was, you figured, an expert at choosing not to see things that frightened him. You found it admirable.

You don't tell me everything, of course. You don't tell me about the long journey north, though I can sense it must not have been easy. You don't tell me how long it takes, or if the man brought you straight there, as he promised, or if he kept you for a few years, trying to find a better use for you and your skills. Maybe trying to find a higher bidder. You don't tell me how you managed to become a student in the famed mage school at the Dageian Plateau. A poor child in that rich place...it must have been a momentous occasion in history. They must have somehow known about your talent, the well of power nestled deep within your soul. The world, after all, does not run on charity, or so you tell me with a note of sorrow in your voice, a tinge of unacknowledged grief. We are not given the things we want just because we asked.

You were older than so many of the others. They looked at you with disdain—this nobody child, dark of hair and dark of skin, daring to walk amongst those who grew up with powerful families. They saw themselves as protectors of their family legacies, bearers of ancient mage gifts; they saw you as an anomaly, a freak of nature who had power that didn't belong to her. Their disdain didn't matter to you—you excelled in everything you did, so much that the others couldn't help but notice. Because your gifts were undeniable, they decided you couldn't possibly be what you said you were. You couldn't be a mere child from a small village in the mountains of Gaspar, couldn't have poor parents, couldn't be in Eheldeth by virtue of your own skills. You didn't fit the world they knew. You must be the bastard of some rich man, they insisted, or at the very least, somebody's mistress, even at your age. The teachers' praises felt like daggers to them. When your spells worked with such potency, when you could conjure things on the first try, you saw the hate and envy in their eyes.

The first person who showed you compassion was... from the last person you expected. The spoiled, rich boy who didn't have a fraction of your talent, who made your first year in Eheldeth a living hell. He switched out your brushes and pens, pretended to drop things down the back of your robes, made jokes at your expense with his many, many friends. You saw him reading alone in the back of the library late one night, a day before the exams, tears in his eyes. You were so surprised that you dropped the books in your arms. He mumbled an apology and then strode forward to help you pick them up from the floor.

He was sent away at the end of that year, and you didn't see him again for another two years. By then, you had gained grudging respect from your classmates, and the boy was not really a boy anymore. He had grown taller, more sombre. There were scars on his arms and his wrists, but you didn't ask him about those. You found yourselves sharing that same corner of the library and then, later, talking beneath the stars after escaping from the yearly school dance. You started calling him by his name then: Raggnar. It felt like fire on your lips.

The day of the argument, years and years later, you spoke his name with venom. "You don't understand," you tell him. "You're a pampered nobleman. I shouldn't have expected you to. Just stay out of my way, Raggnar. Pretend you don't know anything about this. You won't be held accountable."

"I am not worried about me. Forget me. I'm worried about you. You want to create a weapon to destroy the empire. The empire that clothed and fed you and celebrated your achievements all these years, when your own country would've doomed you to a life of servitude! The empire that taught you the very techniques you are hoping to use! You know you cannot just conjure this thing out of nowhere? You need to pull the energy from a source—and the only ready one in Gaspar are people. Are you going to commit mass slaughter, just so you could kill even more? If you weren't the woman I love, I'd—"

"You'd what? Strike me where I stand?" You gave a bitter laugh. "Do it, if you've the courage. But I know you don't. You've always been weak."

"You're a decorated mage of the empire. An officer! Why should you let a little thing like me keep you from protecting your people? It's your duty!"

"Who are my people, Raggnar? The ones you'd see die on the swords of the empire's soldiers, just for an insult? Perhaps you mean the empire yourself. Look in the mirror. Look at me. Do you really think I'm one of you?"

"We gave you everything. Education, a job… a life! I'm not going to stoop down to—"

"Unlike you, I'm not a coward," you hissed. "I have to protect my own."

"I don't even know what that means. Your own? Your own village would have burned you alive if they'd been given half the chance!" His voice dropped to a whisper. "Forget Dageis. Do you care about me at all? Our child? We have a family, Naijwa. We have a life together. Does this not mean a damn thing to you at all?"

You hesitated. I could hear the flutter of your heartbeat in the following silence. It gave me hope.

"You are two," you finally said. "Compared to millions. The woman you loved would not sit idly by as she lets a whole nation die because of a few frivolous notions."

"Frivolous. We're—"

"You know my answer. If you want to stop me, kill me now, or leave."

"I suppose I have no reason to be surprised," he replied, a resigned sigh at the tip of his next breath. He left, and with him, your warmth.

You take me where I can hear seagulls, and where the drumbeat of your heart seems more. I kick, hoping you can feel me, that you can feel the comfort I bring. But you feel as dead to me as you seem to so desperately want me to be to you. I do not know how you manage to erect such an impenetrable wall. You have always been so strong, so firm and unyielding in your beliefs. They have kept you alive all these years. Now I am afraid these beliefs will see you dead. As much as I admire you for it, it also fills me with fear.

"But you haven't been home in so many years," a voice says to you. "You owe Gaspar nothing."

"I don't have to justify my actions to you, Ikius. I hired you to take me home, not engage in arguments."

"I'm not trying to be confrontational. Merely curious."

You sniff. Even now, after all these years, you are not used to mindless chatter nor do you desire frivolities. Even the prestige that accompanied your last few years in the empire had been nothing but a distraction. You wanted to excel because their eyes were on you, because they knew what you were and where you came from, and you always felt they were waiting for you to prove yourself worthy of their attention. Never mind that you left Eheldeth at the top of your class, that you understood techniques and concepts the other, more celebrated mages could only gape at. You felt as if all they could see was a Gasparian trying to be Dageian—mimicking Dageian customs, following Dageian rules, practicing spells the way only Dageian mages were supposed to.

And you? You look at them and see the faces of people who freely follow the empire that crippled your own kingdom for as far as anyone could remember. You see your attempted conquerors, the true slavers without whom the entire continent would've been able to breathe freely. For in Gaspar, the gifted are offered to the temples regardless of where they come from, while Dageis allows you to buy your way to the top. You still don't want to think about what your mother offered that man to bring you here. Not even a woman's body is worth so much.

"It's simple enough, Ikius," you eventually reply. "I never stopped being Gasparian, even though I've been in Dageis all my adult life. Dageis has been kind enough to me, but it has also declared war on my people. Again. Am I supposed to sit back and do nothing? I, who have the power to do something? If I turn away, I will never be at peace."

"It isn't truly your war," Ikius says. "Your family is far enough from the border—chances are, they'll be safe, no matter what happens. And don't you ever forget: we didn't want this. The fact that we're Dageian and you still consider yourself Gasparian doesn't matter. We're your friends, Naijwa. You chartered my ship, but I would've done it for free if you'd just asked."

"I'm not asking you to fight this battle for me."

"And all I'm saying is you're not alone. Raggnar—"

"Don't even speak his name."

"You're carrying his child."

"I made a mistake."

"Your mistake is thinking we don't understand what you're going through."

"You don't," you say after a moment of silence. "You really don't. You can do a good job of pretending, but there is no knife twisting your soul. Thank your gods for it."

You hear the other woman swallow. I think you are wondering if you had gone too far. Ikius means well enough. I have heard her speak to you in the past; I have even felt her touch on my head, how she gave an excited squeal when I turned against her. You were almost amused yourself, weren't you? You didn't know what to think about someone like her expressing genuine sentiment over your affairs. Ikius sar-Enndel is the sole heir of a family even wealthier than Raggnar rog-Bannal; she has no reason to care about you. And yet, part of you knows that she does, somehow, just like Raggnar, somehow…in spite of everything…loves you still. You do not know how to feel about that. Bitterness, straight through, is much easier.

"You don't," you repeat, because apologizing was never your forte, and somehow you feel it is easier to try to explain it to her.

"I know you try to, but you don't know what it really means to try to carve your life in a strange place when you would rather be home. And I can never be home. The empire of Dageis's quest for power has forced Gaspar to make concessions. Here, the gifted are conscripted as mage-warriors for the Holy King—a life of celibacy and servitude worse than what's demanded from the strictest of orders. Can you blame Gaspar? It has to protect itself somehow. Gaspar chose to use us as weapons so our people could better defend ourselves. It's why Gaspar has never fallen. It's why Gaspar continues to resist your empire even as it spreads like a disease."

"I know that must be hard for you to live with," Ikius replies. "But you don't have to let that rage be all you are. You don't have to let this consume you."

You don't answer. You don't want to tell her it already has. Your hands drift from me and onto the railing. I hear seagulls again and then the wind. The cold almost becomes too much to bear, and I try to take comfort from the thumping of your heartbeat. A hollow comfort. Why won't you hold me, Mother? What would you lose if you did?

The winds grow stronger, and the ship creaks as it rides every wave, each one bigger than the last. Storm, you say. I sense your fear, but you push it down. You stay strong, even when the ground seems to break from under your feet. My fear fades. Waves and thunder deafen the world. I try to dream about your soothing voice, back when it existed.

Instead, I remember your argument with the man, with Ragnar. Every night, constantly, the details changing with the turn of the tide. In the last dream, I see him clearly, as if both he and you were standing in front of me.

"Your own? You dare say that, when…" His voice drops to a whisper. "Do you not care about me at all? Our child?"

"What is dead can never live again," you tell him. Your voice cuts like a knife.

I awaken to darkness and hear nothing but silence. You are walking what seems an endless road; some days I think it is all you do. When you finally find others, you speak to them in hushed tones. You tell them about the storm, the shipwreck, how you crawled out of it and survived. They do not respond kindly. Are you a witch? Even when they do not ask, we can hear the accusation in their voices. Only a witch can do such a thing. You laugh. I turn my head, longing for the warm conversations you shared with the ones you left behind. There, at least, you were settled. There, you were happy. Why don't you go back to the comfort of the others? To Ikius, and Raggnar, and all those people who love you?

Here, they fear you. I hear doubt when they ask where you are going and hear them whisper to each other when your back is turned. We are amongst strangers, and you do not talk to me anymore. I wonder if there is a worse hell than this. I, who have not yet been born; I, who have yet to live, have already had what little joy I've known snatched from me.

So, I sleep.

I don't count the days or the weeks—time does not flow for me the same as it must for you. At some point, sunlight caressed my shut eyes. The brightness distracts me. I find myself turning towards it, wondering if it is the same warmth as what I once felt back when you cared.

"You shouldn't be travelling in your condition," a man says.

"My condition is none of your business."

"So it isn't," he laughs. His voice is rumbly, grainy. I can feel you turn away from the unpleasantness of it. "And yet here you are, looking for help."

"I just need you to guide me back to my village," you reply.

"If it's your village, why don't you know the way?"

"Are you going to take my money or not?"

"I could take it anyway," the man grumbles. "I could kill you and take the money, and more besides." There is something sinister in how he says the last part, a note that makes me shiver with discomfort. What are we doing here? This isn't how the other man made you feel.

You laugh. The sound startles me.

"If you mean to frighten me, you're doing a poor job of it," you say.

"Am I?" His voice is so close it is almost as if he is speaking right beside me. "You're alone, helpless in the woods, and you dare give me that—that—"

"You can yell louder if you want," you say. "You're alone, too."

"And so?"

"You need all the help you can get. Because the things you think you can do to me… I can do that and worse to you."

He laughs again. But unlike your laughter, his is tinged with tension. He must have seen something that I can't. I hear his footsteps as he walks away, and you follow him, hands at your sides. It must be so much harder to walk like you don't care. You are still trying so very hard to pretend I no longer exist.

"How long have you been away from Gaspar?" the man asks.

"Long enough," you say.

"The way you speak… there's a foreign lilt to it. Dageian, I think. Am I wrong?"

"You can assume all you want."

"Then I'll assume I'm right. Say, you want me to take you to Hilal. Funny. I know a family in Hilal whose child was taken away. But that was a long time ago, back when I was a boy." He pauses, clearing his throat. "I never met her myself, but my friends talked about her. This child, they say, could make things move. Dolls and figures that she made. They say she even made a dead bird fly over the roofs once. A nuthatch. It reached as far as the second house before tumbling over the eaves."

"What has no life may never live," you say. "What is dead can never live again."

The man gives a grunt of confusion.

"They're rules," you say. "One of the many rules for mages. You cannot create something from nothing. There must always be… a source."

"I don't know that word. Mage."

"The girl in your story. Priests didn't take her."

"You're right. I remember now." He grunts again. "Curious, now that I think about it. They should've come for her. She clearly had the gift. Mages, you say."

You stop. I hear the wind again, rushing through trees the way they do in my dreams, back when we shared those dreams together. "It's a Dageian word," you tell him.

"The Dageians always want everything," he replies. "Our words. Our lands. Our lives. And now they're at our doorstep."

He falls silent. We hear other voices. Your heart speeds up, and I realize that deep inside of you there still exists a part that can hope and feel. You are looking for something, that same thing I look for, now that the dreams are over. I have no name for it; I only know what it feels like as it burns deep inside the both of us.

In one of the dreams we used to share, I would sit on your lap by a window and watch the sun rise over the sea, your heartbeat like a lullaby. Sometimes we would be alone, and I would get the chance to just sit with you and let you stroke my hair while I gazed out the open window. The stars were always so beautiful— yellow pinpricks against the blue-black velvet of the sky. I imagined they were souls, disembodied, weightless, looking down on us with longing and envy. Life is precious: cold, clear water down a parched throat.

I remember one dream where a woman sat cross-legged on the rug in front of us. She looked like you—dark skin, dark eyes with long eyelashes, full red lips.

"I had to do it," I remember her telling you. "You wouldn't listen to me. You wouldn't listen to your father. The priests would've taken you away. They would've taken you away and we would've never seen you again."

"You could've told me. I could've been prepared, at least."

"And what would you have understood, as little as you were? How was I supposed to explain such a thing to you?"

"I would've understood enough to know that my mother cared. You sold me to a Dageian, Mother! He treated me like a slave. The things he did to me… If I had not run away, I—"

The other woman got up and approached us. I curled my hand on your knee, staring at her creased face, greying hair, unshed tears brimming in her eyes. "I didn't sell you," she said. "I wouldn't have done such a thing. I loved you, child."

You turned away, frowning.

"He almost didn't want to take you," the old woman continued. "But the priests would've stolen everything that makes you who you are. They would have turned you into something else."

"Instead, you sent me to the enemy."

"To save you," she said, her voice growing desperate. "Gaspar has more than enough warriors at her beck and call. I would not have you be one of them. I couldn't bear it."

"For our people, I would've gladly become a weapon," you replied. "They look at me, and all they see is a Gasparian trying to be Dageian, nothing more. And now I can't be home. Ever. As far as our people are concerned, I am a Dageian now, which means I belong nowhere."

She touched your face with the back of her hand. "You make it sound like it's the worst thing in the world."

"It is. The Dageians are our enemy."

"And you hate them so much?"

"Don't you?"

"And him?" She glances at me briefly. "The power in him is stronger than yours ever was. Don't tell me you won't try to protect him as I have tried to protect you."

You turned to me then, silent for a long time. And now I remember that this was our last dream together. Maybe that's why I recall it so well—every detail. The way your eyes looked. The fear that stirred in the pit of my stomach.

"He's more Dageian than I could ever be," you managed to say. "This war will go on for years. They will use him. I can't give them that power."

"He is your son."

"Should I let the Dageians have their way with him the way they did with me? Should I let them use him to destroy our people? I still love Gaspar. I can't willingly hand them the thing that will turn the tide in their favour."

"So instead, you will use him to destroy them."

"Use him, Mother? We will work together to protect Gaspar from Dageis once and for all. And then maybe we can all be free."

"You are asking too much from an unborn child. Your man, the father… Does he have no say at all?"

"He will support me on this."

"Will he?"

"He loves me, Mother."

"Do you love him?"

"Mother, I—"

The dream ended there.

I wake now, to the memory of it, recalling the fear in your voice, and I wonder about the worries that must've gnawed at you all this time. I don't know where we are or what we are doing here, but the walls of your flesh are getting too close, too cramped, too suffocating. I am ready to leave this darkness and be by your side.

Suddenly, I hear you scream.

I have heard you scream before—at servants back home when you lived with that man, when they would burn a meal right before a gala, or ruin the man's clothes before a forum. This is nothing like that. This is anguish, and the sound sends a shiver up my spine and a dagger through my heart. I kick at the walls, trying to reach you, trying to tell you I am still here. I am here! Let me comfort you, even if you will not do the same for me. Let me…

"Who killed her? Who?" you scream, and I hear rain falling, the sound of sloshing mud.

"We found her like that…," a woman calls out. "You need to calm down. There's nothing more you can do for her."

"I find my mother in an unmarked grave and you tell me to calm down?" you cry. "My brothers! Where are they? My father?"

"They were sent to the front lines when news of the war first broke out."

"They're dead too, aren't they?" There is bitterness in your voice.

"There's nothing more you can do for them. I suggest you sit down before you hurt yourself. Think about your child."

Footsteps. I feel a tingle run down my arms.

"Tell me what happened to my mother." Your voice has gone dangerously cold.

There is silence for a few moments, heavy enough to break walls, with the potency of poison. I hear you take a deep breath and then hold it.

"It was the men," another woman finally blurts out. "They were drinking, and then someone started blaming her for… for…"

"For what?"

"For being a Dageian sympathizer," the woman manages. "They said they know what she did to make that Dageian smuggle you across the border all those years ago. They called her a traitor and a whore."

"He killed her for that?"

"They followed her out into the night. We don't know. We thought everyone had gone home. And then we found her in the morning…"

"Murdered. Defiled."

"Come to my house. Have some tea. This is not good talk for someone in your condition."

"I am going home."

"Home doesn't exist anymore. Up there is an empty house, and…"

"I am going home," you repeat. There is a finality in those words they must have paid attention to because suddenly there is silence again.

I hear something creak—a door, I think. I turn to my side as I feel you shuffle indoors. The sound of the rain is gone. You sit on a chair.

I expect you to weep, but you don't.

The days pass. The walls tighten. Waves of tension come and go. I can feel your pain with each one.

There is one marked difference since that night you learned about your mother and found yourself home at last. You have started to sing again, the same lullabies you once did back when things were better. You still don't touch me, but at least you sound happy. I wonder at that. Has someone visited you while I slept? Or perhaps you have seen something, heard something that eased your heart. It makes me happy to feel the spring in your step. You have been so sad the last few days, and you deserve all the joy in the world.

"What have you been doing, locking yourself up there?" a woman calls out one day, her voice raspy. "The midwife says it's only a matter of time. Come and live with me for a while."

"I'm perfectly fine," you say. Her voice upsets you, and I want her to leave you alone.

"Is this your first one? Childbirth is no easy thing. And there's—"

The door creaks open. I hear one footstep and then no more.

"It smells something foul in here!" the woman continues. "What in the Holy King's name have you been doing? You'd think this was a slaughterhouse!"

"Leave."

"The others are getting suspicious. They think you're up to no good, that the Dageians have filled your head with nonsense. They haven't forgotten how you left, Nuthatch—"

"Naijwa. My name is Naijwa. I'm not a little girl anymore."

"Well, Naijwa," the woman continues. I hear a grit in her voice, as if she is determined not to drop the conversation even if it's the only thing she wants to do. "I'll be honest with you. After what happened to your mother, it's foolishness to stir suspicions like this. I don't think they'll dare call the priests this time. They'll take matters into their own hands."

"Good," you say. "Let the murderers come forward."

"And then what? How will you fight them? You can barely stand."

"Are you done lecturing me?"

"Your mother was my friend, Naijwa. You don't have to mourn her alone."

"Thank you. You can go now."

The other woman pauses, breathing loudly. I hate her for upsetting you. Everything was so peaceful before she interrupted you, and then…

A wave again. You crumple, heartbeat getting louder, stronger. But you don't cry out in pain, and my attention drifts to the chaos happening around me, to the darkness threatening to choke me. Darkness. Outside, footsteps. "I'll call the midwife!" the woman screams, right before you slam the door behind her.

You bolt it.

There is pressure on the top of my head. My shoulders hurt and my neck. I feel as if I am covered by a tight blanket, one that grows smaller, wrapping me inside of it. I want—need—to break free.

"Not long now," I hear you whisper, and there is something in your voice that calms me. "Not long," you croon, and it is enough. I savor the return of that warmth, relish the sweet honey of those tones. My heartbeat slows. I allow the darkness to come closer. You could call me to death, and I would follow, Mother.

I hear a pop and feel warm fluid gush around me. You scream now, more gut-wrenching than when you saw your mother's corpse. I open my eyes, truly open them for the first time. They burn. And then I see light coming from a lamp near the window and the rafters on the ceiling. I also see the flames from candles. There are so many of them, on the table and on the floor. They look like hundreds of tiny little eyes.

I try to turn and realize there is nothing holding me to you now, nothing but air. Fear strikes me. I open my mouth, and a cry tears its way free from my lungs.

But it is over as soon as it begins. You bend over and pick me up. I see you now, for the first time. You are as lovely as you appeared in my dreams. I can smell the sweet musk of sweat on you, the tinge of milk that hasn't come yet. I turn to nuzzle your neck as you press me against your body, ignoring the sea of blood around us. Is that normal, for you to be so covered in blood? Is it all right for you to have that gaping hole in your belly? Do mothers often have a dagger in hand when they embrace their child for the first time?

"I'm sorry," you whisper. Blue light surrounds us, and the flames from the lantern and the candles begin to dance.

I don't know what you did or what you are doing, but I forgive you.

You are with me as we tear the houses down with my claws, me and all the others that join us as we kill them all. The stench of death, of blood and urine and feces fills our nostrils, invigorates us like the nourishing milk of a mother's breast. We feed on the pain, on the suffering, on the fears. And why shouldn't we? Do the living not feast on these very things as well?

The only time we pause is when the man and his friends arrive. He is a stranger, but also somewhere in the back of our minds, we think that we know him, that we would be sad to see him go. He looks at us with tears in his eyes. The word Father comes to mind.

"What have you done, Naijwa?" he asks.

What have we done?

Only what was necessary.

Only what the world forced us to do.

His friends come wielding spells. We frighten them, but they also frighten us. We try to run. They tear at us with blades and hot, white fire. I pull back for a moment to look for you in the midst of the chaos. I see your shade in the corner, unmoving, distant. Is this not what you wanted? You have nothing to worry about. I know what you meant me to do. I know why I'm here.

Let me sing that lullaby for you, Mother. Let me sing it to the world. Everything will be all right.

K.S. Villoso

I read somewhere
once that grief is not always
about the loss of what was,
but could also be the loss of what
could have been. Lullaby is my attempt
to tackle a story from the point-of-view of one of the
villains in my Legacy of the Lost Mage trilogy at this
intersection of grief—one shared between an unborn
child and their vengeful mother.

Find out more about K.S. Villoso at
www.ksvilloso.com

SKIES ON FIRE

SONYA M. BLACK

To all the chronic illness and pain warriors

SKIES ON FIRE

SONYA M. BLACK

"Lieutenant Colonel Nozaki, the Empire thanks you for your impeccable service in the Phoenix Corp and awards you with this token of our esteem," the man who served as the mouthpiece for the emperor intoned. He bowed low as a servant held out an open box containing a set of finely-crafted daishō. Silver inlay looped from the base of the scabbards to touch the golden phoenix emblem at the top. The exquisite pair of swords were meant to be mounted in my home as a display of my meritorious service to the emperor.

"It is my greatest honor to serve." A hand squeezed my heart as I bowed low. I didn't want this. I didn't want to leave my post, but there was no other choice. My body betrayed me. Slowly, it turned on itself until, at last, I could no longer sit on my phoenix or walk without assistance.

Emperor Matsuoka descended the steps from his throne, stopping before me. "This is a paltry gift for the years of service and friendship you've given me. I wish…" He rested a hand on my shoulder. "I wish there was more I could do."

"You have given me the best care, Your Majesty. That is more than I could ask for." I bowed low. Tears blurred my vision, but I refused to let them fall.

"Come, my friend, let me walk you out." The emperor held out his arm.

I took it, and we slowly walked the length of the hall. My cane tapped the floor, followed by the drag of my right leg. The heavy leather brace kept it from collapsing entirely, as the limb no longer had the strength to carry my weight. Pain burrowed into my lower back and shot down both legs. Each step produced another fiery dagger that raced from my spine to my toes. The world narrowed to a tunnel as I clung to the edges of willpower. The fight to stay upright and mobile consumed everything I had; the shame of collapsing and showing my weakness was more than I could bear.

The emperor held my hand against his arm, the gentle pressure a reminder that he was supporting me. There was a time I would have screamed that I didn't need his help. That I could do it on my own. But pain had long since destroyed my pride and dignity. I clung desperately to anything that kept me upright.

When we reached the doors of the palace entrance, the emperor stopped. "Yoshiko wanted to see you off, but she is hosting the ambassadors from Ongawa, and you know how touchy they can be. Will you join us for dinner next week? We don't want to lose your friendship."

I patted his arm. "I would love to come for dinner."

The emperor smiled, fine creases appeared at the corners of his eyes. Grey streaked his temples. We were no longer vigorous youth eager to take on the world. The years were etched on both of us, wrinkles and scars that told the tale of our friendship. He let go of my arm and motioned for the waiting palanquin. "Don't be a stranger, old friend. I still need your boundless wisdom." He turned back to the palace and returned to the world I was leaving.

I closed my eyes as the crisp spring breeze cooled my skin. Plum and cherry blossoms scented the air, their petals drifting to the ground in a mix of pink and white snow. I stepped into the palanquin, grateful for the chance to finally sit.

I pulled a small vial of pain medication from the breast pocket of my uniform and took a swallow. The fire in my back and legs receded some, but the effect wouldn't last long. I still had a list of things to do before I could rest. The next task was not something I wanted to do, but it was required.

"Take me to the stables," I ordered. The palanquin bearers lifted the chair and headed to the northern corner of the palace grounds.

The Phoenix Stables were a stable in name only. It sat on the edge of the palace grounds with a tall wall surrounding a massive sandy floor with man-made caves built along the wall. The only building in the compound where the riders trained was the hatchery, where the eggs were kept warm and out of the elements before hatching. Recruits and their newly-bonded phoenixes trained in the center area, while the caves provided shelter and homes to the individual birds. Later, they would move to the aeries in the cliffs above the city.

A stable hand approached and offered a respectful bow. "Lieutenant Colonel, I've been sent to escort you."

I took a deep breath and let it out slowly, a poor attempt to calm my quickly fraying emotions. "Lead the way."

"Of course." He showed me to the far end of the stables. "Please enter when you are ready."

"Thank you." The words barely squeezed past the lump in my throat. My footsteps dragged more than usual as I entered the cave. The sounds of training outside died as I passed the magical barrier that kept the cavern at a constant temperature and allowed the bird within well-earned peace and safety to rest.

My eyes quickly adjusted to the dimmed light. Stable Master Asada knelt beside my phoenix, Hisa, stroking her head and crooning. Hisa looked small, curled in a tight ball. Her normally vibrant flame-colored feathers had dulled to dirty earthen hues and her bright crimson eyes were now muddy brown. Hisa's breathing was visibly labored. My heart broke at the sight of her. Her poor state reflected my physical condition. If something wasn't done soon, Hisa would die, and she wouldn't reincarnate.

A young recruit, probably no older than thirteen summers, stood nearby. She rubbed her hands along the front of her pants, plainly nervous as she stared at the bird who was to become her flightmate.

This was a normal part of the phoenix's life cycle, I told myself. Nothing to get upset over. The real tragedy would be Hisa's death. The lump in my throat grew larger. Giving Hisa to a new rider meant she could still soar the skies. Her life would continue.

Without me.

Hisa lifted her head as I approached and gave a forlorn chirp. I knelt beside her, my fingers burrowing into the soft down feathers on her neck. "Hello, beautiful. It's almost time to reincarnate."

She took my wrist in her beak. A precarious position to be in, as she could easily crush a cow's thigh bone with that bite. She offered another unhappy chortle. We both knew this was good-bye.

Tears pricked my eyes, but I held them back.

"I know, love. This is for the best. You belong in the skies and I can no longer—" I choked on the rest of my words as I stroked her head, rubbing at her favorite spot right above her eye ridges. I looked at the recruit. "What's your name and rank?"

The wide-eyed girl bowed. "Private Takeda, ma'am."

"Private, this is Hisa." I stroked Hisa's crown. "She is the most beautiful, loyal mount you could ever have. Treat her like a queen; she deserves it."

The private bowed low in answer.

Stable Master Asada touched my shoulder. "Are you ready?"

"No, but it's time." I kissed Hisa on the beak. "Goodbye, love. Clear skies and fair winds to you, always." Her eyes held mine, soft and trusting, as I pulled on the thread of magic that connected us. "Perhaps we can fly together again in another life."

The cord between us tore free, and a hollow opened in my heart where Hisa once existed. She let out a mournful cry as she rose to her full height, nearly brushing the top of the cave with her head. I moved a safe distance back as flames engulfed her. Jagged-glass memories threatened to cut my soul to ribbons of nothingness while the fire consumed Hisa. Nights spent in the wilds with the stars as our blanket and the world to explore. Fights in the skies where both her blood and mine mingled as we battled griffins and their riders. My heart squeezed as the emptiness in my chest threatened to swallow me. I dug my fingernails into my palms. I couldn't let her see how much it hurt to let her go.

Hisa turned to ash, drifting slowly to the floor. It was over in the space of a breath, yet it felt like I had aged a hundred years. My soul, my body, every bit of my being ached with the need to cry, to scream at the unfairness of it all. I wrapped my arms around myself to hold in the shattered pieces, afraid they too would turn to ash and drift away on the wind.

An indignant squawk pulled my attention back to the moment. In the center of the cavern, surrounded by the dusty remains of

Hisa, a ball of fluff wiggled its stumpy wings, crying indignantly as it tipped over, unable to right itself.

"Help her, Private. She's your flightmate now." Stable Master Asada commanded. "Quickly, or she'll go wild."

The private startled and then dropped to her knees, carefully helping the newly born phoenix to her feet. As she stroked the bird's crown, a thread of magic wove around her, tying her and the phoenix together.

I watched for a few moments as the pair bonded. The lump in my throat returned, larger than before. My palms ached from the pressure of my nails. The memories of bonding with Hisa stabbed my insides as I watched the private and her phoenix, the Stable Master hovering over them offering advice.

The loss of Hisa built into a volcanic-like rumbling in my chest, threatening to erupt any moment. I left without another word, my body navigating me toward home on instinct.

I barely registered getting into the palanquin and asking them to take me home. My vision tunneled from the pain in my body, and I started shaking from the pent-up emotions. The tears I had been holding back all morning burst out in a flood.

What was to become of me? Who was I? I had spent my life as a phoenix rider, and a fine one at that. I had ridden the skies above all of Shinzawa and I'd visited every court on the continent. I had delivered messages that stopped wars and a few that started them. I had fought my way through assassination attempts to deliver the cure for a plague.

Now, I was nothing. A broken woman with no identity or purpose.

Twenty-six years spent flying the skies only to be grounded too early, my wings clipped and my body shackled to the earth. How could I keep going? What was the point in existing? The emptiness I carried stole the breath from my lungs and the strength from my limbs.

The palanquin reached my home, and I climbed unsteadily to my feet. My hands shook as I tipped the palanquin bearers. They offered a bow, their eyes avoiding my tear-streaked face. I wasn't the first broken soul they had delivered to a destination.

I slid the door of my house open and staggered inside. Exhaustion, both emotional and physical, made my body quake. With my thoughts on my futon and the oblivion of sleep, I collapsed into my blankets and let darkness take me.

"Wake up," a grizzled voice said.

I moaned and rolled onto my other side.

"Stubborn woman." Someone shook me. Not hard enough to jar me, but enough that sleep was no longer an option.

"What is it?" I rolled over and opened my eyes.

Renzo Jouon's creased and sun-darkened face greeted me. "You've been asleep for two days. It's time to wake up and face the world again."

"Nonsense." I pulled my blanket over my head.

"I brought breakfast fresh from Kino's stall. She gave me extra when she found out it was for you."

I sat up with a groan. Two days in bed without my tonic. My muscles ached and my joints felt like they were being crushed in a vise. Pain filled my limbs with leaden weight. Losing Hisa sat like a stone in my belly. I crawled from my futon to the table; it felt like I was swimming through thick jelly.

"There's tea and your tonic on the table," Renzo said as he dug through my shelves of food. "Where's your saké?"

"It's too early to drink."

Renzo snorted. "We're not getting drunk. There's something you need to do."

"And what, exactly, is that?"

"Tell me where you keep your saké, then I'll tell you."

"It's on the third shelf." I opened the vial of tonic and tipped the bitter contents into my mouth.

Renzo set the jar of saké on the table, then sat next to me. "It's time to mourn your loss."

"What do you think I'm doing?"

Renzo placed a hand on my arm and squeezed. "You're hiding. You've lost your identity. Everything that made you, you. To move on, you need to fully grieve. You need to mourn your losses."

"And how do you propose I do that?"

Renzo motioned at a cabinet.

I blinked blearily at the new furnishing. "When did that get there?"

"You were dead to the world. Didn't even notice me huffing and puffing while I dragged that beast inside." Renzo helped me to my feet and then steadied me as I wobbled to the cabinet.

Inside the door was a wooden plaque with my name and rank etched on it, a small incense burner before it. The plaque itself sat between the insignia from my uniform and the letter of recognition from the emperor. "What in the devil? I'm not dead yet."

"The old you is," Renzo replied. "The woman who rode a phoenix and saved the empire died when her bond with Hisa was severed. To accept who you are now, you need to grieve her loss."

"You're insane." I limped back to the table and poured a cup of tea.

"Twenty years of comradery and you just now noticed?"

I snorted. "I've always known but this is a little out there, even for you."

He shrugged. "Sometimes the bizarre is what we need to heal."

"Is that what you did when you lost your leg?" I asked.

Renzo shook his head. "I raged and drank and ultimately lost more than just my limb. It wasn't until Suzu left that I sobered up and realized I needed to mourn what was gone before I could move forward."

"And I suppose you are trying to prevent me from making the same mistake."

He waved me off. "You're too smart to give in to that nonsense. Instead, you will hole yourself up in the house and waste away."

"What if I do? It's my choice, isn't it?"

Renzo pursed his lips. "Yes, but—"

"The world tells me to get over it and move on. They demand that I smile and act like nothing happened. I should act like my pain isn't real. I'm tired, Renzo." I squeezed my teacup. "Beyond tired. The only thing I've ever been good at is flying. Now, I'm nothing. I might as well disappear."

"People say that because they are uncomfortable with what you are going through. They don't know how to face the loss any more than you do."

"I don't want to be anything but a Phoenix Rider."

"Fine. You have twenty-six years of knowledge you can impart to the up-and-coming riders."

I shook my head. "I would be a terrible teacher."

"You don't need to decide what to do now. Today all you need to do is grieve. Save the decisions for tomorrow or whenever tomorrow might be."

I offered Renzo a sad smile. "And what if I never decide?"

"That's fine too."

"I can't walk; every step is painful. My body is broken. It will never heal. You want me to move on, to pretend I'm better. I will never be well enough to live the life I used to live. I feel guilty for turning down every invitation. Guilty for asking for help. I am a burden. I will always be a burden."

Renzo sighed. "I don't want you to pretend. Heaven knows I've spent the last fifteen years feeling like I'm a burden. Losing my leg meant losing my ability to do the thing I loved the most. But we aren't burdens. We still have things to offer."

I stared into my empty cup. "Will I ever be at peace with this loss?"

Renzo sighed. "Yes. And no. It will always be there. Little reminders will pop up when you least expect them. But in time, it won't be as raw. You'll be lonely, but you aren't alone. You have me, and others have faced similar situations."

The weight of my disability and disease settled on my shoulders, bending me like a reed. Exhaustion and pain were the dictators that ruled my life. They stole everything and gave nothing back. I was left with the broken remains of a previous life. I didn't have the capacity or will to carry the weight of that corpse.

"I can't do this right now." I laid my head on the table, tears crawling down my cheeks.

"Then do it when you are ready." Renzo patted my shoulder. "Just don't hide forever."

I closed my eyes and let the grief take over. I was too tired to fight it. Wracking sobs shook through me. I cried and Renzo held me, stroking my hair with his callused hands. His firm arms around me, a reminder that I didn't have to do this alone. People cared for me. Some wanted my friendship, even if I couldn't always be there for them.

Renzo was right. Hisa had been reborn, and I could be as well. It was time to mourn my loss and find a new path. It would take time to move forward even if I never fully accepted what I had lost, but time was the one commodity I didn't lack.

I pushed myself to my feet, took three sticks of incense from the drawer in the cabinet, and lit them with a nearby candle. I placed them upright in the dish of sand and bowed to the plaque.

Renzo handed me the bottle of saké. I pulled the top from it and took a small sip before pouring a line of the spirit on the ground.

"Lieutenant Colonel Nozaki, may you fly in peace."

SONYA M. BLACK

Skies on Fire explores the loss of identity, purpose, and independence that comes from chronic illness and pain. Too often, society wants people who suffer from chronic illness to paste a smile on and pretend everything is okay. This story was born from my own struggles with chronic illness and the daily grief that comes from losing my old, healthy self as well as coming to terms with a new normal.

Find out more about Sonya M. Black at
www.sonyamblack.com

A MATTER OF TRUST

ANGELA BOORD

*To my family, who allowed me to write most of this story on the
long drive home from Wyoming*

FOOL
The FOOL

A Matter of Trust

Angela Boord

Bastien was drunk the night his wife dragged him out of her best friend's bed. Maybe that was why it didn't hit him until later how angry Eva was, how a single bad decision could demolish his life.

Be honest, Bastien. It was a whole string of bad decisions.

A long stretch of nights blurred by wine and liquor. Of time spent telling himself that just because he was married and had a child now, it didn't mean his life had to *end*, did it? He could still make the rounds of taverns with his friends and maintain the networks which kept his wife and child *fed*, for the gods' sake. Going out was a *necessity.* Even if he sometimes drank too much and lost the money he was supposed to earn by playing cards, he'd win it back tomorrow. Losing money was an occupational hazard of being a gambler. You had to show you had nerve to play in the big games.

Why are you complaining so much, he'd said to Eva that morning, throwing the few coins still in his possession onto the table amid the bowls of porridge. *I'm trying to move us up in the world! My son won't grow up surrounded by all this common shit, not like I did. My luck's going to turn soon. I can feel it. Then I'll buy you a silver tea set. Silver spoons! Servants! We'll eat bacon for breakfast off a gold platter if we feel like it, just like the Prinze in Liera!*

Eva's mouth tightened into a bloodless line. Men got the same look before lashing out with their fists, but Eva whipped him only with her words. *If you'd get an honest job, Bastien, and stop drinking and gambling all our fucking coin, maybe we could* afford *silver!* Her voice was a vicious whisper, held low on purpose so the baby didn't hear. Cecco patted the table with his pudgy, starfish hands, happily involved in the slapping sounds they made, oblivious to his parents' arguing. But it all threatened to awaken Bastien's hangover. Eva swept the coins off the table into her hand and shook her fist in his face like she might actually hit him. *If I left it up to you, your son would starve! The only thing this coin will buy is bread!*

I'm using the gifts the gods gave me—for you, Eva! I can make more money this way. You've just got to have some faith.

Small hands reached for a bowl of porridge—flipped it off the edge of the table. The bowl landed on the floor with a crash and a wet splatter. Cecco instantly began to wail. For a moment, Eva continued staring at Bastien like they were fighting a duel, but then she cursed and dropped to her knees, pulling a rag from her belt to clean up the mess. Cecco's crying drove a pain into Bastien's head like a hammer pounding on a nail. Putting his hand to his brow, he turned and walked out of the kitchen, out of the house, into the street, where it was quieter. The door slammed behind him—Eva, getting the last word.

He didn't know it then, but the slamming door was a cleaver slicing the ties binding him to everything good in his life. He could have stopped at that moment. Sobered up and apologized. Even taken himself down to the Talos, sold his sword, and become a gavaro, which would have paid enough coin to at least put bread on the table. Instead, he loitered in the courtyard all day, and that night he poured his troubles out to Eva's dark-haired, fun-loving friend like the liquor she kept pouring into his glass. One thing led to another, and all those things led to the morning after and a door that remained closed, this time forever. He'd sat miserably on his own doorstep in the pouring rain amid a pile of soaked and useless clothing Eva had hurled at him, and the door had never budged after that.

He might as well have committed suicide. His weapons of choice had been a bottle and the soft, hungry hands of another woman. From that point on, he walked through life like a ghost.

Dear Eva,

We're stopping to rest before heading into the High Peaks tomorrow. The farther we travel into this wild borderland between Liera and Rojornick, the rougher the road, and the more likely we'll run into bandits. I figured I'd better send my pay now. I don't know if you get these letters, or what you think of them if you do, but I feel better sending them. I hope you'll put the coin toward Cecco's future. I know it's a paltry sum compared to what Mestere Renaldo di Forza is hopefully providing him, but sometimes men don't care for their stepsons the way they care for their own. I'd rather be sure Cecco has something to start on, even if it's small. My employer rewards his gavaros for faithfulness, and I've sold my sword to him for three years now, so my pay may increase soon. But first, we must escort the Lady Lisandre and her children back home to her husband.

She is a delightful woman, he began to write, then sighed and struck a heavy line through the sentence.

She is an old dowager, he thought about writing instead, *mean-spirited with spite lines around her eyes and lips, and I have never once looked at her. I have learned my lesson, Eva. I just learned it too late.*

"Bastien? Are you free to help me a moment?"

He looked up to see Lisandre herself walking toward him. He liked to be alone, mostly, so he was sitting by himself on a flat rock, away from the other guards scattered around the wagons of this short baggage train. The rest of camp was a sprawl of lazy activity on this rest day: playing card games, washing, laughing, talking, doing little chores of mending and repair. All around them, craggy peaks thrust into the sky like the ramparts of a wall, some still snow-covered, though it was warm enough at this altitude for him to doff his tunic and roll his shirt sleeves to the elbows. The oversized landscape of mountains and towering pines dwarfed Lisandre and her children as they approached him, Lisandre holding her small son Jaska by one hand, her infant daughter Dora securely on the other hip. She smiled hesitantly at Bastien, and he fought the answering smile that sprang to his lips. The lady was not old, or a dowager, or mean, and she certainly didn't have spite lines at her mouth. At the moment, she only looked embarrassed and a little helpless. The baby clutched a thick lock of Lisandre's dark hair in one chubby fist, pulling the lady's head down to stuff the hair into her mouth. Lisandre's son, meanwhile, was trying to drag her toward the steep, gravelly slope to peer into the chasm below, but then he caught sight of another gavaro sitting farther down the road next to the lead wagon, polishing his guns.

"Mama, Mama," Jaska said excitedly. "Mama, Mama, Mama, he has guns. Can we see them, can we?"

"Help?" Lisandre asked.

Bastien hurriedly put down his paper and quill, located a rock to keep the paper from blowing away, and went to pry Dora's fingers from the lady's hair. It was harder than it looked; the baby's fingers were sticky with her last meal, and Lisandre had a lot of hair. Bastien tried not to appreciate how thick and glossy it was, or to notice how the brown and red streaks shone in the sun, making it look like polished wood. The sour but sweet baby smell clinging to her made him feel as if someone had rooted around in his chest, carving memories from his flesh. *Remember this? This is what Eva and Cecco smelled like. Only now Cecco is almost the same age as Lisandre's son, and you've missed it. You've missed all of it.*

Gods. Spending time with Lisandre and her children made him happier than he had been in a long time, but the happiness came with an edge that cut him when he least expected it.

He finally pulled all five of Dora's fingers away from her mother's hair. Dora chattered happily and reached for his beard.

"Oh no, little miss," Lisandre said, catching the baby's hand. "I see what you're doing. If she gets hold of your beard, Bastien, she'll never let go."

"It's all right; I'm a big, strong man, I can take it. Here, lady, I'll hold her while you straighten your hair." He glanced around curiously. "Where is your maid?"

"Ah. I gave my maids leave for a rest. They're just over there, beneath that pine tree."

Bastien looked for them, vaguely. He made it a point to stay away from the maids. He didn't want to damage anyone's reputation. There probably wasn't any hope of winning Eva back after three years, but what if there was? It was better for him to keep to himself. "Well, then, I'll take the children, I don't mind."

"Do I really look that bad?"

Tricked into looking at her, Bastien tried not to smile. The fuzzy strands hanging loose from her braid only made her more endearing. "My lady, I am sorry to inform you that the young princess has completely vanquished your hair."

Lisandre sniffed, then blushed in a damnably fetching way. "It also appears that I have not removed all the spit-up from my person. I apologize that you've had to see me in this state."

"Mama, Mama!" Jaska shouted. "Please? The guns?"

Bastien pulled Dora firmly away from Lisandre and settled the baby in the crook of his arm, then reached down to take the boy's hand. "Ser," he said. "Let's give your mama a moment. I'll take you to see Tirello."

"Oh, dear gods," Lisandre murmured in amused horror.

"I'm to learn to shoot once we make it to my papa's hold," Jaska said excitedly. "Papa has guns, too—and three big cannons on the walls! Have you ever heard a cannon? Are they loud? How far off can you hear them? Will Tirello shoot the guns, too?"

Bastien glanced at Lisandre over his shoulder. Her expression was tight and a little worried as she tugged her hair free, then shook it out in a great mahogany curtain. Was she really going to braid it herself without waiting for a maid? He turned hastily, stabbed by another memory of Eva looking just like that, smiling but with worried lines at her eyes as he took Cecco from her and danced around the room…

Had he been drinking at the time? Oh, gods, Eva had probably been afraid he'd drop Cecco.

Bastien sighed and adjusted his hold on the baby girl, held Lisandre's son more firmly by the hand. "Come on, little ser," he said to the boy. "You'll have to follow the rules if you want Tirello to show you the guns. You don't want to frighten your mother, do you?"

Bastien had never been good at following rules. When he was younger, he got around them with a smile and a wink, and people forgave him all wrongs. It began with stealing honey drops from the kitchen in the house where his mother worked and led to long, alcohol-sodden nights in bathhouses and smoking dens.

Eva had seemed so indifferent to his charms, it was almost as if the gods had fated their match. He found her dour, serious face fascinating—found everything about her fascinating—the cynical hook at the corner of her mouth, the way she rolled her sharp black eyes and shook her head at him, sometimes in amusement, often in exasperation. He couldn't help watching the twitch in her hips as she walked away, the way her skirt swung against her calves, how her braid slid over her shoulder when she turned her head…

To see if he was watching?

Not Eva. She knew he was watching.

Well, she said, the first time she invited him up to her room, *I guess if you're going to be that persistent…*

He had been her one weakness, a stress fracture in the metal that shot through her as if it formed her whole spine instead of a mere hand. She and her best friend had fled to the city of Liera as refugees during the war the way so many others had, picking up what work they could… but Eva had always been stronger, more responsible. He could hardly blame Giulieta; it was easy to let Eva take care of things. He didn't understand it then, but now he realized how being responsible for so much must have created a great need inside Eva to lay her burdens down for even one moment. Unfortunately for her, she laid them down with him.

He didn't want to think about it anymore, but he did, too often. What an ass he'd been. What an idiot. What a godsdamned fool to discard such treasure.

But he hadn't known it was a treasure until he'd let it slip from his hands. It was like the stories told by men who panned for gold and gemstones in the high mountain streams. Somewhere inside those big clumps of dirt and rock lay gold, sapphires, garnets, rubies. Dismiss it all as dirt, throw it on the ground, and you missed all the wealth buried inside.

He didn't remember the dirt now. He only remembered the gold.

The little one in his arms tugged at his beard and gurgled at him, watching him with wide, curious brown eyes.

He smiled at her, giving her a brief hug. "Trying to get my attention, are you, love?"

Maybe he enjoyed Lady Lisandre and her children so much because being with them allowed him to daydream about what life would have been like if he'd stayed with Eva. Would they have had a daughter by now, too? But Lisandre, with her uncertain, trusting smile, was also nothing like Eva. Maybe it was because Lisandre had never been hurt. Maybe her life had always gone the way it was supposed to: courting, a proposal, marriage to an important man who took care of his family and would enjoy having them all back under his roof.

How he must miss them.

Bastien walked the children past the guards who'd been contracted at the last minute to replace the ones mysteriously hired away by another Rojornicki lord. The lord had apparently thrown around a great deal of coin and then offered these guards as replacements to Bastien's irate employer. The new guards didn't mix with him and Tirello much. Truth be told, Bastien wasn't sure he minded. They regarded him with the flat stares of trained killers as he walked by.

Bastien held Dora a little tighter and pulled Jaska well away.

"Bastien!" one of them called. "Got a place at the card table if you want it!"

"Can't you see he found a new job as a wet nurse?" another guard called. "He'll be along after he gives the baby her afternoon suck!"

The men laughed. Bastien gritted his teeth. They'd been trying to taunt him into playing cards with them for a long time, but Bastien hadn't played cards in years. It was easier to stay away from the table than it was to trust himself to stop once he'd started.

He left them laughing as he approached Tirello, who was sitting off by himself, too. Bastien had fought beside Tirello, knew his skill in a fight, but Tirello wasn't like the guards. You could still see the man in his eyes. "You'll wear those stocks down to nothing," Bastien said, trying to force some levity into his voice to hide his irritation.

Tirello barely looked up. The guns he was working on were wheel lock pistols, expensive, finicky, with velvety cherry stocks adorned with silver tooling. He cared as lovingly for them as he would a pair of loyal hunting dogs. "We're headed into the Peaks, and I want to be prepared." Tirello darted a glance at the guards lounging around the other wagon with the drivers. They were all barefoot, smoking, talking, their stockings hung to dry on a line stretching into the trees. As with most wagon trains on this stretch of the Spice Road, the guards came from a variety of lands, but the drivers were all Rojornicki, and they knew the High Peaks well. He'd never ridden with them before either; Tirello had recommended him for this expedition, and all the assignments had been rather sudden, not just the swapping of the guards. Even the drivers were new. The wagons were not, though. They were ordinary, stout contraptions of wood and iron which had obviously seen many journeys through the Peaks. Sensible merchant wagons. At least they had that going for them.

Tirello caught sight of Jaska's round eyes and smiled, with a glance to take in the fact that Bastien was also carrying Dora. "Working as a nursemaid now, Bastien?"

Somehow Tirello's comment didn't sound as derisive as the guard's taunting.

"These little ones are deceptively wily and tenacious, Tirello. I'm giving the lady a break. Dora nearly pulled her hair out."

"Ah." Tirello's smile broadened as he looked at the baby, who was now tugging on the curls of Bastien's beard as if she found the spring of them fascinating. Her eyes locked on his face in concentration. The pulling hurt, but he hadn't the heart to stop her. *You have to tell them no, Bastien,* Eva's voice said in his head. *You come in and out of Cecco's life, and all you do is give him sweets and let him do whatever he wants, but that doesn't mean you really care for him. If you really cared for him, you would be there when he needs you, you would take on the bad with the good, instead of handing him to me whenever he becomes inconvenient.*

Bastien still couldn't make himself tell Dora no. He wasn't her father; he didn't have to. He was just a simple gavaro now—a fallen, dishonored man—and he could spoil a baby if he wanted to. He wished he'd been around to spoil Cecco more.

"So, we've got a little warrior woman on our hands, do we?" Tirello said.

"Dora's going to be a princess one day," Jaska blurted out beside him. "*I'm* going to be the warrior. What does *ten-ai-shus* mean?"

"Single-minded. Tough. Determined. Good qualities in a princess, as in a warrior. I suppose you came to observe and approve the shot-making process, young Lord Jaska?" Tirello put the pistols aside and reached for his haversack, methodically pulling out the simple tools for making lead shot: some small lead disks, a ladle, a mold set on crisscross wooden handles like pliers.

The cutter on the mold reminded Bastien of a bulldog, with its flat nose and teeth.

"I can watch—can I?" Jaska looked eager enough to jump out of his skin.

"As long as you stay well away from the fire and the lead."

Jaska nodded like his head was on a bobber. "Promise I'll stay right here."

Bastien adjusted Dora and let go of Jaska's hand. Jaska vibrated like a string on a lute, all his attention directed at Tirello's hands as Tirello jammed the end of the ladle into a long, smooth stick he'd cut for the purpose. Tirello seemed to be making a lot of shot lately, grumbling that he wished he'd picked up magicked ammunition when they were last in Liera. But the Prinze kept everything to do with guns and magic in a tight fist down there. Bastien had no idea where Tirello had come by this expensive and beautiful pair of pistols, since guns weren't exactly common in Rojornick either. At least not guns as beautiful as these.

Then again, Bastien had never asked him. He probably hadn't asked as many questions in his entire life as Jaska asked in a quarter-turn of the clock.

"Tirello, why do you put the ladle on a stick? How hot does fire have to be to melt lead? What would happen if you got molten lead on your fingers? Could you make yourself a metal hand? If you had metal fingers, would you be able to feel anything or would you just punch through whatever you touched? Could a metal hand stop a bullet?"

Tirello answered all the boy's questions patiently without looking up from his work, even the ones about the metal fingers, which he treated in a serious way Bastien admired. He didn't know if Tirello had any children, but Bastien imagined he'd be a good father. When Jaska asked where Tirello had gotten the guns, Tirello finally looked up.

"Your great-uncle gave them to me," he said. "They were the first guns he acquired, along with the cannons on the walls. Your mother has told you the story of those early battles? You know about the Dakkaran captain who smuggled the guns to us, away from the Prinze in Liera?"

Jaska looked a little grumpy. "Mama doesn't tell many war stories."

"It was a frightening time for her. You were born just as the fighting with the Kavol intensified. Do you remember when your great uncle died, and your father became the new lord and sent you and your mother to Consel to keep you safe? You were much smaller."

Jaska frowned. "Is that when we had to go in the middle of the night? When Papa came and wrapped me up in a blanket, and we ran down the stairs? I wanted Papa to come, too, but he wouldn't."

"Because he loves you and Dora and your mother, and for a while, Illichnaya was a very dangerous place to be. He had to make it safe again after Lord Markus was poisoned. He worked hard to clear your family name. The reason people are beginning to know the truth is because of your father's hard work. You'll still hear some say your great uncle was a traitor, and he deserved what happened to him at Vargis Pass, but don't listen to them. Lord Markus was the most honorable man I've ever known."

Tirello's voice grew hoarse and thick with emotion as he spoke the last words. He patted Jaska on the shoulder—a fervent gesture of affection from Tirello, usually taciturn to a fault—then dropped another disk of lead into the ladle and held it over the flames.

"Why did my uncle give you the guns?" Jaska asked. "Did you do something for him? Were they a present?"

Tirello was concentrating very hard on the lead as it turned into a thick sludge. It seemed like an evasion, a way to get his emotions under control. Bastien was familiar with such maneuvers.

"They were," Tirello said tersely. "For faithful service." He darted a glance at Jaska and then up at Dora, and his voice softened as he said, "I feel as if I must re-earn them every day."

Bastien nearly winced. Tirello's words hit him like knuckles in the gut.

Dora poked her finger questioningly into the corner of Bastien's eye, pulling him abruptly from his self-pity. He chuckled as he adjusted her on his arm, trying to keep her from scratching him with her tiny but deadly fingernails. "Little one, you've got hands like an octopus."

When he opened his eyes again, he saw Lisandre walking up the path toward them. She held her skirts with one hand to avoid stepping on the hem and patted her hair with the other. He didn't know how she'd fixed it so fast, but she'd done it up in a braid, smartly wound into a bun at the nape of her neck and secured with a pair of rough sticks that looked as if she'd snapped them off a tree.

She faltered, and he realized he must have been staring. Her fingers fluttered quickly over the bun, the sticks, the shoulder and neckline of her modest dress. "What? Am I still missing something?"

"No, no, lady," he said in alarm, directing his gaze to the ground. He focused on her sturdy, brown leather boots. By now he knew those boots well, every scuff on the toes, the wrinkles the worn leather made where the shoe attached to the uppers. Surely, a lady should have newer boots, red boots with little blue flowers embroidered on them and silver thread stitched up the sides, like the shoes worn by one of her maids. Why would she allow the maid to wear such impractical footwear while she wore a pair of old, worn boots well-suited to mountaineering?

He'd given Eva a pair of beaded boots before they were married. Bastien had imagined her walking down the street, being stopped by other women—*Eva, where did you get such beautiful boots? Oh, Bastien gave them to me. Yes, I am lucky, he takes such good care of me*—but Eva hadn't even worn them once. She'd sold them to the daughter of a local shopkeeper and used the coin to buy chickens instead. He'd been angry at first—stunned, annoyed—but then slowly, the irritation dissolved into curiosity. What kind of woman was so sure of herself that she would throw away a man's attention for a flock of fowl? It made him even more determined to make her notice him.

And here was Lisandre.

"I was just—" Bastien stopped in frustration with himself. "Did you call for your maids? I expected to entertain the children for longer, that's all."

"I think Bastien's trying to tell you that he's enjoying his new responsibilities," Tirello said.

"Oh." Lisandre sounded a little embarrassed. "I didn't want to use up too much of your free time, so I fixed my hair myself. But thank you for caring for the children. I can take Dora now."

She held her arms out for the baby, and Bastien found himself oddly reluctant to part with her, even though Dora kept trying to poke him in the eye. He resisted the urge to plant a kiss on her soft baby curls before handing her back to her mother. Were gavaros allowed to kiss the children of lords? His arms felt emptier and colder after he handed her back than they had before he had taken her.

The lady, however, gave both him and Tirello a bright smile as she hugged the baby and settled Dora on her hip. "I must apologize for my strange ways, sers. I spent my childhood on the deck of a ship, sailing to distant lands. My father raised my sister and me to take over his business. It only lasted until I was old enough to court, but I'm afraid my early upbringing has scarred me for life, according to the women charged with organizing our parties. I learned to do a lot for myself, aboard ship. When we reach my husband's hold, I'll have to be a proper lady and let my maids stuff me into court dresses and pile curls on top of my head until I look like a whipped dessert, but… for a little while, I'll breathe the air."

She gave Dora a brief hug as if trying to make herself feel better.

Tirello looked troubled but turned silently back to his shot-making, giving Lisandre a private moment with her emotions. Jaska soon took over Tirello's attention by bumping into his shoulder and demanding a better view of the melting lead.

Bastien turned to Lisandre. "You miss it then?" The words slipped out before he could stop them. "The sea? The ships?"

Lieran born and bred, he, too, had always lived within sight of the sea or a short walk away from it. The past three years had taught him to love and respect mountains, but he missed the salt tang of the air by the lagoon, the stiff, cool breeze in summer, the way it moved through the marsh grass on the outer islands of the archipelago.

Lisandre regarded him as if he'd lost his wits. "Of course I do. My father was a Caprine trader from Liera. Ships and the sea are bred in my bones. But…"

A broody and distressed expression passed over her face as she looked out at the view, which was, admittedly, spectacular. The lower peaks fell into valleys and foothills that gave way to the rolling hills of Lieran farms and silk plantations farther down. The azure sky blurred into a white Lieran haze as the land neared the ocean. Their wagons would be traveling even higher in the next days, and the view would grow progressively more spectacular as the Irondels themselves rose around and above them. The beauty came with a price; as they traveled higher, it would become harder to breathe, and everyone would have headaches, and the children would probably be cranky.

Lisandre sighed and touched her nose and lips to Dora's downy curls before Dora squirmed away. "But this is my life now. There's no going back."

"It seems a good life," Bastien murmured. "To a gavaro like me."

"I suppose it does, to someone who works hard for their coin, dependent on people like us—"

Bastien darted a glance at Tirello, but the other man was showing Jaska how to hold the ladle. He dipped his head to Lisandre. "Forgive me, lady, but that wasn't what I meant. I meant having a husband to return to. A family. A home."

"Oh," she said in surprise. "Oh, yes." She flushed even more. Dammit, he'd embarrassed her again. "I didn't mean to suggest I don't love my children or, or my husband—"

There was something about the hesitant way she said the last words that made him wonder if she *did* love her husband. Or was she only saying so because she thought she should? He shoved the thought away. Now he was inventing notions. "I didn't mean to suggest you don't love your family, lady. It's only—"

Why was he having this conversation with her? Tirello must be listening, but he didn't move. Lisandre was so far above his station, he shouldn't be talking to her at all. The old Bastien was seeping through again, the Bastien possessed of all sorts of false confidence, who used lies and rationalizations to justify his bad behavior. Sometimes he forgot he was a new Bastien. And sometimes he didn't know who he was, who he ought to be, and that made for awkward moments like this one.

"It's only what, Bastien? Go ahead, I handed you my children like a farm wife."

She seemed earnest, like she really wanted to know. He took a deep breath.

"I enjoy helping with your children," he replied solemnly. "It's just that I have a son, too. About the same age as yours, but I don't know when I'll see him again."

Maybe never. Especially now that Eva had Renaldo di Forza to take care of her and Cecco.

The thought created a hot, painful knot in the center of his chest. He'd been doing so much better, working the wagon trains with Tirello, who expected little in the way of conversation. But now that Lisandre was here, he stumbled into hurts both old and new with every other sentence.

I should be done with this by now. It's been so long.

"You can't go home?" Lisandre asked, not letting the subject drop.

"I could go home. I'm not exiled, I've committed no crimes. But my wife—"

His words lodged in his throat, choking him. Dammit, this was not the way a gavaro was supposed to be. If he kept going, she would lose faith in his ability to protect her and her children, and that would be wrong. He might not be a hired killer with flat eyes who lounged about playing cards, but he was an excellent hand with a sword, and he'd be run through the heart before he let anything happen to Lisandre and her family. Lately, the thought of bandits made him sweat.

Lisandre startled him by laying a hand on his shoulder. "You can tell me, Bastien," she said softly. "I can see it's bothering you."

Her kindness made him feel as if she *had* run him through the heart, with a long blade she twisted around inside him. "It's not important," he replied gruffly. "We've all got our pasts. I'm no one special. Do you need more help, lady?"

Her face fell, and he cursed himself. Then she shuttered the emotion away and put on a neutral, bland smile. "No, thank you. I think we'll be going back to our wagon now. Come, Jaska."

She put out her hand and took her son and her daughter away.

"You know, not being special means you're not alone either," Tirello said after Lisandre and the children had gone.

So, he had been listening. Bastien sat next to him and began picking up cooled shot and dropping them, one by one, into the muslin bag Tirello used to store them.

Clink.

Clink.

Clink.

"It's not my place to speak to her," Bastien said finally.

"If she asks you a question, then it is your place to answer," Tirello replied. "You're not doing anything wrong by telling her your past. The Seroditch have always done things a little differently. The new lord knows he needs a wife who can stand by him. Someone steadfast, independent, and competent." Tirello paused as he adjusted another lead disk in the ladle and put it in the flames. "Though marriages are like a road, aren't they? Some patches are smooth, some are pitted, some are downright treacherous."

Bastien rubbed his brow. "And what if the road crumbles beneath you? What if you do something stupid with the cart?"

"Is that what happened to you? Did you do something stupid with the cart?"

"I wouldn't be here if I was happily married. Would you?"

Tirello was silent a moment while Bastien watched him, waiting for him to say… anything. In that time, Bastien noticed things about Tirello he'd never considered before. A scar, partially hidden by Tirello's beard, that looked as if a knife had almost taken off his ear. The crooked thumb on his right hand, as if an injury hadn't healed right. The steady way Tirello controlled the pour of the ladle into the mold made it seem as if he'd learned to live with it. All these things had been part of Tirello as long as Bastien had known him. For some reason, learning that the poisoned Seroditch lord had gifted Tirello those pistols for his service made Bastien see Tirello in a new light.

"I suppose I'm not one to give advice," Tirello answered finally. "My father was a gavaro. Gone for months. My mother never knew if he'd return. I promised myself I'd never put a woman through that if I had a choice. I found a good lord to hire on with, someone I thought I could give my loyalty to without just selling it for coin. A lord I thought would help me make my reputation. We were both of an age, and it turned out to be more than a business transaction for both of us. Lord Markus got my faith and my service, and I never had time for a wife. Still don't, I suppose."

"My wife has another man now," Bastien said. "A better man than I."

"A better man, or a richer one?"

"Both."

"Would you trust him in a fight?"

Bastien snorted. "Would *I* trust him? Dear gods, Tirello, what kind of question is that? I lost my wife to him."

"Sometimes, when a man fails in his first battle, he works extra hard to make up for it until he becomes better than those who never failed."

How little you really know me, Bastien thought. "Do you have any relationships at all, Tirello?" Bastien asked, hoping he sounded more amused than exasperated. "You'll at least know how hard it is to trust a comrade with your back after he's broken your trust."

Tirello grunted, then moistened his lips and began speaking slowly, as if he had to search for the words he wanted. "After Lord Markus died, I didn't think I would work again. He was more than my lord. He was my friend, too. I blamed myself—

with reason—for his death. He was betrayed by a man he loved, a friend, a—I don't know exactly what their relationship was. We all trusted that man, me included—all of us but one. I should have listened to the soldier who wanted me to be more careful, but I didn't. I should have posted more guards that night. I should have—"

Tirello stopped and wiped his hand across his sweating brow and over his smooth, neatly braided chestnut hair. Then he sighed. "I should have, but I didn't. Sometimes you don't get a second chance. You have to accept, finally, that you can't make it better or different, no matter how awful the thing is. The best you can do is pick yourself up and keep going. Try to be better in the future. To be more than you think you can be, after you've taken that kind of blow."

"You'll pardon me for saying so, Tirello, but it doesn't sound as if you've forgiven yourself."

"No. I still hold myself accountable, and I always will. We achieved some justice, but nothing will bring Markus back. If there had been no justice, though… I would still be stewing in my guilt. More than I already am. Some days are better than others."

"So, you avenged him? Killed his murderer?"

Tirello shook his head. "No, not me. Another gavaro in our company did, the man I should have listened to in the first place. Lisandre's husband backed him, but that's not public knowledge, and he'd deny it if you brought it up. I provided what help I could, but my job was to see Lisandre safe. I was never the single-minded, reckless gavaro a suicide mission needs. Kyris was much more suited to that."

"Was it a suicide mission?"

Tirello looked troubled for a moment. "I don't know. I haven't had news of Kyris in some time, but with the wars ending in Liera, maybe he went home. Something about his past haunted him, too, though he would never tell us what it was." The ghost of a smile touched Tirello's lips. "So, you see, you're definitely not special."

Bastien snorted. "Just another sordid gavaro tale, eh?"

"I'd trust you at my back any day, Bastien."

Bastien didn't know what to say to that. *Thank you? Yessir?* Instead, he pushed himself up and dusted off his trousers. "I should collect my things and apologize to the lady."

"You have to learn to trust yourself, too, you know."

"Pardon?"

"It's part of moving on," Tirello said. "Or so I hear. Why don't you play cards with those guards? Be nice to get some information out of them and to figure out if we could trust them."

Bastien tried not to scowl. It *would* be nice to know if they could trust the guards, though Bastien thought they were probably the kind of gavaros only in it for the coin. Men who worked jobs that didn't depend on reputation or loyalty. It didn't sit right with him, but…

"You're going to have to do that yourself, Tirello. I don't play cards anymore."

Did he want to move on? No, he did not. He wanted to return to the morning when he and Eva had argued over his drinking and gambling, and Cecco had started to cry. He wanted to swallow the pain from his hangover and hold his child close, sing until Cecco calmed, the way his mother had sung to him when he was a boy.

Bastien didn't remember his father. He'd been too young when his father sailed toward the horizon and never returned. Maybe he was dead, or maybe he'd just been trying to escape taking responsibility for his bastard son; he was a minor householder from a distant branch of one of the lesser of Liera's Houses, and Bastien's mother was his mistress, not his *messera*. Bastien spent his childhood alternately hating and idolizing the man. He told himself stories late at night, which always included his father's triumphant return and a shower of riches for him and his mother. During the day, Bastien watched his mother labor in the laundry until her skin was red and rough, her hands knobby, her back bent. Reality eventually scrubbed away his dreams as if he'd never had them.

He was sixteen when he discovered his talent for cards, and it was as if he'd stumbled into a secret passage leading out of his prison of poverty and anonymity.

For a while, when the money was good, his new life felt like one of the stories he'd told himself as a boy. Rich men liked him and his confident grin, his brash, aggressive style of playing—and yes, they liked his looks, too, and some of the old men would play longer when he was at the table, as long as he smiled at them and carelessly brushed his golden-brown curls from his blue eyes. It seemed he could do no wrong, but no one understood he was only bold because he literally had nothing to lose.

Until Eva and Cecco, that is. *Having something to lose* snuck up on him. *Having something* was strange and terrifying, and it was far easier and more familiar to return to having nothing. Except it was impossible to return to the way things were before the *something* because now *nothing* wasn't freedom; it was a state of emptiness, like being constantly hungry and knowing you'd held bread in your hand, but then you dropped it in the mud, and now it was gone. Somehow, the *having and losing* were worse than never having had at all.

And yet… If he could excise all the memories of his life with Eva and Cecco and ease his pain, would he do it? Would he throw away the memory of holding Cecco after he was just born, when he measured only as long as Bastien's forearm? Or the memories of holding Eva and the baby, all of them snuggled up exhausted in bed and smelling of milk, sleeping peacefully in the slanted afternoon light?

He would not.

Bastien sighed as he walked toward the lady's wagon. A few of her maids gathered outside, and he nodded at them politely. He pinned his gaze to the ground and tried to pay as little attention to the women as possible. He barely knew what any of them looked like; they were all a blur of braids and skirts. He probably recognized them more by their shoes than their faces.

"Can we help you, Ser Bastien?" the maid with the red shoes asked him.

He barely brought his eyes up to see the swish of her dress, the flash of blue embroidery along the hem that matched the stitching on her fancy, impractical shoes. "I'd like to speak to the Lady Lisandre, if I could. It will only take a moment."

"Are you *sure* we can't help you?"

The maids standing behind her tittered. It was like they viewed flirting with him as a dare, each woman growing bolder the longer he chose not to respond. Just like the game he'd played with Eva in the early days.

Bastien lifted his head and stared resolutely over the women at the door to Lisandre's wagon. "I'm positive. If the lady is too busy, however…"

From behind the closed curtains of the wagon's window, a baby cried. Jaska whined about something, and Lisandre answered, her voice rising with frustration.

Bastien couldn't help trading an embarrassed glance with the maids. The maid with the red shoes looked uncomfortable and apologetic, as if they'd both been caught spying on Lisandre, as if she acknowledged that she ought to be inside, helping. Maybe Lady Lisandre's independence extended to taking care of her children, too.

He nodded jerkily. "Right. Please tell the lady I was here, and that I'm sorry for the way I spoke earlier." He forced a smile and dipped his head in a slight bow, then walked away, back to his rock and his letter.

Dear Eva,

I don't know if you ever heard me say I was sorry. I tried to say it through the door, but maybe the door was too thick. Maybe the sound of my voice didn't make it through. Maybe you never heard me, no matter how many times I said it. So, I'll say it again.

I'm sorry, Eva. I'm so, so sorry. I just want to come home.

He didn't like the way the guards watched Lisandre. The way Tirello monitored them made him worry, too. Tirello's story about the court intrigue in Illichnaya made him fearful that her husband's enemies might try to harm Lisandre and her children on the road.

A bit too emotionally involved in the fate of a married woman, aren't you? said the ugly voice in his head that liked to berate him with the realization of how little he'd changed. Safest to retreat in these situations. He took his lentil stew and his bread back to his bedroll and ate in lonely peace.

Why don't you join the card game, Bastien? Why don't you find out what those guards are really doing?

Because gambling would take money away from his son. Reconciling with Eva hung on the slimmest of threads, so fine it might as well be nonexistent, but he was going to cling to it anyway, as tightly as he could.

The wagon drivers had built a great bonfire where the guards and maids mixed. Tirello had drawn the watch, or perhaps he'd just taken it. His silhouette moved in the trees while Lisandre sat at the edge of the group. The children had already been put to bed, but Lisandre looked restless.

Bastien looked down to sop up more stew with his bread, and he heard a guard say, "Where's the lady now?"

"Leave her, she'll be fine."

Bastien brought his head up quick. Lisandre was wandering away from the group, toward the road.

Dammit, why aren't they following her? It won't be proper for me to go; I don't need to be alone with her in the dark…

She disappeared into the trees. None of the guards moved.

Bastien put down his stew, got up, and followed her.

Away from the fire, the woods were black as pitch. His vision took a while to adjust. He lost his footing on a slippery bit of gravel, slid down a slope into a pocket made by a tangle of exposed tree roots. In an instant, someone had a knife pressed against his side.

He went as still as he could and raised his hands slowly. He'd *known* there were bandits around the camp. "I'm looking for a woman," he said, heart hammering. His knife hung at his belt; if he could get to it…

His assailant exhaled heavily, and the blade pressing against his midsection disappeared. "I think you've found her. I should have known you'd notice I was gone, Bastien."

Lisandre. How was she always surprising him like this? Popping up out of nowhere when he least expected it.

"It's our job to notice if you go missing, lady. Some of us take it seriously."

"Sometimes I would just like to be alone. Sometimes I *need* to be alone. But that seems to be impossible."

She sounded so tired.

"You're an important woman, and these woods are full of bandits. I'd take care if I were you."

"You're always alone, Bastien. Even when you're near other people."

Her words stopped him. Was that bitterness in her voice? Or was it only his awful hope that she didn't want him to be alone coloring what he thought he heard, making him imagine an emotion that didn't exist?

"Lady, I—"

"Bastien, hush. Walk with me to the wagon, but don't talk."

"We'll be alone together?"

"I said don't talk, didn't I?"

Bastien bit his lip. He wanted to ask about Dora and Jaska, tell her his worries about the guards, but he swallowed his words and fell into step beside her.

"What happened to your wife, Bastien?"

He hesitated a moment. "I thought you didn't want me to speak."

"I've changed my mind."

"Nothing happened to her. She's fine. Excellent, in fact. Married to another man now." He still didn't know if there had been bitterness in Lisandre's voice, but he knew there was bitterness in his.

The scuff of her boots stopped. Bastien stopped, too. He could feel Lisandre staring at him in the dark. The presence of her, the shine of her eyes, the surprised catch of her breath... the warmth of her body in the cool night air.

"I thought you were going to tell me a story about how she died in the war, and your child had been stolen from you, and how you'd vowed to find him again."

Bastien laughed darkly, only because he couldn't help it. "Perhaps I *should* have told you that story. You'd have thought better of me."

"Why should I think less of you if your wife left you? How did she—"

"She found a householder to marry, and he pushed the divorce papers through. It was all my fault, though. We only married because she was pregnant, and well… I had some lessons to learn, I guess. Eva moved on. Now she has stability, which is what she wanted. What I couldn't give her. Genuine commitment, not just empty words."

"You married her, though. That seems like commitment. You didn't abandon her when she was with child."

"I loved her, I just—I wasn't a very *good* person then, that's all."

"Hmm," Lisandre said in a tone he couldn't interpret. "And your wife is all right with this new marriage? She never wishes she had passion, too?"

Bastien felt his skin heat. He didn't know if it was embarrassment or—gods, he was standing too close to her, and that was going to do more than make his skin hot. He took a step to the side. "I don't know what she wishes for, lady. I think passion left her life a shambles. She was just trying to sweep up the wreckage and make the best of it. Renaldo di Forza has a big house, a new land holding granted to him for being on the right side in the wars, a steady supply of coin and food. If he adopts Cecco… Cecco will have a lot more than I could ever give him, although he'll always be known as a bastard's son, I expect."

"Strange for a householder to wed a nobody. Are you sure his intentions were noble?"

Bastien wanted to say no. He wanted to be petty and point out that Lieran nobles could have two wives, and if she married a man who could marry another woman, then throwing *him* out for sleeping with someone else seemed hypocritical. But in his heart, he knew Renaldo was a better man than he was. Eva wasn't Renaldo's first wife, but she was his only wife, and if she'd married him for money, could he blame her?

He sighed. "Mestere Renaldo is a good man. Eva is a minor noble run off her land and Renaldo is older. His first wife died a few years ago, and he's already got an heir, so…"

"So, she was marrying him for stability, and he was marrying her for passion. I understand."

I wish I did. I wish I understood any of it. But maybe he didn't want to understand, because his most fervent wish was that it had turned out differently.

"Is that how it is for you?" he asked Lisandre. "Did you marry for stability? Or did you have a choice?"

"Of course I had a choice. But it seemed a good match. He was handsome—the lord of a hold. I didn't understand the mess Rojornick was, though. I had stars in my eyes, thinking about being a princess. Do you know how many princesses there are in Rojornick?" She leaned toward him suddenly, startling him. "*Five hundred and forty-seven.* Every noble with land, every holder of a rundown keep in an isolated mountain valley is a prince, his wife a princess, his daughters princesses. Five hundred and forty-seven princesses." She laughed in a weary, ironic way. "Being a Seroditch princess is hard work. I hardly know my husband. We come together to have a child, and then he leaves me in some foreign territory, so I'll be safe while he goes away to fight enemies who might be disguised as friends. There's no stability *or* passion in that."

"But surely he cares for you."

"Yes, I think so. I don't think he's only doing it out of a sense of obligation. I think he does care for us, even if he doesn't know us. It's… wrong of me to want more."

She wrapped her arms around herself as if she were squeezing all her wishes and wants and dreams back inside, like shutting them up in a box. As if they were nothing more than dusty mementos to be stored on a shelf until they became forgotten memories instead of living, breathing needs.

Bastien's heart felt like it was tearing itself to pieces. He wanted to put his hand on her arm to comfort her, but one touch could lead to so much more. "I don't think it's wrong to want more from your marriage, to have both stability and passion, to know your husband…"

Shut up, you idiot!

His voice trailed away before he could dig his own grave and jump into it, too.

Lisandre picked up the thread of his thoughts anyway. "To know my husband wants me? Needs me? Not just as the mother of his children? I love my children, Bastien, and I don't want a nurse, a stranger, to take my place in their hearts. But, sometimes, I feel like I'm no longer a woman in anyone's eyes. I give milk like a cow and wash Dora's spit-up from my hair and tell Jaska *no* a thousand times a day, and my ladies-in-waiting treat me like a dressmaker's mannequin. To the noble families in Rojornick, I'm just the Queen card in an indij deck. And here I am, unloading on a hapless gavaro as if that will do anything but make you think I've come unhinged."

"I don't think you're unhinged, lady. I think Eva would have sympathized. I'm sure she thought I didn't regard her the same way I did before Cecco was born. Honestly, I was an idiot."

He remembered the gravid swell of Eva's belly, the heaviness of her breasts. He had wanted to touch her all the time. And when he laid his hand on her stomach and felt the baby kick… it was as if the three of them formed their own little world.

It seemed important to make Lisandre understand she might feel like a cow, but she hadn't lost her beauty. She'd merely gained a different kind.

He gathered his courage and went on.

"Eva was beautiful when she was pregnant. I loved the shape of her body, the glow of her skin. After Cecco was born, she was just as much a woman to me as before. But she was tired so much of the time in a way I didn't properly understand. And there were days she couldn't bear another touch, but I felt like I was starved of touches, and gradually those days added up and I wondered if she even wanted me anymore. I got... lonely."

Lisandre's gaze settled on him as if it bore weight, but he took a deep breath and plunged onward. As long as he didn't look at her, he was all right.

"I thought admitting it would make me weak, and I was afraid of being weak. I was afraid I was too weak to shoulder all my responsibilities, and they terrified me, so I hid from them. I blustered around, consumed with projecting bravado, only to find that my bravado had gotten me in over my head, and I was drowning. Maybe I expected to be saved, but some mistakes are forever. You just have to live with the consequences. As I am." Bastien swallowed, turned. "Your husband, lady... give him a chance. Don't assume he doesn't want you just because he's not here. Or that no one sees you as a woman—a beautiful woman— and wishes..."

Gods. The words just kept dripping out of him. Like blood.

"Wishes things could have been different," he finished in a whisper. "I don't want to make another mistake."

He was shaking now, trembling like the leaves in the trees all around. He'd said too much, crossed a line. *Why* hadn't he stayed on his bedroll, eating his stew?

But Lisandre's eyes shone in the darkness, her face turned toward his. He couldn't see much, just the curve of her cheek, the lines of her lips as she leaned forward and rested a hand against his face. "Thank you, Bastien," she said. "Thank you for that."

Her fingertips were cool and light, but her touch scalded him. He closed his eyes, clenching his hands into fists at his sides. He wanted so badly to touch her, to catch her hand and pull her into the shelter of his arms, to press his lips to hers, to taste and feel her, to give her all the passion she craved and that he had been fighting for years.

He didn't, though. It took all his willpower, but he dug his fingernails into his palms and stood so still it felt as if his bones would break with the strain of it.

Lisandre's fingers slid slowly away from his cheek. He felt so much colder without them there. Then she walked away into the darkness, alone.

Bastien strode up to the card game by the bonfire and threw his coins viciously on the table, watching them bounce the way the coins had the morning he'd argued with Eva.

"You bastards," he snarled. "You let her go into the woods alone. *Anything* could have happened to her."

The men sized him up. Bastien didn't care. He was so fucking angry. They weren't doing their jobs, and they'd forced him to follow Lisandre in the dark, to admit things, to *feel* things, to change his relationship with her in such a way—

He couldn't move on *or* go back. He was stuck, stuck in this no-man's-land of grief and guilt and sorrow.

All he could do was take out his anger on these stupid fucking guards. If one had touched steel, he would have pulled his own sword and welcomed the fight. Maybe it would have cut through this gray, numb haze that had paralyzed him for so many years. Then he'd show them what killing meant.

Instead, he was going to play some fucking cards. Show them exactly what kind of godsdamned nursemaid he was. Loving a woman and taking care of children didn't make him *weak*. By the gods, they were going to pay attention to Lisandre from now on.

He throttled his anger with an iron grip. Anger was just as bad as drinking when playing cards. And this game mattered. The drinking had always been a large part of his problem. When he was sober, he was a damn good card player, and he knew when to fold and go home.

If he'd been sober—if he'd had the fucking fortitude to stop the drinks and say *no*, he wouldn't have taken Eva's friend to bed, either. That decision had been fueled by a great deal of alcohol.

Giulieta was the kind of woman who *seemed* to care about you, but she'd also never met a boundary she recognized, and she moved through men like she was trying on clothes. And he'd *known* that. He saw her at the tavern all the time. He knew how she operated. But dear gods, the woman had been Eva's *best friend*. Why had she even considered sleeping with him in the first place? Eva had fled in the night with her, set her up with a job at the tavern as a barmaid, so Giulieta wouldn't be forced to whore herself out for food, the way so many other refugees did. If only he'd been sober, he would have realized how much more that betrayal would hurt Eva—how much worse it was than if he had slept with anyone else. He wondered if Eva ever wished she'd left Giulieta to her own godsdamned devices, left her back on the ravaged, plundered land of her inheritance to make her own damn way in the world.

But he couldn't think about any of that now. He shoved it all aside and watched how the other men played. He counted cards and figured probabilities in his head, kept an eye on how much the men were drinking…

Then he took them, hand after hand, ruthlessly, until all their coin belonged to him.

"You'll do a better job watching the Lady Lisandre, do you hear? I can show you my skill with a sword, too, if you like."

"That's all right, Bastien," one of the men said, shuffling the cards and grinning a wide grin as he moved away. "Don't get your knickers in a twist. The money's nothing."

Bastien stood frozen, feeling suddenly cold and shaky. What did the man mean, *the money's nothing?*

It took him a long time to fall asleep that night, with the dregs of fight and anger turning to anxiety. When sleep finally came, it tormented him with a dream that had recurred over and over again for the past three years. He was in bed with Eva's friend, Giulieta. She leaned over him, laughing in her flighty, intoxicating way, watching him with those wide brown eyes that made him feel as if every word he said was important. In the dream, she was touching him, unlacing his shirt. He kept wanting to say no, kept wanting to catch her hand and move it away, but he watched as his dream self caught her arms and lifted her on top of him. She slid astride him, her breasts spilling from the loosely laced bodice of her thin chemise as she leaned down, smiling hazily. *Get up, you idiot,* he thought to himself, *get up, get up,* but he pushed his hand under her chemise and stroked her warm thigh, while she pulled his shirt from the waistband of his trousers.

"Bastien! Wake up!"

A hissing voice. Male. Not in his head. A hard shake to his shoulder snapped him against the pack he used as a pillow. Bastien blinked in surprise and found himself staring at Tirello, who was barely visible in the faint moonlight.

He swiped a hand over his eyes, trying to wipe away the hot, guilty muzziness left by the dream, and pushed himself up. "What's wrong? Bandits?"

"No," Tirello replied. "Worse. Traitors." He rose from his haunches. Something behind him fluttered pale in the trees.

"*Gods' balls*." Bastien fought out of his bedroll to his feet. It was a man, blindfolded, gagged—hanging by the neck, swaying from a tree branch, toes pointed downward like a dancer twirling slowly, slowly, around.

"I had everything out of him before I strung him up," Tirello said. "The guards were impressed with your card playing, but they figured that game meant you were going to be a threat when they did what they'd been paid to do. So, one of them came to get rid of you. Good thing for you I was keeping my eye on them."

"But—Tirello—you—*why?*"

"Because they've been paid to take Lisandre and the children hostage. Lord Seroditch suspected this might happen if the other lords found out where Lisandre was. They were going to wait until they were deeper into the Irondels, but apparently, you're such a pain in the arse they decided it would be better to make their move tonight. You don't have much time to get the lady out of here."

Sleep wouldn't leave him fast enough, even with the shock of seeing the corpse swaying from the tree branch. "What, Tirello—me?"

"You know the way through the forest. We used the trail for that job last year when the slide blocked the road. And you demonstrated tonight what kind of man you are."

Bastien swallowed. He did know the way—knew it in his bones, because last year wasn't the first time he'd used it, or the first time he'd had to fight his way along it. But it wouldn't be easy for the children. Hell, it wasn't easy for *him*. As for what kind of man he was—not one of those fucking guards, at least. "What are you going to do?" he asked Tirello.

"Lisandre's maids and I will take care of the rest of the guards," Tirello replied. "They're waiting for this man to come back. Cocky bastards, assuming everything would go well." A twig snapped and leaves crunched, and Bastien felt like he was going to jump out of his skin. Two oddly shaped forms moved in the dark—the women with the children.

"Your horses are there, already provisioned. I couldn't risk saying anything before. I didn't want to give it away by accident. But Bastien, I think the guards have connections to the outlaw bands in the mountains here. They probably have reinforcements in the woods. Be careful."

"The children have had sleeping draughts," the maid whispered as she and Lisandre stepped into the puddle of moonlight. To Bastien's surprise, it was the maid with the red shoes. Lisandre's eyes were glimmers of fear in the dark, but a glimpse of her face revealed pale determination. She wore Dora wrapped tightly against her chest, curved into a comma with her thumb in her mouth, her short brown curls damp and messy, long lashes resting peacefully against her pudgy cheek. The maid held a sleeping Jaska in a similar position, the thumb at his mouth a reminder of how young and vulnerable he was, regardless of how many questions he asked about metal hands and guns.

"I misjudged you," Bastien told the maid.

"Flirting was part of the ploy," she whispered. "It's how I learned what the guards were planning. All the maids were in on it, so we could protect the lady and the children."

"I'll take Jaska," he said, then turned to Lisandre. He tried not to think about how she had left him earlier in the woods, what he had been dreaming about when Tirello woke him. "We'll ride back down the road to the last switchback. Then we'll have to dismount and walk. There's a path, but it'll be treacherous in the dark. There are rock formations where we can hole up, though."

"Put as much distance between you and the wagons as possible, as quickly as possible," Tirello said.

Bastien nodded curtly. "Understood. I'll do all I can."

"No, Bastien. You'll do *more* than you can. I failed my lord once, and he paid the ultimate price for it. I won't fail him again, and neither will you. I think you know what failure would cost."

Tirello's hands moved inside his cloak. They came out with his pistols. The metal parts glinted wickedly in the moonlight, the polished cherry stocks a dull gleam. The guns were ugly and beautiful and dangerous, and when Tirello offered them to him, Bastien realized the full weight of what he was undertaking.

He paused. In the moonlight, Tirello's eyes were hard, but they weren't the eyes of a killer. They were the eyes of a man sharing a deep, unforgiving knowledge of the meaning of his words, a meaning made flesh there in the darkness…

Lisandre and those two vulnerable, sleeping shapes.

Bastien gave a short, firm nod of acceptance and took the guns, tucking them into his belt. "That's understood, too." Then he let the maid wrap Jaska securely onto his chest and went with Lisandre to find the horses.

The trail was narrow and rocky. Giant firs and craggy granite and black basalt formations rose around them, strange in the silver light, as if the rocks and trees had transformed into creatures from fairy stories and myths. At night, the whole mountain felt as if it were alive, a malevolent presence looming over them, lying in wait to spring its many traps—hidden crevasses, loose gravel, fallen trees, wolves, bears… Stone murder markers jutted up unexpectedly out of the landscape, ripe for haunting by the ghosts of the dead they commemorated.

Bastien's mind catalogued all the dangers. He tried not to think about how the guard's body had twisted in the night and that it had again been his godsdamn card playing that set this in motion.

This time, it wasn't my fault.

The threat against Lisandre and her children had been planned long ago, before the caravan had left. His card playing had nothing to do with it.

But they showed their hand too soon, and Tirello took care of it. Now, I just have to do my job.

He watched for the landmarks that would let him know to dismount and lead the horses. A tall spire of rock marked the place where the trail suddenly plunged down a steep, rocky slope skirting close to a cliffside. The trail was hard enough to navigate in daylight, but at night…

He wished he could speak to Lisandre, but he daren't. He wished he could apologize for the too-familiar way he'd spoken to her earlier. He wanted to assure her she could trust him, even though receiving that trust was more frightening than the thought of fighting off bandits. The night was alive with the feeling that came before a lightning strike; he was restless and jumpy, trying to take in everything at once. He just wanted to bolt, to get out of here—

A sharp *crack* yanked him from his thoughts.

Gunshot!

His body reacted before the realization of what had happened became a conscious thought. He threw himself flat against the horse's neck, shielding Jaska with his body as he fought the horse into the trees, where it absolutely did not want to go. Lisandre exclaimed behind him and did the same—

Another loud *crack* split the air and then a thump as the shot buried itself in a nearby tree. Bastien swore and slid off the horse as quickly as he could. He should have known the men would also have guns if other Rojornicki nobles had paid them to capture Lisandre. "We can't ride these horses through here at night," he whispered urgently to Lisandre as she scrambled off her mount. "We'll send them in different directions to confuse the gunmen—"

A gun exploded again, this time close enough to see the cloud of smoke lit by a shower of orange sparks in the rocks above them. They had to get out of range, lose themselves in the dark—

Another gunshot from a different position. Fuck, *two* guns—he forced himself to breathe, to think—probably arquebus. More range than the wheel locks, but inaccurate the farther away the target was. They had to put distance between themselves and these guns. Bastien pulled one of the wheel locks, loaded it, and handed it to Lisandre.

"You don't need to light one of these pistols," he said raggedly. "You just thumb back the dog—"

"I've handled a pistol before," she said. "Give me more shot, quick."

He complied, dumping a few of the remaining lead balls into her outstretched hand. "If we get separated," he said, loading his own gun, "remember you're looking for that spire of rock. It goes up high, just like the tower of a building. You can see it from leagues away." He stopped and pointed. "Run only in *that* direction, not the opposite, else you'll run off a cliff. Understand?"

Lisandre's voice was tight with fear when she answered. "Yes, but Jaska—"

"I've got him, and I'm right behind you. Now, go!"

Sparks lit up the night, too close for comfort. Lisandre cried out, and he lurched toward her voice, heart pounding. But dammit, he had to protect Jaska, too. In the dying flash, he glimpsed the shooter, and he tried to think.

All right—fuck—I can use this, fucking hells, I hope Lisandre is all right... Son of a bitch, just breathe, breathe... One breath, two, and he moved quietly behind a tree. He extended his pistol, shakily counting down the time it took an arquebusier to reload, light, and shoot. The gun belched fire and smoke again, lighting up the vague black silhouette of a man standing before the rock face. Bastien was ready. He thumbed back the dog of his gun and pulled the trigger.

The pistol exploded in a roar of orange and white, the smell of gunpowder burning Bastien's nose. The kick of the gun drove his elbow back, but in the instant before the sparks roiled up, blinding him, he glimpsed a man's face: a wild black beard and wild black eyes. Then, the wet thud of impact and an animal cry, and Jaska was stirring against him, waking with a whimper as he fought the sleeping draught, his eyes huge flashes of shine in the night.

"Mama?" he asked. "Mama!"

"I've got you, Jaska," Bastien said. "I'm going to keep you safe."

It was a long, crashing run through the trees, sliding on gravel, tripping on roots and rocks, praying he wouldn't fall on top of Jaska, or—gods—fall off a precipice.

The other gunman was so close now, Bastien heard him curse and then his boots crashing through the brush as he followed Lisandre. Bastien couldn't shoot in that direction for fear of hitting Lisandre and Dora; to use his sword, he'd have to take a hand off Jaska or put his gun away. Jaska was getting heavy now, hiding his face against Bastien's chest, but not speaking, not crying, not even sobbing—just clutching Bastien's shirt as tightly as he could. Bastien felt like every breath he took ripped a new pathway through his lungs, he was breathing so hard.

"Jaska," he panted. "Do you want to be a man today?"

"Uh—mmm—"

"Your mother and your sister need help."

"Oh—oh—yes."

"You have to be brave, Jaska."

"Yes!"

Bastien took his hand off Jaska's back. He stopped and grabbed a branch. Bark and broken twigs drove into his hand, but he snapped the branch loudly and the crashing stopped. He hurled it in the direction he thought the man had gone, heard the strike of a match, smelled a burning wick and gunpowder—threw himself behind the tree, making sure he was turned so Jaska would be doubly protected by both the tree and his body—stuffed his shot down the barrel of his gun as fast as he could, fumbling—

The night lit up with the other man's shot. Bastien pulled the trigger as soon as he saw the flare, shooting directly into it. The guns roared, spitting sparks. Everything happened at once. Something hit him hard and hot in the fleshy part of his arm, and his body shouted with pain as he curled tight around Jaska. The boy whimpered in fear, and a man cried out, but the man's shout ended in gurgles as if his throat was filling with blood.

There was a rustle, a crash, a thud. And then—

Silence.

Only the wind in the trees, his own ragged breathing, and Jaska's quick, frightened rabbit breaths against his chest. Bastien suddenly realized how tight he was holding Jaska, his arms locked around him with the gun still gripped in his hand.

"Did we do it?" Jaska asked in a small voice, muffled by Bastien's shoulder—the shoulder of his hurt arm. "Did we save Mama and Dora?"

"I don't know," he answered.

Gods, his shoulder was on fire. Carefully, cautiously, he moved. He didn't want to risk Jaska if the man wasn't dead, but he had to see. If the man got up and went after Lisandre—

Suddenly, another gunshot split the air—a flash of light and the overwhelming smell of gunpowder. Bastien jerked, covered Jaska with his body again. Jaska cried out, his voice muffled in Bastien's chest.

"He's dead now!" Lisandre called out. "I got him!"

In the morning, they found the trail again, and Bastien led them to Tirello at the waystation. The bandit's lead ball had lodged in the flesh of his arm, making it look like pounded meat, but Lisandre heated her knife in the fire and dug it out with the tip. Pain made the memory hazy, like a dream. He barely remembered her cleaning the wound or wrapping it with a strip of cloth she must have cut from her dress. His injury cost them some time, but at least it hadn't hit the bone. It was a small price to pay for keeping Lisandre and her children safe. Jaska stared at him, wide-eyed, as if Bastien was some kind of hero when he was really just doing his job—trying to do more than he was able.

Blood loss and altitude left him feeling giddy. Lisandre and her children were safe, and he would get Lisandre to her husband. Somehow.

In the morning light, he got his first good look at the wound. It was ugly, scorched with black soot marks like ink from a tattoo. Lisandre patiently cleaned it again, picking out the remaining scraps of shirt fabric the passage of the ball had embedded in his skin. He must have fainted, because it seemed like she was in a different place every time he blinked. And then, suddenly, she was stitching him up, like she was mending a dress.

"Stay with us, Bastien," she said as she worked. Jaska sat behind her, his eyes wide but dutifully doing his best to hold Dora in his lap and keep her from eating fistfuls of dirt. "We still need you, you're not done yet."

Bastien put on a brave smile for Jaska. Or tried to. Maybe it came out looking more like a grimace when Lisandre stabbed him with the needle again. "I won't let you down," he said.

He got woozily to his feet when she finished, but not for long. It seemed like he blinked, and then he was looking at her face too close, and her jaw was strained with effort, and he realized she was pushing him back upright.

"Come on, Bastien," she gasped.

"Just a little fever," he murmured. "I'll get through it."

Fevers were the worst part of healing, but if he made it through, the wound would heal eventually. The pain would dull to a sore ache, and then it would fade to memory, leaving only a scar.

Like Eva. That wound was messy, and it had been open for a long time, but he realized now they weren't meant for each other, and he hadn't known what it was to be a man when they met. He'd thought it had to do with strength you could show off and brandish at other men like a weapon. But that kind of strength was sorry and weak when it came down to it, like a cheap disguise he used to cover all his fears. It was so much harder to take responsibility for the care of those most dear to him. That responsibility was terrifying and utterly necessary, and he understood now how much actual strength it took to do it. He didn't know if he would ever have enough.

But he was learning. Knitting the wound, dealing with the pain, walking through the fever.

"Bastien," Lisandre said. "Just put one foot in front of the other. We're almost there. I can see a roof on that slope. You've almost made it. You're not going to have come all this way only to give up now, are you?"

He wondered if he shouldn't tell Lisandre to go on without him. But then who would help answer Jaska's questions? Who would guide them all away from the crumbling, dangerous edges of the path? Who would make sure they found their way through the forest?

"No," he mumbled.

He was stumbling, unsure where he was, and gods, his arm hurt. But he tried to do what she said. One foot in front of the other. In the end, he thought she was holding him up, and it was only Dora's babbling and Jaska's constant, enthusiastic chatter that kept him in the world—*what kind of tree is that? Oh look, a fox! I can't wait to tell Papa how we fought off the kidnappers.* But finally, they stepped out of the trees, and there was the waystation, with its walls hewn from giant firs and its cedar shake roof. And standing framed in the doorway—Tirello and the maid with the red shoes, now wearing sensible boots and a split skirt for traveling, waving at them.

Bastien fought Tirello's guns out of his belt and extended them toward him, stock-first.

"Thank you for the pistols," he rasped. "They were very helpful."

And then—finally—he collapsed.

"Bastien!" Lisandre exclaimed.

Tirello knelt beside him and examined his arm, then gave a satisfied nod. "No, lady. I think he's going to be all right."

Dear Cecco,

I hope you are taking care of your mother, and I hope you are learning everything your stepfather can teach you. I'm sending you this coin so you can lay it by, just in case. One day, when you're older, you may want to take a wife. Find a woman who is strong and independent and self-reliant... and then stand by her as her partner, holding her up when she needs it. Tell your mother I hope she's happy. I miss her very much, but perhaps now I under-

stand why she put the bandage on the wound I made and encouraged it to heal. Perhaps now my healing will start as well.

With all my love,

Your father

ANGELA BOORD

Angela Boord writes giant fantasy novels that blend genres—from romance to historical, epic and beyond—at her kitchen table surrounded by her kids' Legos and Nerf guns. She likes to take broken characters in need of redemption, patch them up, and give them a little hope in the darkness. She also likes mercenaries, Renaissance weaponry, and twisty spy plots.

"A Matter of Trust" is set in Angela's *Eterean Empire* series, and there might be a few Easter Eggs for *Fortune's Fool (Eterean Empire Book 1)* scattered here and there throughout the story…

Find out more about Angela Boord at angelaboord.com

A Recurrence of Jasmine

Levi Jacobs

To Sarah H—for the world we shared, and the ones we never got a chance to

A Recurrence of Jasmine

LEVI JACOBS

They lock my son away and send me before a dying god. I am not the first sacrifice: I watched their last attempt fail, the famous bard from lake country whose shanties and epics echoed in the vast stone chamber, sweat rolling down his brow and voice cracking from exhaustion.

He sang for two days, then froze solid where he stood.

I must do better, or leave Alexhy an orphan.

"Your Holiness," I say, falling to one knee as women of this land do. "How can I be of service?" The flagstones are coated in frost, and cold seeps into my bones.

"You cannot," he says, voice rumbling from all directions. A blue gem glows at the end of his scepter, lines of power running up his arm, illuminating his eyes. Through it, he kept this wintry mountain valley lush for a thousand years. It is refreezing now, returning to ice as he loses his will to live. "How will you change this taste of dirt and death on my tongue?"

I don't know. Poets, philosophers, and courtesans have all failed. In desperation, they've begun throwing servants from the kitchen before him—like me—hoping something works. What can I do that they did not?

Well, wit never hurt.

"Why, with sweetmeats, Your Grace."

"Meat comes from dirt and tastes already of death. If you had lived as long as I, you would know its flavor."

I have no idea what a thousand years feels like. I have lived twenty-two, and already I feel old. "Then perhaps some fresh air, Your Grace. When did you last walk your gardens?"

His Grace snorts. "When last I smelled their dirt and death as well. Do you know how long I kept those trees alive, held in perfect youth?"

He gestures at the soaring windows. Frost begins to crystallize on the forest of bare branches outside, and my skin prickles with fear.

Not good.

"Ah—long! Clearly, quite long."

"Yes." The god shifts on his seat, chin slumping forward onto his chest. "Quite long. Too long."

I wait with nails biting into my palm, wondering if I have failed, if this is when he loses interest and freezes me like the bard. If this is when my son loses his mother.

Instead, a soft snore emerges from the god's mouth. The knots in my stomach loosen. Divine snoring. I will take that over death.

"Good, good," Vizier Chalmes says, gliding up to take my elbow. "You did well, young Thaylea."

His gaze is distant, however, and I know I didn't do well. No one has, in the six months I have been here. There is a funeral for a frozen corpse nearly every day, sometimes two. Meanwhile, the divine empire falls apart.

And with it, any hopes of saving my son.

They wake me when the god rises, despite the late hour. It's a cruel reminder of the days after Alexhy's birth when our patterns of wake and sleep had little to do with the sun or stars. Father gave my son and me eleven days in the caravan—just enough to build up my milk—then sold us into indenture. *For bringing shame on our family*, he said.

For ruining his chances of a profitable marriage alliance, more like. But what would my father understand of love?

The god has not moved from his throne, though the air carries the scent of lavender soap, and the floors have been swept. The moon casts gray shadows that catch in the frost on the floor, and the chill scrubs any lingering fogginess from my mind.

"Sandwalker," he rumbles when I step in. He's noticed my dark hair and eyes, then. "What could I possibly want from you?"

I don't know, but I need to answer, so I say what comes first to my tongue. "My name, to start with, Your Grace."

Silence. I wince. Father always said I speak too quickly.

"Names," he rumbles at last. "These are as repetitive as the seasons and years. I want nothing of it."

"But you had a name once, didn't you? You were not always 'Your Grace' or 'Holy One.'" According to legend, the scepter was passed from parent to child, so this god must once have been a child. He'd had children of his own, though they were murdered centuries ago. He never had more.

The god grunts at this and shifts on his massive granite seat, looking strangely small. "I did. None know it now."

"Do you?"

"*Wretch!*" he shouts, starting forward. The scepter flares, and veins of frost shoot from where it touches the floor. "Think you I've forgotten my own name? I know it!"

I run.

The vizier blocks the door with an iron arm.

I beat at him. "Let me out!"

"Back, back, child," Chalmes murmurs, eyeing the god. "He does not kill out of anger. And your child yet needs you."

"Don't use Alexhy as a bargaining piece," I spit, anger burning past the fear in my breast.

"It is only a statement of fact. Without you, the palace has no need for an infant."

The thought of Alexhy turned out of the palace in the bitter cold shuts my mouth. I would face anything to keep him from that. Even for a few days. Even for today.

So, I turn back to the god, feet numb from the cold, and force myself to walk closer, steps crunching on the circle of frost. My question made the god angry, but anger is better than apathy. Anger might keep this god alive. I take a deep breath.

"Will you tell me that name, Your Grace?"

"For what purpose?"

I try a smile. "If only to avoid calling you *Your Grace* all the time."

He waves a tired hand. "Do not seek to seduce me, young one. The best and most beautiful have tried, for centuries. I am beyond such things."

"I have never sought to seduce another. If a man does not want me for who I am, I do not want him either." The words bring up memories, of the fifth son of a minor trader with a limp to his gait and a smile like all the diamonds in the sky. Alexhy's smile.

I push them down.

"That is admirable," the god says. "I loved such a girl once. She is dead now."

Frost melts, and I feel a spark of something I have not felt since they pulled me from the kitchens yesterday. Hope. "Will you tell me of her?"

He hesitates, and the dead vines climbing the audience hall begin to green, leaves unfurling in the moonlight. Yes. Maybe this is what he needs.

The question hangs between us, air warming. Then, the god turns away, and the leaves wilt. "No. Leave me. I must attend her shrine."

He stands, and I go, before the frost can come again.

Vizier Chalmes catches me in the door, bony hand on my elbow. "What was *that*?" he hisses.

I shake him off. "It was all I could think of. I am a caravan daughter. I do not know pretty songs or dances."

"No, fool girl. He has not been that alive in months! The vines *greened*!"

I swallow my surprise. I despise this man, but I can't let that cloud my judgment. I have apparently done well, and I am too much a merchant's daughter not to realize that's worth something. "Then perhaps you will let me see my son."

"In time." He releases me, voice cooling. "I am afraid there are still things we need from you."

"Is appeasing your god not enough? Saving his vines?"

"It was good, but you must continue. Do more." He fingers something beneath his robes. "He must see that I have brought him comfort in his old age."

"You? *I'm* the one doing the work." I let some snap come out in my voice but keep a firm hand on my real anger. I am only a servant, after all, and he the top of the theocracy. *Poor men must bargain with a subtle hand*, I can hear my father saying.

"Ah, but *I* am the one who chose you."

"From a line of scullery maids. You picked me because I'm from the sands, the most expendable of your expendable servants. A quick distraction while you searched for someone better." I take a breath. I do not know what drives this man—whether ambition or devotion—but I know *something* does. The passion in his eyes is for more than duty. I need to find out what it is.

"You have no idea what you're doing," I say. "No idea what will work."

"I know that *you* are working. And that you will continue working until His Holiness is ready."

My ears perk up. "Ready for what?"

"To choose an heir."

Ah. Here is the reason he cares—but I need to know more if I'm going to use it. To bargain with my father's *subtle hand*. "But there is no heir. They all died centuries ago."

"There is a ritual." He draws himself up, gaze going distant. "An old ritual, but still part of our faith. His Holiness can name an adult heir. Naturalize one of us into the royal line."

"One of the viziers?"

The spindly man starts and glances down the hall. "We are the only ones who could handle the power—but that is none of your concern. Just be ready. I suspect he will call you again, soon."

He spins and strides away, indigo robes billowing behind him.

I mull his words as I walk back to the kitchens, fitting them into what I've seen in the last few months. Aykuna has been outdoing herself in the kitchens, Chalmes in the audience chamber, other viziers in diplomacy and agriculture—but not to try to save the empire, as I'd thought. To try to prove their worthiness and be chosen as heir.

I shudder. From what I've seen of the viziers, I want none of them taking that power. But this is not my nation, and I have more immediate concerns. If Chalmes sees me as his ride to divinity, I will gladly accept the yoke, so long as I pull Alexhy out, too.

This is my bargaining chip. Now I just have to stay alive long enough to use it.

The god summons me just after dawn. "How was the time in your shrine, Your Grace?"

"Do not call me that."

The room grows cold, and fear shakes off the last fringes of sleep. "Then what shall I call you?"

"Verenal. Call me Verenal."

It is an ancient name, one of the eight words of power used in Haylen's Epic. More importantly, he trusts me with it. "It is a good name."

"It means nothing. It belongs to someone who is dead."

"But Verenal," I say, testing the word like a stretch of boom-sand, "you are still alive."

"Out of duty."

"Nothing more?"

He shifts, skin the color of old parchment. "You have not told me yours."

I flourish skirts in the way of my people. "I am Thaylea Ash-foot, of the Twelve Dunes Dynasty."

He tilts his head back. "Twelve Dunes. Your father is Aylen?"

I stifle a gasp. Aylen was my father's father's grandfather—but maybe better not to tell him that. "You have been to the sands?"

"I have been everywhere, seen everything. It has all changed but remains the same."

He sounds so tired. Or bored? But courtesans and bards have not kept him entertained. Does he want philosophy? "Surely it cannot be both."

"Look at these flowers." The god—Verenal—extends his hand, and the vines climbing the north wall burst into white pinwheel blossoms. My nostrils fill with heady jasmine, and I cannot help but stare in awe. He made life with a wave of his hand.

"Have you seen these flowers before?" Verenal asks.

"No. They are newly blossomed."

"And yet you have. Jasmine grows in the shade of your oases. You grew up with it."

"That's true, but—these are not those flowers. These are new and beautiful." My heart beats faster. This is what I need to show Chalmes, to get leverage in our next conversation. His god making things green again. "Is that not worth keeping alive?"

"I once thought so. Perhaps I still do. But thoughts do not desire make."

"Do you not remember the first time you admired jasmine?"

"I remember." His voice echoes in the empty chamber. "I was a child then, and my father held the scepter. But that vine is dead, as this one will be, as is my father."

"And has your desire died too?"

The blossoms close, and he looks in my direction, but there is no anger in his gaze. "What meaning is there in repeating the same things, time after time?"

I think of my son, who hasn't yet smelled jasmine or held the waxy petals in his hands. "The meaning is born again with each new life."

"For centuries, I believed that. Tried to experience that meaning again with each new planting, each new vizier, each new monarch in the low countries. But they form patterns, and the patterns themselves make patterns, until in each part you see the whole."

"That sounds wonderful." I would like to live to see such patterns.

"It was, for a few centuries more. Then everything began to look the same and to smell of dirt and decay."

I hear the desolate tone in his voice from yesterday, after he froze the bard. Not good. "But it isn't! That pattern can change."

"I have waited for that to happen. It cannot. Only death releases us." The gaze he gives me is both terrifying and wholly disinterested. It's the gaze of a god at milkthistle drifting in the breeze. "I tire of you."

My stomach knots. My breath frosts. *Say something.* "You said you see the pattern in each part, each person. Which parts do you see in me?"

His chin flexes. "It is hard to describe."

"Try."

"I see pride. Impetuousness. The passion of youth, and the dedication of motherhood. The quick wit of your people, and the anger, too. The love for one who is gone."

I suck in a breath, feeling suddenly stripped. "You're wrong," I say, needing him to stop, to cover myself. "The only one I love is here, in the nursery."

"Not for your child. For a man. The child's father, perhaps."

"Rolend? I loved him, yes. But I do not love him now."

Verenal watches me calmly, a light in his eyes—amusement? Is he *enjoying* this?

I should be pleased—an amused god is not one about to freeze me—but it's irritating. There is no space in my life for lovers anymore. "It was just for a season, a thing of passion. We could never have been together."

"Why not?"

"He... wouldn't have fit in. He wasn't a trader, not properly. More like a tinker. Or a juggler. Or—I don't know. He was many things. But Father would never have accepted him into the wagons."

"And you would not leave your wagons?"

"Of course, I would," I snap, then realize I never considered it. And that Verenal is asking *me* questions now.

"But you didn't. Why?"

That's personal—but the jasmine blossoms are reopening along the walls, and Chalmes watches from the side entrance, gaze intent. If this is what it takes to earn Alexhy a future, so be it. "They are my family. And Rolend—I loved him, but he was not family."

Verenal nods as if this is sage wisdom, and I wonder again what pattern he sees in me. "And where is your family now?"

"They sold me," I say, unable to keep the bitterness from my voice.

"And yet you love them?"

I don't know. Yes. "They are my family."

Verenal nods again. "I had a family once. A wife who loved as you do. Go now. Be with your child."

"But—Your Grace," a voice starts from the side door. Chalmes.

"Do it, vizier," Verenal rumbles, just a hint of displeasure in his voice. "I care not for your schemes. Let this woman be with her child."

"Yes, Your Grace! Yes. Certainly."

I surprise myself with tears. I told myself I would never cry in front of my owners, no matter what they did to me.

They never tried kindness.

Chalmes waits in the hallway outside the entrance. "You did well today, young Thaylea."

I wipe the tears from my cheeks, not wanting this man to see me cry. "Well enough to get you named heir?" It's blunt, but I'm not in a state to mince words.

He sucks air, glancing at the door. "I do not wish to be heir. I wish for His Grace's speedy recovery and that He will reign another thousand years."

I almost laugh, despite everything. I take a breath, forcing myself to think strategically. I've proven my worth. Now I need to use the leverage it gives me. "And if he doesn't? *Some*one must take the scepter."

Chalmes glances around. "Yes. Well. May the worthiest of us be so blessed."

"Like the one who brings him comfort in his dying days?"

"Perhaps, yes." He steps closer—a good sign, according to my father. The signal that posturing has come to an end and the bargaining begun. "If you can keep it up."

I recognize this for what it is: Chalmes seeking his own leverage, trying to weaken my position with doubt that I can keep doing the impossible. Maybe trying to string this out until he *is* chosen, without making a deal, leaving Alexhy and me none the better for it.

Fortunately, I have levers of my own.

"I think I can. If I choose to continue."

"Choose?" His eyebrows rise. "You have no choice."

"Even those of us under indenture have a choice. We can choose life or death. I am already risking my life going in there, when no one has ever survived it. To refuse is not so different."

His smile is oily, but I read worry in the crinkles of his eyes. "But your life is not your own. You must stay to care for your child."

Anger flares in my chest—*this is why you will never be a caravanser,* my father once snapped at me. But I have never been able to change my heart or even to hide it well. So, I have to use it.

"Better he die," I snap, "than live under indenture's yoke. No. If I do this for you, you must do something for me."

The lines deepen around his eyes, the crow of time sinking its claws in. "And that is?"

I take a deep breath. "Make me your queen."

"What?" the vizier spits, eyes bulging.

"When you assume the scepter, you will marry me and name my son your heir." It would not be a union of love, but I have had my fill of those. And this is a better life for Alexhy than I could make elsewhere.

"Have you lost your wits? That—that's impossible!" the vizier splutters.

"Nothing is impossible with that much power, vizier. You would be a *god*. But not without me."

The muscles of his jaw work. "Freedom," he says at last. "The best I can give you is freedom."

Hope blooms in my chest. I ignore it. I didn't expect him to take me up on marriage, but the promise of freedom is too vague. Specifics. The profit and loss of a contract are decided in the specifics. "Tomorrow. I keep him alive until tomorrow, and you release us, me *and* my son."

"Two more days. I need you for two, at least."

"Two, then. But we'll need money. Enough for a year or more. And safe passage out of this nation." In case it *does* freeze over once I'm gone.

"Fine," he snaps. "Done. But first, your two days."

The merchant in me relaxes, deal made, but the servant in me is not done. "My first owner promised me freedom once, in return for a favor. You know how well that went. Proof. I need proof you will keep your word."

"My word is my proof, girl. I am a vizier of Chuali."

I would laugh if everything didn't ride on this. "Then you will not mind a witness. Vizier Aykuna. Call Vizier Aykuna, and let's have her witness the arrangement."

His face darkens. "You would question my—"

"This, or no deal, and you can go back to freezing lake country bards while your nation starves." It's a bluff—I would not actually risk Alexhy's life—but I have seen the avarice in his eyes. He will do it.

His mouth puckers like he's bitten a lemon rind, then he snatches a serving girl and sends her for Aykuna. I feel better when it is done and better yet at the pleased smile Aykuna wears, witnessing Chalmes' oath. She will hold him to it.

They leave, and I hurry toward the nursery.

Two days. Two days to freedom. Two days to a better future for my son.

Two days to keep a god alive.

But first, my son.

Alexhy is crying when they open the door, the nursemaid attending another child. I scoop him up, chest aching, not wanting to hear another moment of his torment. He wails louder, chubby arms clinging to me, and my tears come too. "I've missed you," I whisper into his soft brown hair. "Oh, how I've missed my boy."

"One turn of the glass," Chalmes grumbles behind me. "You have one turn with him."

"I have as long as I want," I spit, rounding on him. "Or do you want me to go back and ask your *god* for clarification?"

A silence. Then, "Until His Grace needs you, then. But no longer."

"Fine," I snap. "And I want them gone, all the rest of them." I wave my hand at the four or five other children in the room and the nursemaid.

They go. I collapse on the soft carpets, tears flowing again, but they are tears of joy this time. "My sweet fig," I whisper, pressing his soft cheek to mine. "A day is too long without you, even a minute. Come here."

I do not know how much time passes. Alexhy gets hungry, and there is still milk in my breast, and I lay back on the cushions, talking of the stars visible from the sands, which are so different than those painted on the ceiling. He gazes at me with wide eyes, one pudgy fist clutching my scullery maid's dress, and eventually sleeps, tiny chest rising and falling against mine.

I can't sleep. Every moment is precious. Before I know it, they summon me back.

Verenal greets me not from his throne but standing in the center of the darkening chamber. It is nearly night, but the vines still bloom along the wall, white pinwheels against dark stone. "How was your time, young Thaylea?"

"It was heaven," I say, already missing Alexhy's weight on my chest. Already hating the nursemaid who came in as I left. Already haunted by Alexhy's confused wail.

Verenal nods, blue eyes intent on me. "Good. Come. I would show you something."

I glance at Chalmes, but he only shoos me on. "Of course."

The god leads me to a long hallway behind the throne, sunset burning gold and orange out the west windows. "What is his name?" he asks as we walk.

"Alexhy," I say, not needing to ask who.

"A good name," he rumbles, and even here the stones seem to speak as much as his voice. "Though not of the sands."

"No. I did not want to name him such when we can't claim my family's title. A sandwalker without title—"

"Is a sandwalker without honor," Verenal says. "Yes. It has ever been such. I tried to change these injustices, but they are beyond my powers."

"The injustice of culture?"

"The injustice of the human heart. That one should imprison another, deny another, judge another based on any criteria but their actions."

We pass into a circular chamber, open to the chill evening air. I take a deep breath—how long has it been since I was out of doors? "And yet you perpetuate injustice now. Take slaves. Kill bards. Oppress the low countries."

"I did not mean to kill those people, I was only… so tired. But yes. I am not the man my father was. And there is no changing the pattern of time. If I did not do it, another would."

"But you *can* change that! You hold all the power in the world."

He turns, gesturing to an arched wooden door, and a sad smile plays on his lips. "No. I have no power over human hearts. Not even my own."

I glance at him, but his arm still points to the door, and the man *is* a god after all, or nearly so. I go through.

Into a desert bath. I suck in air—sweet, warm, dry air, spiced with jasmine and smoldering frankincense and the thousand scents of home. Date palms sway to each side, warm sand gives beneath my toes, and a clear, sparkling pool stretches between high marble walls. "Wh-what is this?"

"It is your home," he says. "Or, the best version I can make of it here."

I turn to him, bewildered. "Did you make this for me?"

He smiles again, and though his face is ruined and ancient, his skin the color of ash, I see a nobility there. The echo of a handsome man. "I made it for another. For one who wanted to see all the nations of the world, but whom I would not let from my side.

It has been unused for centuries now. I want you to stay here, if you wish."

I stop. Does he not know? "Verenal. Vizier Chalmes promised me my freedom, in two days' time." Nearly one day now, I realize. "You will honor that?

His face stiffens. "Yes. Of course. For those days then. I want you to be comfortable." But his voice does not hold all the warmth it did, and I realize I've hurt him somehow. Apparently, mindreading is not one of his abilities.

And apparently, he cares. That would be a first, among my captors.

"Go," he says gently. "Enjoy it."

I smile despite myself, despite the uncertainty of the situation. No sandwalker can refuse a bath, and it has been so long. I leave him, sand deliciously hot between my toes, and bend down to drink. The water is pure and cool, refreshing in the heat of this place, so different from the endless chill of the palace. The pool is shallow at this end, and I wade in up to my knees, closing my eyes and remembering my family's palace in the desert, the rose quartz stones and red woven tapestries on the walls. A small tray of dates and hard cheese waits at the far end. I devour it, the flavors of my childhood, and for a moment I almost feel at home.

Until, of course, I remember how I left home.

"How," I ask, to distract myself from the memories, "did you know?"

He still stands at the entrance, leaning on his scepter. "I told you, I have been all places, seen all things. Your people have not changed so much in six hundred years."

I feel kindness for him then and a desire to offer him something in return. He is a god, and I an indentured servant, but that only makes his gift the more unexpected. "Come," I say. "Cool your feet in the water. Or sit here on the sands, and let us talk."

He comes and sits, stiff in his robes.

"No," I say, smiling. "You don't know us so well, if you would sit like that. Lean back—use these pillows. You are in your oasis. Among family. No one can hurt you."

He leans awkwardly. "Like this?"

I can't help but laugh. "Something like that. Here. Try one of the dates. This one." I pluck the finest from the tray, a dark medjool, its papery skin shredding, the meat soft and honeyed beneath. "I can't believe you grew these here."

"I can grow anything," he says, without a hint of pride.

"Eat it," I say, nodding to the date. He takes a delicate bite, and I smile and dangle my legs in the water, enjoying the feel of it on my skin. "Well?"

"It's good," he says, having barely taken the tip from the thing.

"Eat it *all*," I say.

He glances at me almost guiltily, then puts the whole thing in his mouth. It's a big date, and I can tell he hasn't stuffed his mouth in a while. Do gods even need to eat?

"There's a pit! There. Tell me that tastes of 'dirt and decay.'"

"It does," he says, spitting the pit awkwardly into his hand.

"And?"

"And what?"

"And what else? Do you not taste honey and sunshine in it? The soul of the date palm?"

He chews a moment longer. "Yes. Perhaps I do."

I smile. "Good, then. You see. You just needed some perspective."

He finishes chewing and swallows, throat bobbing behind his ridiculously high collar. "I just needed *your* perspective."

My stomach clenches at that. The vizier promised. And Verenal knows. And even so, even as much as I feel some trust with this ancient man, I am afraid to believe he will follow through.

"Tell me of the one you built this for," I say. "Your wife?"

He hesitates. "She was perfect. Not actually perfect, but perfect for me. The only woman I met who didn't care that my father was the god-king, or that I was next in line for the scepter. A loving wife to my children."

"And you made this for her?"

"Yes. Because I could not let her travel. Could not let her from my sight, and at that time I felt I had so much to do here that I could not afford to leave. She died never having seen the world."

His voice is heavy again, though the air holds no chill. "And that's when you started traveling?"

"Yes. And seeing the eternal recurrence of all things."

I take a fig from the tray. "Does not the good also recur with the bad? Why do you see only dirt and death in it, rather than sunshine and honey?"

Verenal stares over the water, late evening sun playing on the surface of the pool. "The truly good is so rare and so fleeting. Death is the only constant."

"Except for you," I say around the fig, juicy and soft. "Maybe that's why you don't see it. Death has no meaning for you. Alexhy and I have been staring at it every day since we left the wagons, and every day it doesn't come feels like a blessing."

"Even here, living as an indentured worker in a foreign temple to a dying god?" There is a hint of humor in his voice.

"Even here. Look at this place you built." I gesture at the bath around us. "Isn't it wonderful? Here. Try this."

I hand him a black fig and smile at his thoughtful expression. There are olives and flatbread and honeyed pistachios yet to try.

Verenal tires after a time but allows me to bring Alexhy to the oasis when he leaves. Alexhy loves it. My child is still a sandwalker deep down, and he laughs and throws sand and gets wide-eyed at the morsel of date I feed him. It is his first, and my heart swells despite our situation, despite the uncertainty of it all. I can't help remembering Verenal's face fall when I said the vizier promised me freedom in two days. Nearly one day, now that night has come. Verenal could stop it all.

But he won't, I think. There is a good man in there, behind the world-weary bard-freezing god. A man like my grandfather was. When the servants call for me again in the morning, I ask them to bring Verenal here instead.

Their eyes go wide at my use of his name, but they bring him, and I quell the fear that worms in my belly, exposing my child to this man. We spend the morning and afternoon together, Verenal content mostly to watch Alexhy and me play. He even joins in, sprouting goat's weed and yucca from the sands to Alexhy's delight, or dropping dates from the palms for Alexhy to run screaming after.

"You… are leaving tomorrow," Verenal says, after we've finished a meal of curried lamb and flatbread. The kitchen does not do as good a job at replicating sandwalker foods as Verenal does, but it's still delicious.

"We are," I say, trying to sound confident, even as I shove down the hope that flutters in my chest. I have been disappointed too many times. And I don't know how Verenal feels about all this. If I've fixed him, or if he will go back to freezing bards when we leave. I hope he has changed. But mostly I just pray he lets us go. My son's future is not in a dying nation.

He nods and looks away, as though searching for something. I have never seen him lost for words. "Thank you," he says at last. "For sharing your time with me."

"I didn't have much choice," I say with a smile. "But you're welcome. I… enjoyed it."

Alexhy coos, pushing a wooden wagon with deep concentration, and we sit on the sands as the sky purples overhead, the god and my son and I.

Verenal stands with the first star. "I will not keep you. Go tonight."

I look up in shock. "Tonight?"

"Tonight." His voice holds the certainty of an immortal.

I stand, hands trembling. It's happening. It's actually happening. "Thank you," I stammer. "Thank you for everything."

He turns away, voice rough. "I have done nothing. But I will send guards with you, to see you safely to the edge of the valley or as far as you wish them to go."

And then he is gone. Guards come in time, bearing packs loaded with clothes and supplies, and we are laid in a wagon made for a queen. A sandwalker wagon, with henna-painted canvas stretched over a mesquite frame. Verenal has thought of everything.

I realize I will miss him.

We make it as far as the eastern palace gate.

The wagon stops, and I hear voices outside. Alexhy is sleeping, but I poke my head out the dowager's flap.

Vizier Chalmes is there, arguing with one of the guards, a squad of men behind him. His eyes snap to me. "You. You cannot leave."

I am not surprised. I'm crushed but unsurprised. My hope is a broken thing that has been stepped on many times. Somewhere, deep down, I knew it would get stepped on again. It always does.

Still, I run, grabbing Alexhy. Still, they catch me, Alexhy wailing, and still the vizier's eyes glitter in the darkness. "Just for another few days," he says. "Until we understand what he needs. You should be honored. His Holiness likes you."

"To *hell* with you," I spit, struggling against the thick arms taking my son. "To hell with your *holiness*. This is no honor. This is slavery, and you're a hypocrite, and it's no wonder this nation is falling to ruin. You—"

They gag me then, and soon enough the fight goes out of me, Alexhy's panicked wails squashing my anger like a boulder on my chest. I would do anything for him, to soothe him.

Even this.

I am slumped in the wagon, the vizier's men dragging us back inside, when a light fills the torchlit courtyard, brilliant blue.

Verenal.

I look up to see him striding through the palace arches, all semblance of frailty gone, gem in his scepter blazing. "What is this?" he roars, and the stones shake around us, dust sifting from the mortar. Vizier Aykuna stands in the doorway behind him, looking pleased.

Chalmes goes pale. "M-my Lord. Your Grace. The sandwalker woman was escaping, and I thought—"

"*Quiet*," Verenal thunders, and the vizier stumbles back as though struck by a giant palm. His men scatter behind him, and the wagon guards flee. My bonds fall away, and I snatch Alexhy from the man holding him.

The god approaches.

I pull my child to my breast, fearful and relieved at once. He *is* a god—I see that now. How could I have ever forgotten it?

How could I have ever thought they'd let me leave?

"What did they do to you?" Verenal asks, stones still shaking, but his voice is gentle, the gem's blaze dimming.

I make sounds behind the gag. He pulls it out with a touch as gentle as his last was violent.

"What they always do to indentured people," I say when it's out. "Give us hope so they can crush it out." It comes out angry, a challenge. Better that than the despair inside.

"No," the god says. "This is not their kingdom. Not their decision to make. You should go."

I look up from Alexhy's tear-streaked face, searching for the trick. "You will let me?"

"I am done with trying to hold what should be free." His eyes soften in the dim light. "But you could stay. Help me to find your perspective. To… enjoy the pattern, as I leave it."

He is ready to die, then. I feel a flush of happiness for him, but it does not change the facts. "I would. I want to. But I have to think of Alexhy. There is no future for him here."

"I could make a future for him, before I go," the god rumbles. "For both of you. Someone needs to take this." He gestures with the scepter.

Chalmes bristles at that, stepping in as if the god had not just struck him. "Only trained viziers can handle the power, Your Grace. As you yourself were once trained."

"Silence!" Verenal roars, and frost shoots up Chalmes' legs, freezing him to the flagstones.

"Something has gone wrong with our training," the god says in the quiet that follows. "And I do not relish passing the nation to any of these viziers. But Alexhy is young enough, you could steer him clear of that." He suddenly looks so old. "But you would have to deal with my viziers, until he comes into his majority. Even staying another fifteen years sounds… far too long."

I glance at Chalmes, frantically rubbing his icy legs, and catch a measuring gaze from Aykuna. They will each try to break me, if I stay. As they have broken so many others. As so many others have tried to break me, starting with my father. It is easier to run.

In my arms, Alexhy gazes wide-eyed at the blue glow of the gem. "What would you have me do, my love," I murmur to him, my fear a sandstorm inside. "Do we run, or do we hope?"

He doesn't answer. It's an impossible question—no one knows the future. But holding the perfect curve of his body against mine, I know which mother he would want to raise him. Which mother I want to be. I raise my head. Maybe what I have not been able to do for myself, I can do for him. For us.

Alexhy coos, reaching toward the scepter. The god smiles and, to gasps and cries of dismay all around, dips it toward him.

I smile too, feeling a knot untie deep in my chest. This is not the life I would have chosen, not the security I long for, but it is a chance, at least. A chance I am going to take.

Levi Jacobs

Levi Jacobs was born in North Dakota and grew up in Japan and Uganda, so he was bound to have a fantastic take on modern life. Currently marketing his award-winning epic fantasy *The Empire of Resonance*, and at work on the quick-but-intense *Tidecaller Chronicles*, he runs a small fruit company to pay the bills.

Find out more about Levi Jacobs at
www.levijacobs.com/free

TWICE–DOMESTICATED DRAGONS

Intisar Khanani

For every child who has had to grow up too fast and carry more than they know how

Twice-Domesticated Dragons

Intisar Khanani

"**N**o!" Baba's voice echoed up the stairs from the kitchen, the sound of it unnaturally high, edged with terror.

It was a sound she had heard before, would never forget, and it brought with it a dizzying wash of panic. Yusra set her toothbrush on the edge of the bathroom sink, telling herself there was nothing to fear here, in this land they'd come to. Nothing at all.

But then her father cried, his voice getting quieter, "Get away from there! *Yusra!*"

"Coming!" Yusra sprinted down the hall, took the stairs at a run, and burst through the kitchen entry as her little brother pulled himself up to place his palms against the screen door—

which, thankfully, had been dutifully locked the night before. Baba grabbed Ilyas a moment later with shaking hands, calling for her other brothers—*Haroon, Dawud!*—his voice fading to a labored whisper. Much good that would do if the boys couldn't hear him.

"What's wrong?" Yusra demanded, her voice sharp. Baba's beard was scruffy, his shirt rumpled and bearing coffee stains from three days ago even though she'd done the wash. She took Ilyas from him, wrapping her arms around his wriggling form. He was her charge, and she wasn't going to risk his safety to their father if something really was wrong. "Haroon! Dawud!" she called, just in case they were needed.

"Don't look away." Baba turned his wide eyes to the backyard.

Look away from the *yard*? Baba hadn't even been watching Ilyas, who needed watching first! She couldn't depend on her father. She knew it; had known it for a lifetime, or perhaps only a year that felt like one. Murmuring endearments to the squirming, brown-haired toddler in her arms, Yusra looked out the window just as Baba said, "There's more now!"

Yusra's stomach sank as the realization hit her. She knew what she'd see through the window long before her eyes found their small, sturdy forms. Of course there were more. Again. The things were a nightmare, and Yusra knew all about nightmares. She forced herself to assess the yard as Dawud and Haroon ran into the kitchen.

Gnomes. Everywhere. At least two dozen this time, their scarlet pointed caps glinting in the sunlight, their sinister sneers wide beneath hard ceramic mustaches and beards.

"How are there so many already?" Haroon cried, looking out the screen door. He sounded so much older than his seven years. "We cleared them out only a month ago!"

"You know what happens if even one escapes," Yusra said.

Everyone knew how gnomes bred, skulking through dumpsters, gathering discarded stoneware and ceramics, and molding them together—somehow, without water or a kiln—to form new gnomes. A single gnome could fashion an army in the space of a few weeks if left unchecked. Yusra shivered. To think people had once considered garden gnomes *cute*.

"We need a dragon," Dawud finally said, breaking the dismal silence. "We can't risk missing any again."

Yusra slid a sideways glance at him. Dawud was the eldest of her brothers at twelve, still a year younger than her. If they needed a dragon, she'd be the one to manage it. Not Baba with his shaking hands and whisper-soft voice, and not any of her brothers, all of them younger than her and placed into her keeping.

Stepping forward, she pushed the toddler into Haroon's arms. "You'd better stay home from school today. Watch Ilyas and help Baba keep an eye on the infestation."

Haroon wrapped his arms around his baby brother.

"Baba, you call Haroon's school while we're all helping watch so they know he won't be coming in."

Baba nodded, pulling his cell phone from his pocket with evident relief, glad to be doing something, to be told what to do. Oh, how she wished she didn't have to be the one to make these decisions!

"I'll go, Yusra," Dawud said, as she knew he would. Why couldn't Baba offer? But he had the phone to his ear as he spoke with the school receptionist, as she'd told him to do.

She shook her head. "And be late for school again? You know Mrs. Hanlin will forgive me. But your teacher, Mrs. Reynolds? She hates us all. You can't be late."

He hunched his shoulders. "Mrs. Reynolds can—"

"Dawud," Baba said, his voice heavy with warning as he lowered the phone.

"Go suck an egg!" Dawud shouted.

Stunned silence.

And then Ilyas giggled just as Yusra realized none of them were watching the yard—and a garden gnome crashed through the kitchen window.

Baba screamed, a high fluting sound that caught at the back of his throat. Under their collective gaze, the gnome lay perfectly still on the glass-littered floor, the gleam of its white-glazed teeth beneath its beard a warning of the horror to come if they looked away.

But this wasn't the only one.

Yusra tore her gaze away to stare out at the garden. Their small patch of tomatoes and cucumbers had been destroyed. The grass was turning brown already, as if the gnomes were toxic, and one of the boards in the privacy fence had been torn free. She could just glimpse the green of the woods beyond. And now the window was broken. How would they explain such damage to their landlord? Again, after the last episode only a month ago? They needed a dragon. Now.

"Dawud, watch this one! Baba, Haroon, watch the rest! I'll be right back!"

She tore out of the kitchen, passing through the living room with its two cushions and blanket on the floor, and into the so-called garage, where affluent people kept cars, and where her father kept his bicycle, and where the last owner had left a rusted old dragon cage, amongst other discarded items. She snatched it and raced back to the kitchen, and there was her family, still safe.

Dawud stared grimly at the gnome on the floor. Baba looked out the broken window, and Haroon had taken up a station at the screen door, Ilyas resting quietly against his chest. The broken glass gleamed on the floor, but they'd have to clean it up later. She'd make sure everyone had shoes in the meantime.

But first, the gnome. She set the cage on the floor beside the gnome, worked the rusted hinges open, and *kicked* the godforsaken thing into the cage. It clattered like a broken dish over the metal floor, but still, it didn't break. If only it were trash, and not whatever garden gnomes were in this country she had come to. This haven that remained safe from all the wars it started. Magic might exist in the world, but not even the most advanced scientists or wisest elders knew how to harness it, or how it ended up inhabiting such creatures as these. At least they were one thing she hadn't had to deal with back home.

"Got it," she said savagely, slamming the door shut. The old latch fell into place. The rings for a padlock to fully secure the door remained empty. Yusra didn't have a lock to use, but she doubted the gnome would be able to open the latch while she carried it.

She hefted the cage, testing its weight. The muscles of her right arm twinged. She switched hands and said, "Keep watch. I'll be back with a dragon shortly."

Baba hesitated. "We… don't have money. And if we request additional funds," he shook his head, gaze focused on the nightmare of gnomes outside. "Our application could be blacklisted."

The boys shot nervous glances at her before returning their gazes to the backyard. They couldn't afford to have their application blacklisted. They were only here on a provisional status. If it was revoked before they received full residency… no.

Yusra straightened her back. "We're not asking for anything. There are dragons in the woods. I'll just lure one back here."

Baba risked a glance at her. "Yusra, you don't know anything about dragons!"

"I just studied them at school, Baba. It will be fine." A lie, of course. They all knew that nothing was guaranteed. But she had studied dragons; the gnome in the cage could attract at least a small one. She'd have to hope she could handle it from there.

She stepped out to gather all their shoes from the front door and brought them back to the kitchen, even her baba's beat-up old sneakers.

"Yusra." Baba's voice was agonized as he took the shoes from her. He glanced from the boys to the garden, then back to her. For just a moment—just one impossible heartbeat—she thought he'd offer to go in her stead. Then he said, "You'll be careful?"

"Yes, Baba. You take care of things here. I'll be back soon. And make sure Dawud doesn't miss the bus! Haroon, you keep watching the garden, no matter what."

Haroon nodded. She almost took Ilyas with her... but she couldn't manage him as well as the cage. Or run with him if the dragon turned nasty.

She lifted the cage and hurried out, leaving through the garage, hoping all the while no one would see her.

The edge of the woods was a wasteland of old fencing and broken things. The gnome rattled around in the cage as she made her way through the low-growing brush to the shadowed reaches of the deeper woods. She could hear the cursed creature gnawing at the metal bars when she wasn't looking. Once, its little, clawed fingers even managed a swipe at her jean-clad legs, but she held it at a distance and glanced at it often enough that it couldn't affect any real damage. Ceramic against iron wasn't a winning gambit anyhow.

Last time, she and Dawud had gone into the garden with the spare baseball bats (also found in the garage) and smashed the gnomes to pieces. They'd bagged up the remains, but it had been difficult, too many of them shattered, the fired clay mixing with the dirt and grass. And clearly they'd missed at least one of the cursed creatures, which had led to this second invasion. No doubt a few of the gnomes in the backyard had been reconstituted from the remains of their predecessors. Yusra's skin crawled at the thought.

This time, they'd get rid of them for good. No dark looks from the neighbors, no whispered rumors at school about how they naturally attracted horrors. Yusra didn't know why the gnomes had picked their yard—whether it was a coincidence, or if someone who knew how to lure them had chosen her family as their target. Either was possible. But she wasn't going to let more rumors spread about them if she could help it.

So, she stepped carefully around the heaped trash, not a bit of it ceramic or stoneware, and made her way deeper into the woods. It was still early morning, sunlight dappling the leafy floor here and there, most of it caught in the tops of the trees. Dragons liked water, that much she knew, however counterintuitive it seemed to her for fire-breathing creatures to prefer wetlands and swamps. Especially twice-domesticated dragons, which were what she was hoping to find.

As their name implied, valiant efforts had been made to domesticate this particular breed of dragon not once, but twice. The breeding and training programs had leaned toward creating smaller, more compact dragons, with gentler demeanors and an omnivorous diet. To a certain extent, the programs had succeeded, and twice-domesticated dragons were known to have a taste for garden gnomes and other stoneware.

The dragons were also wily creatures, twice the size of ferrets, and only sometimes able to communicate telepathically. They were still wild at heart and could not be fully trained to respect household pets, or not attack strangers, and so researchers had given up trying to domesticate them. Then, some noble-hearted employee left the back door of a facility open one evening, and the whole of the final population of twice-domesticated dragons escaped before they could be exterminated.

Whatever their name was, Yusra blessed them as she hiked through the forest, searching for a stream.

Unfortunately, twenty minutes of hiking brought no sign of a stream or even a little puddle from the recent rains. Yusra came to a stop beside a large oak. She could keep going, but she wasn't sure she'd be able to find her way home if she did. She'd also been gone long enough that what gnomes Baba and Haroon couldn't see might easily band together and cause more trouble.

"I've a whole garden full of gnomes for you, don't you know?" she called, frustration pushing her to use her mother tongue, a language she hadn't let touch her lips in nearly a year. It tasted sweet and rich and full of heartbreak, a forgotten delicacy. The birds fell silent. "Dragons! Won't you come eat them?"

She waited, as if the dragons could understand her. As if they cared. Maybe they would attack her, drive her out of their territory. In which case, she'd just throw the caged gnome at them and be off. Surely that would be enough of a distraction?

She glanced down at the cage, aware suddenly that it really *was* quiet, the gnome neither clawing at the metal nor grating its teeth at the bars. It lay on its side, completely still.

Very slowly and very carefully, Yusra set the cage on the ground, unlatched it, and stepped back. The forest remained still, but Yusra was certain she was no longer alone—and it wasn't the gnome she counted as company.

Still moving slowly, she backed up to the oak tree, reached for a branch, and then quickly clambered up. When she turned back, the gnome still lay unmoving in the cage. She settled on the branch, watching.

Little girls shouldn't try to trap dragons. The voice was low and growly and entirely in her mind.

Yusra started, a scream welling in her throat, and looked straight up into the glinting gaze of a dragon.

She fell out of the tree.

It wasn't a long fall, and the ground was soft and springy and covered with a thick layer of leaves, but it still knocked the breath right out of her. She lay on her back, her mouth gaping, and stared as the dragon smirked down at her. It was a mottled brown, lizard-like, with small sharp teeth and reptilian eyes—what else would it have?—and the quintessential vestigial wings lying flat against its leathery hide.

Forgot your firestick, did you?

Firestick? Oh. She took a wheezing breath, enough to spit out, "I'll *never* use a gun."

The dragon dropped, landing on her chest, its claws cutting through her T-shirt to poke holes in her skin. Its weight sent her breath right out of her again.

Don't believe you.

But it did bring a tasty gnome, another voice said. This one was decidedly lighter, more amused. *Have a bite.*

I'm not going in there, the brown lizard said, a snarl to its mental voice. *You shouldn't either!*

Too late. The other chuckled, a soft raspy sound she heard with her own ears.

Yusra managed another breath and turned her head sideways just in time to see a mossy green dragon nip into the cage, open its mouth, and envelop the gnome in flame. The creature's hard glaze began to run, and then the clay beneath cracked apart with a pained cry. The green dragon happily crunched up the broken clay. Yusra shuddered.

If that cage closes on you, the brown dragon began ominously.

Then I'll open it after I finish. It doesn't have a lock. Didn't you see? Or if you like, you can just sit on the girl until she agrees to help.

The brown dragon turned its gaze upon Yusra. She looked up at him. A mated pair, her brain told her hazily. Also, clearly telepathic and far better at speaking than her textbook seemed to think possible. Admittedly, its publication date was a good ten years ago. It probably required updating. Or had been updated, and the school simply couldn't afford a revised edition.

"There are more," Yusra rasped, since the brown was still staring at her. "In my garden. At least two dozen. Please, can you help me?"

A likely story. You probably plan to trap us there.

How? With her old lockless cage and a regular stick, perhaps?

Yusra shot a grateful look to the green dragon who was now sauntering out of the cage.

Trust a human and you'll regret it, the brown said, but there was an edge of defeat to his voice.

It's just a young one. The older ones are worse. Come, little one. Where do you claim this feast is?

"I can show you," Yusra said.

The brown dragon looked to its mate, heaved a sigh, and stepped off Yusra.

His expression, however, went from grim to wide-eyed when they finally reached the rickety old privacy fence that surrounded Yusra's backyard. The two gnomes skulking about outside met a quick and fiery death. Then the dragons topped the fence and sat back to gaze in astonishment at the sight within.

Feast! The green crowed, and dropped into the garden. The brown spared Yusra a single, warning glance, and swooped down after its mate.

Yusra smiled, listening to the hiss and crackle of fire-bathed gnomes. And then there were other sounds: whistling cries that accompanied the hisses, the shriek of breath through pierced lungs, a crunching like bones breaking, concrete crumbling on impact. Yusra's throat closed, even though this was different.

These were clay gnomes, little evil sneering menaces crackling and breaking. There were no missiles here, no broken buildings and shattered streets, no cries for mercy from ragged throats. There were no soldiers with hard stares and harder bullets. But still, her world darkened, terror screeching through her that she could not stop, could not reason with. How can memories be reasoned with?

She gave a single gasping cry and turned, shuffle-running away, away, her shoulder slamming into something, and then something else—trees? Posts? She could not tell; she heard only the screams of the dying, the gurgle of death, her mother's voice somewhere beneath it all, and she could not get away, could not stop the horror surrounding her, could not help. Could not, could not, *could not.*

She fell somewhere further on, pushed herself to her knees, and kept going until something hemmed her in, beige walls and brick, and there she stayed, huddled and shivering, her eyes unseeing.

A long time later, or perhaps it only felt that way, a voice said, *Little girl.*

Yusra curled into a tighter ball, but now that she wasn't alone, the sobs came. They shook her whole frame, shattered her heart.

Little girl, the voice said again. She blinked away tears to see the brown dragon crouched beside her, its nose barely a handbreadth away from her own.

She nodded.

Why do you sorrow?

She closed her eyes, but she didn't have any words.

It's because of the firesticks, the green dragon's voice said, almost gently. *Isn't it?*

Yusra nodded. Slowly, shakily, she reached out, hiked up her sleeve, and there was the scar, round and small on one side of her arm, and wide and ugly on the other.

Ah, child, the brown said sadly and licked away her tears with the soft leather of his tongue.

We know that pain, the green said. Yusra lay still, her sobs quiet now, but her tears still flowing. The brown sat back, and for the first time, she saw a faint scar on his tail. She knew how it would look on the other side.

"My mother died," Yusra said into the quiet, her voice rasping. "I couldn't save her. She helped me up, and then she gave me Ilyas and told me to keep going, get my brothers to safety. Baba was too far away to help. And I did, *I did*, but the bullets didn't stop, and then she wasn't behind me anymore."

Oh, little child, the brown said again and curled against her chest. The green came and settled at her back. And there they stayed until Yusra heard a sound she didn't expect.

It was her father's voice, reedy and uncertain and scared, calling her name. She sat up, and there he was, his face sallow beneath the natural olive of his skin, one arm holding a somber-faced Ilyas, and the other hand gripping a baseball bat. Haroon hurried along in his footsteps.

"Yusra, my Yusra! Are you okay?"

"Baba," she said, and all her anger and resentment at him, all the fury she had harbored in her chest at his helplessness and fear, drained away completely. He was here, terrified and shaking, but here. He'd come for her, and she knew what nightmares he faced. She knew.

She stood as he hurried across the ragged earth to her, dropping the bat as he reached her so he could fold her into a hug. And then Haroon wrapped his arms around them both, and Ilyas's hands patted the tears on her face. And finally, Yusra could breathe again.

Tell us if you have more gnome trouble, the brown dragon said. *We'll come.*

Thank you, she thought back at him and rested her head against her father's chest.

Intisar Khanani

Twice-Domesticated Dragons started out as a story about the "natural" predators of garden-gnomes-gone-rogue, but it very quickly became something else: a story about resilience and survival; about loss and grieving; about the scars we carry with us, and the healing we can find among those we love as well as those we have just met. This story was deeply influenced by the ongoing refugee crises around the world, my reflections on how hard it is to be a child in such a situation—and the deep vulnerability and strength such children carry with them.

Intisar Khanani writes mighty girls and diverse worlds. She's the author of the Dauntless Path novels, beginning with Thorn, as well as the Sunbolt Chronicles.

Find out more about Intisar Khanani at booksbyintisar.com

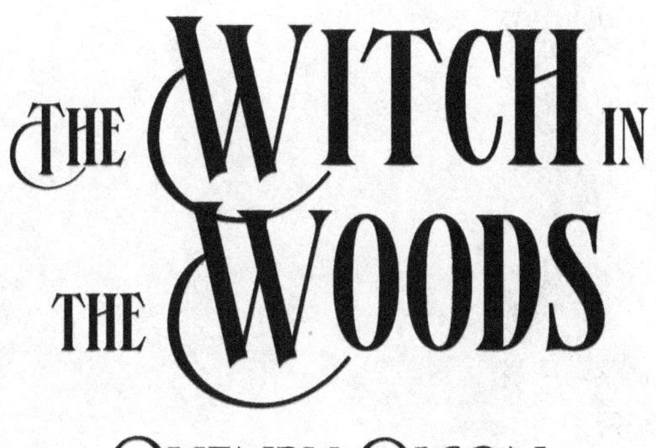

QUENBY OLSON

To Ola—I'm so thankful you're still here

THE WITCH IN THE WOODS

QUENBY OLSON

A storm's coming.

The leaves turn over, showing silver as the clouds roll in, as the hills in the distance disappear under a haze of rain. It's not raining here yet, where the gnats still swarm in great black clouds over the fields, where the sweat sticks to you like a second skin, something no amount of washing seems capable of completely scrubbing away.

You used to glory in afternoons like this, the cloying heat like a living thing. Made you feel vital, bright and shining somehow. But then the fussing begins again, and now the heat is something to wish away. To curse if you had it in you to voice such a thing.

"She won't settle," you say to no one in particular. The house lies quiet, and Birgit's downstairs, far enough away she can't hear you unless you yell. And you don't want to yell, don't want to raise your voice and disturb the babe from her rest. What rest she can get.

The babe…

You haven't named her yet. Mikkel's still out in the field, scything the hay before it's too late. And you're standing here, worrying about the babe's name, as if somehow you might have brought all this on by not naming her, as if you were too frightened to claim her as your own.

She's there in the cradle, the one Mikkel built last month, the wood still pale and unfinished because the babe came too soon. That's why you didn't have a name picked out, because she came early. Or perhaps you and Birgit read the signs wrong, since this was your first, and you didn't know what to look for. And she was small, but not too small. All pink and screaming and ready to suckle at the breast like any other healthy creature.

Another cry, softer this time. You wish it was louder, that there was more fight in her. Should you fetch the doctor? Send Birgit to find him? But you balk at that. The man most likely would've killed you if he'd been there to oversee the birth. Probably would've killed the babe, too, judging by how many mothers and children have been lost under his negligence. That's why you pray, every morning and night, thanking anything and everything that the old man was too drunk to attend you that evening, that the babe came quick before he sobered up.

Now, you wonder if you prayed too much. If you've gotten prideful, somehow. Relying on the old gods and your own faith, as if the strength of it alone could spare you and yours from harm.

You shuffle to the foot of the cradle. She's asleep again, but restless with it. Arms twitching, her face mottled and pink. Pinched, you think. Like she's in pain. But nothing you've done seems to help.

She's light in your arms. Three weeks old, and you would think she could float away if you let her go. All the babies you saw when they were carted around by their mothers and nurses were big, bouncing things with thick thighs and fat cheeks. You forget that you never saw them when they were this small, looking more like a doll than a living creature, something that could be broken to pieces should you hold it the wrong way.

Her mouth puckers as her eyes flutter open, and you hope it means she wants to nurse. Almost a whole day now, and she's hardly eaten, only sucked a little and then pulled away as your breasts began to ache and leak down the front of your blouse.

You open your top and offer her your breast, but she doesn't latch on, simply noses it and turns her head away. She feels warm. Warmer than the heat of the day should warrant.

"Oh," you say. A puff of sound from your mouth, yet it carries the weight of all your fear for her, heavy enough to drag your voice down like it's fallen into quicksand.

Her blanket, a spare nappy... You snatch them both and slide your feet into your boots without even bothering to lace them up.

Downstairs and Birgit's in the kitchen peeling something, carrots or parsnips, you don't look long enough to see.

"I'm going—" You stop yourself when you don't know how to say the rest of it.

Birgit drops what she's doing, a chunk of root vegetable rolling off the edge of the table and thunking onto the floor. Her hands find their way into her apron, wiping and wiping until you realize her fidgeting has nothing to do with cleaning bits of food off her fingers. "The doctor?"

You breathe. The air tastes sick and hot on your tongue. "No, no. Not him." Anyone but him. He might as well smother the child and make it quick. "I need... I need Mim."

Birgit's hands go still in her apron. "Surely, you can't…" Her lips draw into a line and there's a look on her face, words written there she'll never speak to you out loud. "Not yet."

"I have a sick child, and I don't know how else to save her."

"Mikkel has the horse," she reminds you. "All the way out by Stemson's lake."

Too far, too far. There's no time to fetch the horse, to tell Mikkel what you're planning. No doubt he'd try to talk you out of it, too. The same way Birgit wants to but won't let herself do it. Not when she sees how your mind's already made up.

"I'll walk," you say.

"Do you want me to go with—"

"No." You cut her off before she can finish speaking, before you're tempted to accept. It would be too easy to turn back with someone else at your side.

She nods once, a slice of her jaw and there's the end of it. "Take your shawl," she tells you, her voice harder than before. She helps you wrap the babe inside of it, cradling her against your chest and leaving your arms free.

She bends down and ties your boots when you realize you can't manage it with the baby at your chest, with your hands rattling until you think she might hear your bones shake. She leaves only long enough to wrap a parcel of food for you: bread and cheese and fruit and carrots. But the thought of eating any of it makes fire rise in the back of your throat.

"You need to keep up your strength," she says, pushing the food into your hands. "For the babe and for yourself." A kiss then, a quick brush of her lips across the child's fevered forehead. And a kiss for you, too brief and too light, like a single drop of water on a parched bit of earth. "Go now. Before the storm arrives. Before the sun sets and the way is closed to you."

You don't run, though your legs twitch beneath you with the urge to take off as though at the blast of a pistol shot. Out on the porch, the screen door slams shut behind you. Down the steps, to the path that takes you past the sunflowers drooping under their own weight, the corner fencepost sticking out of the ground like an old tree half-pushed over by the wind.

The road is nothing more than two ruts in the dirt, dead grass and chicory decorating the mounds between them. The stones bite at your feet through the soles of your boots, and you fear you'll have blisters before you've gone too far. The baby's made you soft, you think. Your hands are less callused, and your muscles aren't as firm as before. The pregnancy was hard, and Birgit took up all the extra housework, leaving you with little to do but let the panic of motherhood settle over you like a cloak.

You pause after a few yards and wonder about turning around. Not to go back inside, but to head for the Stemson's, to find Mikkel. It shouldn't make you hesitate. Birgit can tell him where you've gone. It'll be better that way, rather than risk seeing him, just his presence enough to maybe make you change your mind. But still, you linger for a moment, staring at the horizon like you can latch yourself onto it, string a cord between the two of you no matter how far you travel.

The walk shouldn't take long. Four miles, or thereabouts. No more than two hours at the most. But you've forgotten the weakness in your legs, the heavy ache in your thighs and your abdomen, the way your body feels like it could still turn itself inside out since having the babe. But you trudge forward, your teeth clenched and your arms wrapped around your hips as if you could hold yourself together by strength of will alone.

The woods creep up on you, indistinguishable from the haze in the distance until you're right there, the branches arching overhead, poison ivy and jewelweed battling for your hem. The ache in your legs has changed to a steady throb at the last mile, and you wonder if you've done too much, worry you'll take to bleeding again. Still wrapped in your shawl, the babe fusses and squirms against your chest. Angry and ill. You wish she would cry, that you could hear that plaintive wail tear from her throat, a scream of life and the strength to hold onto it. What you would give to—

You close your eyes, bow your head, and breathe in the scent of the babe's skin, the soft tickle of her hair against your nose. What you would give, to hear her voice again.

Rain finds you just as you step under the cover of the trees. It spatters on the leaves above, filters down to errant drops that land on your head, your shoulders, out of rhythm with the storm building all around you.

"Let me in." Your voice is a quaver, a rustle of bird's wings. You need to be stronger than that. You take a step forward, and it's as if the trees back away from you, regaining their distance, keeping you at the edge of things.

No, not like this. You close your eyes, though you'd rather not. You breathe, inhaling the scent of green things and wet things, of life and the decay of it beneath your feet. You can't be afraid. You remember her telling you that, years and years before, that when it was time, you couldn't recoil from it.

"I need Mim." Strong and unwavering, a voice meant to be obeyed.

The trees answer.

You move forward. One step, and then another. The emptiness of the fields and the leaden sky are left behind you. The ground is both soft and hard, last season's leaves and dying things blanket fallen logs and tree roots. A glance behind you and the road gone, the fields swept from existence. Only the woods stretching into the distance, miles of trees just waiting for you to lose your way under them.

You walk for too long, or perhaps not long enough. The rain beats on the leaves, thunder rolls in the distance, but always in the distance, never finding its way to the woods.

The babe writhes, struggling to push an arm free of the shawl, struggling to whine but without more than a whistling breath from between her puckered lips.

"Please," you say. You cry.

And there, the outline of a small house, not much more than a shack hidden beneath the choking vines and weeds. There's the edge of a wall, and just a little farther, you can make out the corner of the roof, partially collapsed on one side. Another step, and you see rows of wasp nests, long abandoned, stuck to the eaves. Another step, and there's the remains of a porch, a door, the wood coated with white and purple streaks of bird droppings.

The knocker is warm and rough in your hand, red rust flaking away onto your fingers. You remember the last time you were here, when you weren't even tall enough to reach it. Three knocks, and you wait. You could kick the door down and force your way inside, but you know that's not the way of things.

The rain picks up, working its way through the canopy. You don't want the babe to get wet, so you tug at the edge of the shawl, folding it just so. A brim over her head, over her cheek, and her lips begin to suckle in her sleep, eyes dancing behind their shining lids.

You fight with the buttons of your shirt, hope flaring through you with the speed of a brushfire. Maybe it's enough, just to have come this far, to show that you're willing to make the sacrifice. You struggle to draw your heavy breast free and touch the nipple to her lips while her mouth still works. A prayer that she'll latch on, that she'll nurse, even for a moment. But her mouth seals shut, and she turns her face away, as if the very smell of you is distasteful.

"Just a little longer," you say. A promise you're not certain you can keep. Or a prophecy you pray doesn't come true.

The door opens. An inch or so, hinges creaking.

Leave now, you think. *Turn around. Go back through the woods. Onto the road. To the house. To Mikkel and Birgit and the comfort they may give. Let the sickness do what it will. The babe might survive. She might.*

It's the "might" that sways you.

You push on the door, hard enough to ignite an ache in your shoulder, muscles already tensed against the world. The wood gives way, enough to let you slip through, stepping sideways with the babe tucked to your bosom, your hand cradling her tender head.

The room inside is cozy. Warm, but not too warm. You smell a fire, hear it crackling like footsteps in the underbrush, but look around, and there's nothing there. Just the cold, swept stone of an empty grate. Everything is clean and tidy with a place for all of it. You try not to think about how the shape of the room doesn't match the outside of the house, how the windows are clear and unbroken, how the view through the glass is of late evening, the sun down, lightning bugs flickering like starlight.

Turn around, and there's a chair that wasn't there before. The woman sits in it, a bucket on the floor at her feet, a potato in one hand and a knife in the other. She pays no attention to you, her fingers turning the potato, long strips of peel falling into the bottom of the bucket with a hollow sound.

She looks different. That's what you tell yourself even as you recognize the tracery of veins beneath the skin of her hands, the stoop of her shoulders, the sharp line of her jaw as she keeps her face turned away from you.

"She's sick," you say. Because what else can you say?

The woman nods. Her hair is thick and gray, grayer than before, brushed and plaited so it hangs like a rope over one shoulder.

"I need your help," you say. Because she won't answer.

"Why should I help you?" Her voice… It claws at your memories, deep and hoarse, like she hasn't said a word to anyone since she last spoke to you. The chair creaks as she leans back, tipping it onto its rear legs. Her gaze settles on you, and you take a small step back at how it pierces through you, that look.

"I can't…" But you don't want to finish. Because you realize you don't need to.

She sets her knife on the table, the one that appeared with a blink of your eyes. The potato is rolled in her hand, her fingertips searching its surface, scraping at a missed bit of peel with her thumbnail before she sets it aside as well. "Here, now. Give her to me."

No, not that. Not yet. You hold the babe against you, wishing she would fuss at the pressure.

But the woman's fingers beckon. "I won't know if I can help if you won't let me see her."

You unwrap the child from the shawl, hating how warm she is, how there should be more sweat on her brow, how her eyes are half-open, showing you a sliver of the whites veined with red.

The woman takes her with practiced care. "Ooh, chicky," she croons and rocks her for a minute. She lifts a gnarled finger and prods at the dimple in her cheek. Mikkel's dimple, like a stamp of his fatherhood on the infant's face.

The woman's eyes lift again to meet yours. She looks tired, and you wonder if it's sincere or simply a reflection of the expression on your own face. "You know I can't fix this," she says. "You know that."

"But I hoped," you reply. That it wouldn't be time already for you to come here, that there might still be years left before it was your turn. If there is more to say, the words won't come.

"I'm too old." The woman shifts the child in her arms, smiles down at her. It should be a comforting sight, one to take up residence in your heart. An old woman and a young child, the line continuing unbroken. But instead, you want to recoil from it, want to tear down the house around their heads and run, run, run until the storm catches up with you.

The woman clears her throat, the low rumble of breath and phlegm like the first skittering of rocks before an avalanche. "Years ago, I might have been able to. Well, almost certainly. But now…" She lifts the babe and presses her lips and her nose to her scalp, breathing deep. "She'll die," she says, a murmur of sound against the child's skin. "I'm sorry."

No, no, no. The apology hits with the weight of a fist. You'd rather she not say it at all. Be cruel and harsh about it. Give you a reason to hate her.

"But you could try." Anything, you think. Better to try and fail than… what?

She looks up at you. You wish you could read something in her eyes, but all you see is grief long worn down, an acceptance of things that can't be changed. "It's not my time anymore. The power's shifted."

"No," you say. As if that one word can change your fate.

"You'll still have Mikkel," she tells you. "And Birgit. More love than most in that house, I'd say."

You wonder if she said these same things to herself, how she might have tried to talk herself out of it. If she held you in her arms and imagined things going a different way.

"Please." Your entire world is twisted up in that word.

But she shakes her head. And you hate that you knew she would, that you came all the way out here carrying a hope that it might be different for you. Chasing a chance that disappeared like a wisp in the sunlight.

"I've told you before," she says. "Make your choice."

You swallow what you want to say. Bitter words with spiked leaves catch in your throat, crowding out the things you should say. "Is there a chance?" you manage, at last, cobbling the question together from scraps. "If I take her home, if I care for her, if I…"

She doesn't nod or shake her head. She offers you nothing, and it's worse than anything.

You close your eyes, and the house goes quiet. The sound of the fire dies down, and you feel coolness on your brow, on the back of your neck, drying the sweat you hadn't realized was there.

It's yours, you know. This power. This curse. It sweeps across your skin, like fingers trailing through the water of a farm pond on a silver sky kind of day.

The magic is there, ready for you to take it and to take from you in return. Just slip below the surface, and it's all yours.

You open your eyes again, gasping.

And there she sits, your child in her arms. Still breathing, face flushed, the color at its brightest before it might drain away completely.

Might.

But not if you stop it.

"Give her to me." You don't wait for her to hold out the babe. Just scoop your arms beneath her, wonder at how light she is, as if her life is already slipping away. Your fingers grip the fabric of her little shift, the one you sat up late sewing when your legs were too restless to allow sleep, while Mikkel snored in the bed and Birgit brought you cups of warm milk before lying down beside you.

And there were the later days, with your belly swollen, your ankles swollen, all of you seemingly too large for your own skin. And the child shifting around inside of you, feet and knees and elbows where you would have thought they couldn't go. Mikkel with his hands on your belly, his ear pressed against you. Listening. Just listening. And the smile on his face, the light in his eyes. Eyes just like the babe's.

A sigh slips out of you. "Tell me what to do."

"Here." The woman stands up, all lithe sharpness despite her age. She pushes you into the chair, and you set the child on your lap, her head on your knees, her curved feet tucking against your abdomen as though she still shares a familiarity with that part of you, even weeks separated.

"But what do I—"

The woman puts one hand on top of your head, the other on the head of the child. "She's yours. You'll know. Just as I did."

You look into the old woman's eyes, eyes that are so much like yours you could be staring at a smudged version of your own reflection. "Mim," you say, repeating your first word as if you're learning speech all over again. "I'm scared."

She smiles. "So was I." She leans down and kisses your forehead, her lips dry as dust on your skin. "But I would do it again, for you."

You cradle the child's head, tucking her chin against her chest, her lips pursing in displeasure at the change in position. You want to say you're sorry. You want to say a thousand things, but all the words of wisdom and kindness and frustration will have to be the burden of Mikkel and Birgit now.

Close your eyes. You tell yourself not to fret, as if you can tell a raging river not to overflow its banks. The coolness comes so fast you wonder how long you've been holding it at bay, and you wonder for how long you must have known this was how it would be. In the end.

Your heart pounds against the inside of your ribcage as the power leaves Mim and slips into you. A magic with roots in the earth, older than anything you can imagine. How many have there been before you? How many had let this power rush into them, one person after another, from mother to daughter over the centuries?

Beyond the house, beyond the woods, the storm sweeps through, over and done with a burst of hail and rain and thunder. Only the wind is left, chill in the room without the warmth of the old woman's fire, without the heat and the hum of the gathering storm.

"I'm trying," you say. The babe squirms in your arms, the fever reaching a pitch that floods her cheeks and chest with color. But you imagine the magic like a scythe in your hands, shearing off the sickness before it can take her from you. A chill runs through you, from your heart to your fingers where the babe's head is cradled. It hurts at first, like your limbs waking up after sitting for too long. And then the pain fades, and the child stops fussing, her little fists relaxed as her fingers unfurl like petals.

And just like that, she's sleeping. The blooms of red have already faded from her cheeks, the purple bruising gone from her eyelids. Her heart beats strong and true, no longer frantic, no longer missing the occasional thump until it would've stopped entirely. Your fingers skim across her scalp, over the soft spot in her skull. Angry and swollen before, smooth and placid now. She sleeps, quiet and peaceful, lips suckling at the air, slightly sunken in that way before her teeth come in.

She's asleep, but you open your blouse anyway, nudge her cheek against your breast. She turns to you, seeking you out, latching on hard and strong. You wince when the milk comes down, but you let her drink, let her have her fill. She'll need it, to hold her until she's home again, until Birgit can arrange a way to see her fed.

"It's time," the old woman says, once the babe is finished and settled down to rest.

She's so soft and warm in your arms, her fingers a bit cool. Her nails will need a trim, and she'll need a clean nappy, and she'll need…

All the things you won't be able to give her. Not anymore.

You kiss her forehead and her cheek, touch the soft whorls of hair on her head. You tell her you love her, as though she might not know it if you don't say it. As if you haven't given up everything for her already.

You hand her over, so slow you wonder if you'll change your mind at the last minute, break down the door and escape with her. But it doesn't work like that. You belong here, and she doesn't. At least not for some time, you hope.

"There you are, chicky." The old woman takes her and tucks the ends of her shawl around the babe, pausing long enough to caress the soft, wrinkled soles of her bare feet with the pad of her thumb.

"What will you do?"

She doesn't look at you, doesn't take her eyes off the babe. "I've enough left in me to see her home. After that…"

You think she might not finish, and you're to fill in the blanks on your own. But she heaves a deep breath and drags the rest of the speech out from her lungs. "I'll linger, for a little while. Won't be long."

"Can I…?" You stand up from the chair, nearly knocking it over you're on your feet so fast. She doesn't hold the child out to you, just tips her head a bit, lets you lean in and kiss her, your nose to her temple, lips to her ear. "I'll see you again."

A promise and a curse, all twined together.

The old woman pauses at the door, her hand on the latch. Her mouth works around something she doesn't want to say, like a bit of cud she can't dispose of. "I'm sorry," is what she does say, those two words carrying the weight of a thousand other things she couldn't tell you while you were apart.

You nod and swallow, unable to trust your voice anymore.

She leaves then. No more goodbyes or awkward words. She steps out, lets the door swing closed. Then it's just you, all alone.

And you think that in different circumstances, on a different day, you might come to like it, this strange new solitude.

It doesn't find you right away, the grief. Or the joy of it, either. Perhaps neither of them will truly touch you, so tangled up in themselves as they are.

You look around, and you notice the changes already. The bucket is gone. The potatoes. The knife. The house is cooler now, as if there's a window somewhere letting in a draft of evening air.

The chair is still there, and the table. The sound of the storm reaches you through the walls, faint and fading, the worst of it rolled past. But the smell of it holds. The air brushed clean. You walk through the house, into other rooms that shiver and change when you think about what you want from them. Come to a window and look out, at a silvered moon and a darkening sky pricked with stars. And there's upstairs to explore, this rambling place your entire world now.

Your forehead touches the glass of the window, as though you could push on through and leave this place. The heaviness is there, the weight in your breasts, in your belly, enough to drag you all the way back home if you'd let it.

You thought you had some time yet, maybe years before it was your turn to come here. Your fingers pressed into the wood of the sill, your grip so strong you think you could tear the house to splinters if you wanted. It's all there, your rage and your sadness, threatening to split you apart if you let it. And then you sigh, the release of a breath held within you since the day you were born.

How did Mim do it, you wonder? All those years ago, when she let go of your hand, when she took her place here, away from you, away from everything. You didn't think to ask her, could only look at the babe as she left, your insides wrenching as though the labor pains had started all over again.

But now your thoughts stretch outward. The babe. Mikkel and Birgit. The home you'd built together. All of it ripped away from you. And it's the ignorance that gets you, like a shiver of weakness in your knees. That you won't know how they'll fare without you. You won't hear the babe's first laugh or watch her take her first tottering steps. You won't even know what name they'll give her until she comes back to you, when it's her turn to find her way into the woods and look for the crumbling house in the middle of nowhere.

You tip your head back, looking at the ceiling, seeing nothing. The house is as large as you want it to be, but the emptiness is suffocating. The drip of a tap, the thump of a footstep, of a dropped book, of a word, a touch, a kiss. Anything, you think. You want to hear anything that's not the flutter of your own heart, the ringing in your own ears.

You'll see her again. You tell yourself as you step back, as your nails scrape over the windowsill, some of the paint stripped from the wood. And she'll have Birgit and Mikkel until then. Mikkel's strength and Birgit's wisdom. And you hope…

A catch in your throat. Thick and heavy, along with the pressure behind your eyes.

You hope she'll know how much you love her. And that she won't ever blame you for it.

Quenby Olson

Quenby Olson
writes what she knows,
which is utter chaos and cake.
(And all of her rampant
thoughts in parentheses.)

Find out more about Quenby Olson at
quenbyolson.wordpress.com

VIRGINIA MCCLAIN

For Mom—You may have loved me more, but I miss you every day and always will

Thief

Virginia McClain

"On second thought, a magic sword is probably not enough to save my ass," I mutter, as blood drips down my hands. I grit my teeth against the wounds tearing the skin of my arms and spit on the rocks at my feet. Ignore that the spit is mostly red, as I adjust my grip on the sword that probably won't save me. When I inhale, the sting of sulfur hits the back of my throat and sweat drips down my face.

I shift again, trying not to look at the corpses surrounding me in various stages of decay. Some look barely cold, like they might hop up and rejoin the fight if not for the gaping wounds that mar them, others are little more than bone-colored dust. My grip is weaker now, the hilt of the sword slipping, and I utter a low snarl as I muster the energy to raise the blade once more.

"You are persistent, small one," a voice growls from above me. Her crimson, plated skin is slick with seeping green fluid from the few gashes my sword has managed to inflict. "But it's clear you've never done battle with that weapon. Why do you not admit defeat? I will even let you live if you turn away now."

"You're the Time Guardian, aren't you?" I ask, even though I already know the answer. I wouldn't be risking my ass fighting her with an ancient, rune-covered short sword if she weren't.

I crane my neck to catch the gaze that towers at least ten feet above me. She nods but makes no move to attack.

"Then I have to get past you. You can stand aside if you like," I offer. "I don't have any particular interest in fighting you."

The Guardian emits a low rumble that shakes the cavern walls and has all the menace of an approaching storm, and it takes me a terrifying moment to realize the sound is laughter. The horns that top her enormous head are as long as I am tall, and I'm not short. Not for a human anyway. Clearly for a… whatever *she* is, I'd be laughably small. Then again, maybe her outlandish size is how she got this job. I have no idea. She's the first Guardian I've ever seen. Hopefully, she'll be the last. In addition to being enormous, horned, fanged, and bleeding an alarming shade of green, she is also faster than someone her size has any right to be, and her claws are as sharp as my sword.

I'm surprised I'm still alive.

"You have not even trained as a warrior, yet you would throw your life away just to reach a treasure you cannot possibly understand?"

Her voice, and her words, send fear clawing up my spine.

"Oh, I understand it well enough. And you're wrong about not training as a warrior. I've never trained with a sword like this," I pause and gesture with the short sword I hold, though my grip is steadily weakening. The gash in my upper arm isn't making me any stronger, that's for damned sure. "But this isn't my first fight."

The Guardian tilts her head to one side and nods ever so slightly.

"You surely would not be alive if it were," she admits.

"I was told that nothing but this sword would penetrate your skin. I figured fighting awkwardly was preferable to dying."

"You do value your life, then?"

"Of course, I do. I'm not here to die. Only…" I think about what I *am* here for. "I need Time."

"Time cannot return you to the way things were," she says, and now her voice, which had been a distant, angry thunder before, is more like a soothing caress.

"I know," I reply. The steadiness of my voice surprises me, but I didn't spend a year searching the world's oldest libraries and the past month scouring the most remote mountain range just to have this Guardian tell me nothing will change. "I'm very aware of its limitations."

"Yet you would still fight me for… what, precisely?"

"Just a few more minutes," I say.

The Guardian looks at me and flames flare behind her enormous black eyes. I can feel heat prickling all over my skin, and I flinch but I don't step back. If she can set me on fire with little more than a thought, running isn't going to help. This is either a test, or it's my death and I'm not moving unless there's a tactical advantage to it. In three heartbeats, the heat vanishes.

"You speak the truth," she says, stepping aside.

I won't lie, I gawk for a minute. I mean, I came in here expecting to have to fight some monster to the death, and now the monster is just letting me waltz right past her? It's got to be a trick.

I look pointedly at the myriad corpses around me.

"You expect me to believe I just get to walk past you?"

"You expect me to have been slain repeatedly by the thousands who have challenged me? There is but one Guardian, small one. There has only ever been but one."

"But the legend says—"

"The 'legend' is meant to give hope to the hopeless, be a warning to the careless, and a deterrent to the thoughtless. I cannot be defeated with *any* weapon, though some may tear my flesh," she says.

When I still don't move, she sighs, and that noise from such a huge and intimidating being is almost comical. If I hadn't known she was an immortal Guardian, I would have sworn she'd just rolled her eyes.

"I grant you access. Do you no longer wish it? It will change nothing, you know."

"Nothing but *me*," I reply.

The Guardian's lips curl upwards around her giant, pointed teeth and I'm surprised to recognize it as a smile.

"Nothing but you," she agrees.

I drop the sword on the ground and take a hesitant step toward the narrow stone bridge that leads across the chasm below.

"Sorry," I say, turning to her as I pass by. When she raises an eyebrow at me in response, I clarify. "About the cuts. I didn't want to hurt you, I just… thought it was the only way."

Both of her eyebrows rise then, and she shrugs.

"Part of the job," she allows. "They will heal soon enough."

I pretend I don't see her step on the short sword covered in runes that I'd brought with me, the one I'd spent months seeking out and weeks practicing with just to be competent enough to even get a few cuts in against the Guardian. I ignore the crunch it makes as enormous hooves grind it into the stone. Instead, I focus on the bridge that spans the chasm, doing my best not to look at the endless depths below. There are no guardrails, of course, just sheer death on either side.

"Low risk, high consequence," I mutter.

I point my feet ahead and keep my eyes on the rock in front of me. The bridge is so narrow, I can't imagine the Guardian crossing it. I wonder if she ever has but decide it's none of my business. Maybe she has wings. Maybe she never needs to cross this thing. Maybe she has exceptionally good balance. I'm not even sure why I'm thinking about it except to distract myself from the seriously pants-shitting void to either side.

Before I can come up with more inane distractions, I find I'm across the bridge, on the opposite ledge of the chasm.

Relief floods me, the rush of finding myself still alive with two feet on a carved stone floor. It's hard to believe I'm standing in another part of this night dark cavern instead of splatted at the bottom of an unfathomable void or skewered on the end of a razor-sharp talon. I did it! Which means there's nothing left between me and…

My eyes focus through the darkness. Ahead of me is a small, brightly glowing gem suspended in a column of light. The gem is every color the human eye can behold, sometimes all at once and sometimes in cascading succession. The space around me is so dark that it's as though nothing else exists but me, the gem, and the column of light. Not the chasm. Not the bridge that spanned it. Not the Guardian before the bridge. Nothing. I don't dare turn around to see if it's true or not. I have no interest in knowing if the Guardian is watching my progress or off sharpening her talons, and I'd just as soon forget the chasm exists.

I place one careful foot before the other, ignoring the sharp pain in my sliced arm, and the dull ache in my tired legs. One painful step at a time, the distance between me and the gem falls away and I reach out. I know I can't take it with me, but I need to touch it to do what I've come here to do.

The moment my fingers graze the gem my body goes rigid, and I don't even have time to register the sensation properly before everything fades to black.

I open my eyes and find myself in a hospital room. The constant beeping of monitors is the only sound besides the rasp of a CPAP machine forcing air into reluctant lungs.

There she is.

Lying with her eyes closed, the clear mask over her nose and mouth doing its best to give her life. I know it's not enough; I know that all too soon it will be a tube instead of a mask, and that won't be enough either.

I sit in the chair beside the bed and reach for her hand with trembling fingers.

"Mom?" My voice is far steadier than it has any right to be.

Her eyes open and she smiles at me. I can see the smile in her eyes even though I can barely see her mouth beneath the mask.

She reaches up to pull her mask down, but I stop her with my free hand and hold her hands with mine.

I can see her mouth my name, and I nod, forcing back tears.

"I think you're supposed to keep the mask on, Mom."

She rolls her eyes, as though the whole thing is just some silly inconvenience and I laugh. She looks me over and smiles again but then frowns when she sees the cut on my shoulder.

"You're hurt." I can just barely hear the words through the mask, but I know she's not supposed to take it off for long and there's more I want to say.

"It was hard to get here." I don't know how to explain any of this. Getting here was impossible, not just hard.

Mom's eyes darken, so I smile and squeeze her hands. "Totally worth it, though."

The smile returns to her eyes, and, not knowing what else to do, I catch her up on everything that's been going on lately. I tell her how her grandkids are doing, how her kids are doing, how I'm doing. I skip the bits about finding the Guardian, the sword, the fight. It's the kind of story she'd love as long as it happened to someone else, as pages in a book. But it won't make sense to her now, and I don't know how to explain it as anything more than a story I've written, and there are other things I want to say.

I take a deep breath. I want to tell her the important parts: how she made me the person I am today; how I can never thank her properly for everything she taught me; what I learned from the challenges she faced, all the obstacles she overcame... and the ones she didn't. I'm so grateful for the love she gave me and the love she gave my daughter. I wish that we could see more of her, that my daughter could still grow up with her. But I can't say any of that. The same reasons that held my tongue the first time stay it now. She's still trying to get better, and she refuses to believe that there won't be a hundred more tomorrows, a thousand, a lifetime of them and I'm not going to break the fragile hope that's keeping her afloat by saying something that sounds far too much like goodbye, even though that's exactly what I came here to do.

"I love you, Mom."

She reaches for the mask on her mouth, and I let her because as much as I want to stretch this moment out into forever, I know it's time for me to go.

"I love you more," she replies, with what little breath she can get.

I don't argue. I used to. We'd go back and forth like a bad rom-com couple trying to say goodbye, right up until the day that I had my daughter. The day I realized that my mom absolutely loved me more than I loved her, even though that had never seemed possible.

"I know," I agree, grinning even while tears spill down my cheeks. "But it's pretty close."

"No, it isn't," she says, as we both laugh. "I thought you couldn't get here?"

I can tell it's a question and it's not one I know how to answer.

"I couldn't. The borders are closed. I came anyway." That's true enough, in its own way.

She smiles again, and her eyes close for a second.

"I thought this was a dream," she says, smiling.

I hold her hands and lean forward to kiss her cheeks.

"Maybe it is," I whisper.

I settle the mask back on her face and her smiling eyes open again.

"I love you," she says again, through the mask.

"I love you too, Mom. So much."

She nods and closes her eyes, and I know she needs to rest. I give her one last hug. I try not to think of how frail she feels in my arms and focus instead on how good it feels to hold her. She's already asleep again by the time I let go.

Suddenly, I'm standing in front of a sparkling gem within a column of light, surrounded by darkness.

I turn to find the Guardian standing between me and the bridge.

"I guess you can cross that thing, then," I mutter.

She ignores me and gestures at the gem.

"Did you do what you intended?"

I nod, wiping tears from my cheeks and my nose on my blood-soaked sleeve.

"Did it help?" she asks.

I shrug.

"You were right; it didn't change anything."

But even as I say the words, I know they aren't true. My heart feels a bit lighter, despite the tears that wet my cheeks. Holding her one more time helped. It isn't enough. It could never be enough. But that is the fuckery of death. That is the thievery of time.

I half expect the Guardian to cut me down, or at least bar me from leaving, but after considering me for a moment, she simply steps aside.

I walk past her but stop just before the bridge.

"Was it real?" I ask, not turning back.

"Does it matter?"

I shrug and start walking again.

"It was as real as I am," she says to my back.

I nod and walk on, my eyes already turned toward the world that awaits me beyond these dark caverns; a life I love, a partner who loves me, and a child who argues whenever I tell her I love her more.

Virginia McClain

Virginia McClain is an author who masqueraded as a language teacher for a decade or so. When she's not reading or writing she can generally be found playing outside with her four legged adventure buddy and the tiny human she helped to build from scratch. She enjoys climbing to the top of tall rocks, running through deserts, mountains, and woodlands, and carrying a foldable home on her back whenever she gets a chance. She's also fond of word games, and writing descriptions of herself that are needlessly vague.

Find out more about Virginia McClain at
virginiamcclain.ca

Thicker Than Water

Carol A. Park

Thicker Than Water

CAROL A. PARK

Danton glanced out the window at the darkening sky. "Come on, Loena. We need to *go*."

Danton's younger sister flicked her hand at him. "Ugh, you're as bad as Mama."

"Sit still," Freena said through pins in her mouth as she wound a lock of Loena's hair around the mound already placed. "I almost have it."

Danton exhaled. "Freena, Mama told me to come get her," he said, trying to reason with his oldest sister. There were six of them altogether in his family, ranging from twelve to twenty years old, and Freena was the oldest and recently married. Appeals to her newfound maturity usually worked. "The sky-fire is going to start *any minute*. You can play with her hair another day."

Freena slipped a final pin triumphantly into place. "There." She handed Loena a hand mirror. "What do you think?"

"For Temoth's sake," Danton said. "I'm leaving. If you want to be eaten by bloodbane, be my guest." He turned and headed toward the door.

"Go on then," Loena said. "I'll stay with Freena this sky-fire." She glanced at Freena hopefully.

Freena sighed. "Mama wants you back with the family. Maybe next year. Go on. Shoo."

Loena handed the mirror back to Freena and stood. "Gods, I can't even remember the last time a bloodbane appeared *here*," she muttered.

Danton pulled her out the door and onto the street, one eye on the sky. Even in their little country town, bloodbane appeared nearly every year at the sky-fire, but normally no one saw it happen because they were hiding in their cellars.

He remembered the last time someone *had* seen it, though. "Three years ago."

"It was just one of those bird things. So, some cattle got dragged off. *Big deal.*" Loena rolled her eyes, clearly annoyed at being contradicted. "You're *such* a bore."

Right, big deal. Unlike Loena, Danton had seen what remained of those cattle. Whole cows, ripped to shreds. Body parts and entrails strewn across the fields, bloody bits and chunks *he*—thirteen at the time and deemed old enough—had had to help clean up.

All that by a so-called *bird*. "Mama said to come get you, I came and got you. Quit dragging your feet before you get both of us in trouble."

They approached a dilapidated house, the door broken, chimney crumbling. Also, unlike her, he remembered the rumors from six years ago, when the sweet old couple that had lived in that house had just…disappeared.

After that sky-fire, neither husband nor wife had been heard from again. Some said one of them had been changed to a Banebringer—someone given unnatural powers by the illegal gods they worshipped—then murdered their spouse and ran into the night. Some said they'd already been secret Banebringers, and they'd been torn to shreds by bloodbane they'd summoned at the sky-fire. But no one could remember if they'd ever seen one of them bleed.

Still others said one had been changed and apprehended by the Conclave in the night—and the other executed for trying to stop them. The Conclave was ruthless in not only hunting down Banebringers but also punishing those who harbored them.

All they knew was that blood was found on the floor of their house in the morning, and some of it was silver, which was a trait shared by both Banebringers and bloodbane.

Their house was an eyesore among the otherwise well-maintained homes along the road, but since that day, no one had dared set foot in the house, as though it might be cursed.

He shuddered, quickening his steps as they passed; it was creepy, and the sky had turned inky black, a dark canvas waiting for those first streaks of angry, glowing red—a sure sign the sky-fire would begin any moment now.

"Quit dragging your feet before you get both of us in trouble," Loena mimicked, interrupting his thoughts.

"Temoth, you're annoying," Danton snapped. "I hope you do get eaten." His steps quickened as their house came into view, but Loena skipped ahead, outpacing him, then turned at the front door and stuck her tongue out before going inside.

Great. Now she was going to tell their mother it was *his* fault they were late before he had a chance to give his side of the story.

Not that it wasn't sometimes his fault when they got in trouble. But not the night of the sky-fire.

He entered the house after Loena and slammed the door behind him, relieved to be back inside the relative safety of his home.

By the time he reached the kitchen, his mother had already loaded Loena down with a basket of food. His sister was disappearing out the kitchen door while his mother waited for him, slapping a towel against her thigh. "I don't even want to know," she said. "Just get down into the cellar."

As if her words were a cue, they both turned to look out the window.

The first embers were falling, fiery claw marks against a black sky.

He didn't need any more encouragement than that.

Loena could dismiss the bloodbane all she wanted. Now that they were all huddled in the cellar, tension was etched on every face— including hers. It broke when his father shut the cellar door with a loud thud, and everyone jumped.

Then Lakyn, Danton's only brother, challenged him to a game of cards, and as with every sky-fire Danton could remember, his family settled in for a long, watchful, and ultimately uneventful night.

Out here in the country, bloodbane pulled through the veil between the human world and the abyss usually ran away. Most of the time, the only evidence that one had spawned was a missing chicken or an upturned water trough.

It was worse in the cities. When tears in the veil appeared—as they did everywhere, by the thousands, during the annual sky-fire when the veil was at its weakest—the bloodbane that broke through had nowhere to go. Driven mad by walls and buildings on every side, all but the most benign caused property damage, and the gods forbid they run into people.

And the worst of them? They just wanted carnage.

So he'd heard from the stories traders told when passing through. He'd lived here in the endless plains of Arlana his entire life, so he didn't know *personally*.

Lakyn snapped his fingers in front of Danton's face. "Come on, it's your *turn*."

Danton blinked. "Oh. Sorry." He set a card down, not paying attention to his move. He shuddered, an unseasonable chill running through him; the cellar was cooler, but not *that* cold. Then he began to sweat.

Temoth. He hoped he wasn't getting sick.

Suddenly, Loena shrieked. Danton didn't turn, expecting she'd lost a pin from her hair or some such nonsense, but when his mother gasped and called his father's name, he paid attention.

He turned and saw it.

A dark slash rent the air near the year's first harvests, in front of the shelves and to the right of the door. The tear grew longer and wider as he watched, as if giant, invisible hands were ripping the space in two. The baskets of peas and early potatoes were a dark, distorted blur behind the hole, and black flames licked out of it.

"What's that?" one of his younger sisters, Kija, asked, her voice shaking.

"Oh, gods," another sister, Kataryn, said. "Papa? Is that—?"

Their father was already striding toward the cellar door, giving the tear a wide berth. "Out, get out—all of you—now!"

Then Danton understood. Panic sent him in the wrong direction, backing into a far corner rather than the now-open cellar door.

"But," Loena protested, "it's the sky-fire!"

"It's a tear! Get out! Get *out*!" their father shouted, which was unusual for him. He never yelled. Their mother was the yeller in the family.

The tear now stretched from floor to ceiling, and no sooner did his father finish speaking than the first rat emerged from the hole.

Not just any rat. It was a bloodrat, a demon rat from the abyss —twice the size of the largest rat he'd ever seen, with white, pupilless eyes and a mouth lined with razor-sharp teeth.

One bloodrat was dangerous enough, but they never came alone. Instead, like normal rats, they traveled in packs. Two or three could swarm a grown man and gnaw him to the bone—so said the traders, anyway.

The rodents poured through the tear until there had to be more than half a dozen.

For a split-second, the rats thronged around the tear in confusion. Danton, or any of the others, might have used that time to make a break for the door. But the unnatural shrieks emitting from the rats' mouths kept most of his family petrified. Their father stood outside the door shouting, but his words were lost in the haze that had become Danton's mind.

Then, as the traders said, the demons went mad. Their lips curled to reveal their teeth, like snarling, feral dogs, and they charged Loena.

She screamed.

The sound roused everyone. His mother, who had been paralyzed with shock along with the rest of them, now sprang into action. She grabbed a broom, leapt in front of Loena, and began whacking the creatures with strength Danton didn't know she had.

The door was only a few feet away, and yet Loena still stood, slack-jawed, face pale.

"Move, stupid!" Danton shouted at her, and when she just swiveled her head to stare at him blankly, he launched himself at her, pushing her out of the way.

Just in time. One of the rats bypassed his mother's valiant efforts and skidded to a stop right where Loena had been.

Danton could have sworn its shriek was angry as it turned and lurched toward them. He tried to kick at it, but Loena clutched him so tight he had a hard time getting leverage. His foot landed, but not hard enough to fling it away; instead, it bit the end of his boot, just missing his toe.

He shook his leg frantically, and the monster let go, if only to better screech at him.

Then, *finally*, his mother managed to whack one of the rats through the door and out the cellar. Following that one's unintentional lead, like a flock of birds scattering from a tree, the rest of the rats scampered away.

His father slammed the door shut behind them. The sound seemed to echo, despite the dampening effect of the dirt floor.

Silence reigned for a long moment. Loena, trembling, still clung to him, and Kija to Kataryn.

Danton drew in long, shaky breaths, as though he had been the one engaged in martial broom combat like his mother, though the whole nightmarish scene must have taken less than thirty seconds.

Lakyn ran to an empty bucket and vomited.

The sound of his coughing and hacking and the smell of bile broke the spell.

Loena pushed Danton away at last, though she still trembled. "Gross, Lakyn."

"I'm sorry," Lakyn said, wiping his mouth. "I just…I'm sorry."

"It's okay, sweetheart," his mother said, stepping toward him.

"Mama, I'm *fine*," Lakyn snapped.

"We're all okay," his mother said aloud, as if to reassure herself rather than them. His father stepped over to her, and she turned and pressed her face against his chest.

Danton tried to relax now that the danger had passed, but he found himself unsteady on his feet, his limbs quavering. He'd heard about the tears between worlds at the sky-fire, but never seen one himself. He had always been tucked safely in their cellar with the rest of his family.

Though, safety was relative. It wasn't so safe if a tear formed in your cellar or safe room. The best you could hope for was to get out—or get the bloodbane out—before someone was maimed or killed.

"It could have been worse," his father said. "Just some bloodrats. It could have been far worse."

Just some bloodrats.

He shuddered at the thought of how close they'd all come to being gnawed to death by those tiny teeth. He'd rather go in one big chomp than that. A bloodwolf would do the job.

"They'll be in the grain," his mother said, and the concern struck Danton as oddly out of place.

Danton's siblings roused themselves.

Kataryn set Lakyn's smelly bucket near the cellar door and tossed a rag overtop.

Lakyn settled himself on his crate, picked up his hand of cards and stared at them blankly.

Kija shadowed Kataryn. Loena went back to playing with her hair, though her hands shook.

But Danton watched his parents, his neck crawling. He couldn't shake his feeling of trepidation, even though the immediate danger had passed.

His father was murmuring to Danton's mother, too quietly for Danton to understand the words, but there was something… *something* in his tone.

His mother's voice rose. "We can do it later. Not now. Let's just get through this night."

Huh? Do what?

"Better to be armed with the knowledge than taken by surprise," his father replied.

His mother closed her eyes. "I don't want to know."

What in the abyss were they talking about?

His parents shared a cryptic look, then turned toward their children. Tears shimmered on his mother's eyelashes. "It was random," she said softly. "It had to be."

"Perhaps," his father said, "but the odds are so low…"

The prickles in Danton's neck intensified, spread through his whole body, as he finally realized what they were talking about.

There were two reasons tears formed at the sky-fire. First, tears were created by Banebringers to summon bloodbane from the abyss to the human world while the veil was weak. The Conclave said the demonspawn didn't have control over where the tears were formed; they created them to cause chaos.

And second, some tears were caused by the creation of new Banebringers, those chosen by the heretic gods themselves to carry on their work in the mortal realm. Some said they were secret followers of the forbidden gods and had performed some ritual to gain their powers. Others said they were those who had such strong evil in their hearts, it called to the gods at the sky-fire.

The Conclave said both could be true.

His mother insisted the tear had to be random; one of those created by a Banebringer far away, which just happened to form on their tiny square of the continent.

His father thought that was unlikely. Which meant he was suggesting that one of *them* had been chosen by the heretic gods.

Danton dismissed his father's opinion. It couldn't be true; his mother had to be right. None of *them* were followers of the heretic gods, and while Loena was annoying, she wasn't *evil*. It was coincidence. *It has to be*, he thought, echoing his mother's own words.

Then why, despite his mother's words, did she look so distraught?

Loena had started paying attention to their parents as well. Her eyes darted back and forth between them. "What odds?" she asked. "What are you talking about?"

Their father drew in a deep breath. "Everyone, gather round. We're going to have to test the whole family."

Test? *Test?* They were going to draw blood? It was the only way to know for sure, because Banebringers had silver blood, but still…

He wasn't the only one who balked at the notion; multiple exclamations of protest filled the cellar.

His father held up his hand, and they quieted. "It's better to know."

Danton stole a glance at his mother. Her eyes were downcast, but she didn't argue.

"Your mother and I will go first. Loena, may I borrow one of those pins?"

Loena mutely withdrew one of the pins from her hair, and a lock fell, framing her face. She handed it to their father.

He pricked his finger and then Danton's mother's. Tiny drops of blood welled. They stared at them, holding their breath, but both drops were a deep ruby red.

"Oldest to youngest, then, quickly," his mother said. "Let's get this over with." Her tears were gone now, her face pale, her jaw set.

They quietly arranged themselves in order, and his father moved down the line, pricking each of their fingers in turn.

A few seconds passed, and all their little drops welled up red. "Well, see? Just a random—" his mother began.

"Look at Danton's!" Loena shrieked.

What? Danton thought. He looked down again at his finger, along with the rest of them. Where once there had been red was now silver. He stared at the silver dot, his mind slow to process. It had been red seconds ago!

He tried to wipe the silver away, but it was no longer liquid; it disintegrated into dust. Another red drop welled up—*see, red*! But as they watched, it *shimmered*, changed to silver, and hardened.

No.

No.

No.

His mind latched onto the single-word refrain. There had to be a mistake.

His father's hand moved to his mother's forearm.

"Danton?" his mother whispered, a plea for an explanation he didn't have.

Danton flicked the silver away, rubbed the spot desperately, then pressed his finger against it to keep more awful silver dots from appearing and glanced around the room. Everyone was staring at him. "I-I don't worship the heretic gods," he protested. "I don't." He *didn't*. Even as he said the words, he doubted himself. Had he done something, said something, *anything* to draw their attention? He couldn't have. Yet, that silver blood was undeniable evidence that he had been chosen as a Banebringer.

No. No. No. He couldn't comprehend it. He couldn't think it. He couldn't accept it. The consequences were too much to bear.

"You said earlier you hoped I would get eaten by a bloodbane!" Loena accused.

He held his shaking hands up. "I-I was *kidding*."

She backed away from him. "You set them on me! They came straight toward me! Didn't everyone see?"

"Loena," Danton said over a strangled chuckle, "that's ridiculous. I tried to *save* you—"

"Mama saved me," she said. "*You*—"

"All right," his father said. "I'm sure Danton didn't set anything on you, Loena." His voice was calm, but there was the slightest catch.

Just the slightest. It was enough.

Desperation welled in his chest. His mother—his mother would help. "Mama? You have to believe me. I don't worship the heretic gods. I'm not evil. I don't understand why this is happening."

She shook her head, a hand to her mouth.

"He *is* evil," Loena declared. "I always knew it."

"*Loena*," her father said sharply.

Danton backed into the corner of the cellar and searched every face, desperately seeking some assurance, for someone to concede it had been a mistake, to stand up for him, side with him.

But his father's eyes were to the ground, despite his reprimand to Loena. His mother avoided his gaze, as well, and that subtle lack of acknowledgment, to match her lack of reassurance just moments ago, was a blade slipped between his ribs.

As for the rest of them—

Lakyn's eyes were wide, curious. Kija gave him an uncertain side-eye. Kataryn's face was pale.

Loena—her eyes were daggers. Gods, he'd been horrible to her sometimes, but only because she was horrible to him! He didn't *actually* want her eaten—how could she think that? What about the time he'd carried her a mile home when she'd broken her ankle after jumping a fence?

When she'd fallen ill with a dangerous fever, who had done her chores without complaint for a month? *Him.*

And when Kija, who was normally Loena's choice of playmate, had fallen ill with the same fever, who had been the one to play her silly pretend games with her? *Him.*

She was annoying, but she was his *sister*, for Temoth's sake.

He had to have drawn the heretic gods' notice by what he had said to her. It was his fault—somehow—what other explanation could there be? But he didn't want this. He didn't *want* this! Why would they have chosen *him*? *Take it back!* he wanted to scream at the sky, but his throat had closed tight.

"Well, there's nothing we can do about it right now," his father said, as if there was anything they could do about it, ever. "We still have to wait out the rest of the sky-fire. We'll discuss it in the morning."

The night had been long.

They had spoken little, and Danton found himself huddled on his blanket in his corner of the cellar, alone amongst six other people. The night of the sky-fire was never restful; that one had been a nightmare. At times, he wanted to reason with his family, convince them he had nothing to do with this, figure out what was going on, but the furtive looks he received when he even dared glance someone's way were enough to stop his mouth.

Stopping his mind was much more difficult. The Conclave was kind to neither Banebringers nor those who harbored them. When his mind wasn't racing with all the outcomes the next day might bring, he found himself silently pleading with the heretic gods—whichever one might listen—that this had been some mistake, they'd chosen the wrong person. And then he realized, with no small amount of horror, that that might qualify as *praying* to illegal gods.

If he'd managed to fall asleep, he might've dared believe it had actually been a nightmare, but he hadn't even closed his eyes.

Dawn broke, and the moment his father opened the cellar door, Danton escaped into the room he and Lakyn shared.

He sank down onto his bed. Despite the fear that tiny dot of silver had engendered in him the previous night, a morbid, desperate sense of hope led him to find his pocketknife and prick his finger once more, just to make sure…

He stared at the blood that welled up. *Stay red, stay red, stay red…*

It changed to silver, then hardened.

He clenched both fists, one around the pocketknife and one around that dot of silver, crushing it against his hand. It wasn't fair. How could they look at him like that, like he'd committed a terrible crime and they no longer knew him? Like they'd *never* known him?

The creak of the door opening made him look up.

Lakyn stood in the doorway of their room, now frozen in place. His eyes flicked to Danton's knife, then to his face.

Danton flicked the knife shut and set it on his bed. "What?" he snapped.

Lakyn edged into the room and shut the door. "Can I see it again?" he whispered.

Danton stared at him. "See *what?*"

"You know." Lakyn gestured vaguely. "Your silver blood."

Danton gritted his teeth. He'd been changed into a Banebringer, and *that's* all Lakyn could think about? What was he, some sort of circus curiosity now?

"What did you have to do?" Lakyn asked eagerly, voice low.

Danton blinked, taken aback. "What?"

"Did you have to exchange something in blood sacrifice or something?"

Danton stood up, fingernails digging into his palms. "I didn't do anything!"

Lakyn cast him a look askance. "Right, right. Come on. You can tell me."

The implication that Lakyn didn't *believe* him cut deep. "*I didn't do anything!*"

Lakyn backed away from him. "Just calm down, okay?"

"Calm *down?*" Danton asked, his voice rising despite attempts to control it. "You want me to calm *down?*"

With a frightened glance at him, Lakyn fled the room.

Danton stood, clenching and unclenching his fist, his blood boiling.

He shuddered. It literally felt like his blood was boiling, but without the pain. His flash of panic at *that* lasted until he glanced down at his hand, and—

Was that *light* coming from his hand?

Gods—yes, it was. His entire hand shone with light, except not red or orange like fire, but more like a sunbeam piercing clouds.

He waved it around frantically, trying to get it to stop, and it did, along with the uncomfortable bubbling sensation inside of him.

As though he could flee from himself, his feet took over and his knees buckled as he bumped into the bed behind him. He sank down onto it and raised the offending hand, trembling, and turned it back and forth. What had that been? How had he done it? Burning skies, what was happening to him?

There was no one to ask, no one to turn to. No one could help him.

His entire existence was now anathema.

Fear choked his throat; for a moment, he couldn't breathe. He swallowed until he could gasp for air, then gulped until his breathing settled into a steady rhythm.

He leaned forward, his hands gripping the bed on either side of him, his eyes closed.

They'd figure out what to do in the morning, that's what his father had said. He'd see what they were going to do. That was all. They'd figure this out, right? Maybe no one needed to know, or…or…

His mind scrambled for more options and came up frighteningly blank. And that was why he needed to talk to his parents. They'd have a plan.

He left his room with new determination, walked to the top of the stair, and nearly ran into Kataryn on the landing.

"Wha—" he exclaimed.

She put a finger to her lips and jerked her head toward the bottom of the stairs, which ended in the kitchen.

He halted and listened; his parents were speaking in hushed voices—he had to strain to hear.

"…in danger if we're found harboring him," his father was saying.

"No one knows but us," his mother said. "We have some time."

A long silence, then: "Yes," his father said. "We have some time, but he can't stay here for long; you know that. We have to think about what's best for our family."

There was a rustling sound, and then his mother's voice again, this time muffled. "…don't understand…"

Danton backed away from the stairs. He didn't want to hear more. It was all about the danger *they* were in, what was best for *them.*

What about the danger *he* was in? If the Conclave found out—

But, no. He couldn't think about that right now. It was bad enough to realize that his parents weren't discussing how to help *him,* how to save *him.* Only themselves.

And he wasn't part of *them* anymore.

He put a hand on the banister, a solid post amidst shifting sand.

How—how could that be—how could that change so quickly—

"Run, Danton," Kataryn said, her voice low.

"What?" he said, dumbfounded.

"You have to run." Her eyes were serious, her face pale.

"I—but—" His head spun.

She shook her head emphatically. "If the Conclave finds you, we're all in danger. Get out of here before it's too late. This doesn't end well, for any of us."

His chest squeezed, and he gripped the rail tighter. "Any of us?" he choked out. "Am I included in that '*us*'?"

Kataryn looked to the side. "I don't understand what's happening, but I know you. You're my little brother." Even so, she avoided his gaze. "And I've heard enough stories to know they'll find you. Papa's right. If you're found here…"

She didn't have to finish. Danton *knew* what could happen. They'd all heard the stories. They'd heard the traveling priest preach against the evil Banebringers—and warn that Temoth's wrath would fall upon those who helped them.

"I don't want *any* of us hurt," she finished quietly.

By that you mean the rest of you, he thought bitterly. Just like Mama and Papa. Because, obviously, *he* would be hurt, one way or the other.

"Where would I go?" he whispered, not because he didn't want to be heard, but because his voice was stuck in his throat.

She looked as helpless as he felt.

His so-called family left Danton alone for the rest of the day. Whether that was out of fear or respect for his privacy, he didn't know. Either way, it wasn't what he wanted. He wanted his mother or father to tell him it would all be okay. They'd get through this, together, as a family. Like they always had.

He lay on his bed, staring at the ceiling, Kataryn's words echoing in his mind. *Run.*

Run? It was unfathomable. How would he survive? He knew nothing but this little town; he'd been born and raised here, sixteen years. His family, his friends…how could they stand by and do nothing?

How could it all disappear, just like that?

He didn't need to run. No one knew about his change, just like his mother said. Only their family. As long as no one said anything…

He sat up. He'd been lying in bed all day. He'd missed breakfast, and lunch, and now the sky was deepening and he was hungry. They'd left him alone, but no one brought him food. He supposed they thought evil Banebringers didn't need to eat.

When he made his way to the kitchen, he found his mother standing at the kitchen table, peeling potatoes, and talking in low tones to Kataryn, who sat chopping carrots.

"Can I help with dinner?" he asked, trying to sound casual, as though this was any other day.

His mother jumped, and the knife clattered to the ground.

Danton picked it up and held it out to her, handle first.

His father appeared at the doorway. "What's going on?" he asked, and then he strode to his mother's side, as if…

As if to protect her from him? Surely not. What kind of monster did they think he was?

Hand limned in light. Boiling blood. *Silver* blood. *Was* he a monster? Maybe…Banebringers started out fine, then snapped. Maybe—But no. That couldn't be, could it? The heretic gods chose people who were already their followers, already evil…

He had no answers, and the only ones who did were the priests. And *that* was right out.

Chest squeezing once more, he put the knife on the table and took a step away, clenching his fists. "I only wanted to help," he said. "I'm not—I'm just Danton. Nothing has changed."

It was both a truth and a lie. Nothing had changed, yet everything had changed. He knew it. It just hadn't sunk in yet.

"I think you should stay in your room for now, Danton," his father said. His tone was gentle, but he still hovered near his mother, body partially in front of her. His actions spoke loudly enough, and they nullified any effort on his part to soften the blow. "We'll bring you dinner."

A knock sounded on the door.

Everyone in the kitchen stilled, all faces turned toward the door.

Run. Kataryn's words echoed in his ears.

His father broke the spell, moving to open it.

Danton held his breath, but it was only Freena.

Only Freena?

She halted when she saw Danton, and her look caused Danton's stomach to drop to his toes. It was the moment of fear, the moment of guilt—then, the way her face shuttered, as if closing him out.

She knew. She knew, which meant someone in their family had told her.

Then two Watchmen moved into their kitchen behind Freena, one older with a full beard, and one younger and clean-shaven.

Fingers of ice wrapped themselves around his chest. No one moved except his mother, who stepped reflexively toward Danton. Hope guttered briefly. Yes, his mother, surely his mother… *Mama*, he wanted to plead. *Please. Do something. Fix this.*

But she stopped short of coming to him. That stutter of movement spoke louder than any words, a punch to the gut—his hope snuffed out like a candle.

His father didn't move. Neither did Kataryn. And neither did Danton, his feet frozen in place, his breath loud in his ears, and the world around him at a standstill.

Freena stepped out of the way of the Watchmen, her hands wringing her apron.

"Da," the bearded Watchman said to his mother. "I'm looking for a young man named Danton."

His mother was pale. She glanced at his father, then at Freena.

"Loena told me," Freena said. "I… had to…" She swallowed. "Papa, we have no choice." Her face was pleading, her voice cracked. "You must know that."

Danton's limbs started to quake. Try as he might, he couldn't still them, and his teeth began to chatter as though he were freezing. His heart jumped about, skipping every other beat, and the room swam in front of him. *This can't be happening. This can't be happening.*

They'd not only found him, but his own sister had turned him in.

The ground roiled beneath him. He stepped back and put a hand on the table, fearing he might fall; his entire body was wracked with tremors. Why couldn't he stop shaking? *Stop, stop, stop!*

His movement drew the attention of the Watchman who had spoken. Apparently, the guard needed no further confirmation. He moved swiftly toward Danton and placed one hand on his arm. "Don't fight it, son," he said, "or we'll be forced to report that to the Hunter when we deliver you. Let's make this easy on everyone." His eyes swept the room. "Anyone have any objections?"

While the Watchman's face was placid, a hint of danger bled into his tone. His other hand rested on the hilt of his sword, as did his partner's.

No one spoke. Not a word in his defense.

"Mama?" Danton asked, a plaintive note in his voice. "Please." *Something. Anything. Scream, sob, fall to the ground pleading for my life, even if it makes no difference in the end.* Anything but this suffocating silence.

Her response was to turn away from him, tears trickling down her cheeks.

Kataryn avoided his gaze, choosing, instead, to stare at the ground.

"Papa?" he tried, his eyes blurring.

"I'm sorry," his father choked out, but it rang hollow.

"You're sorry?" Danton rasped in disbelief. "You're *sorry?*" That was it? He was *sorry?* Anger flowed through his shock, molten metal pooling in his gut, and his ears began to ring.

His father held out one hand, palm up. "I'm—Danton, Freena's right. It has to be this way. They'll—our family—" He cast a hurried look at the Watchman and fell silent, as if afraid to even voice what the Conclave might do to them if they resisted.

"Our family." Of which he was no longer a part.

It had only been theory until this moment. Danton finally knew, finally *believed*, that they were going to let them take him. No one was going to lie for him. No one was going to fight for him. No one was going to stand for him. No one was even going to protest, to ask for more time—make a distraction so he could get away.

He had been sacrificed for the greater good of the family.

Family. The people who were supposed to stick together no matter what. Who *had* been there, no matter what, up until that moment. Snatches of desperate examples flashed through his mind. His siblings' games and good-natured teasing, his mother's lullabies, his father's strong hands, a kiss to the knee when he fell, a kiss on the brow after a nightmare, sky-fire after sky-fire, huddled together, together, *together.*

His family was his refuge, his sure place—no matter what, he could return to it. How could a fortress that had felt so unassailable suddenly crumble like this? No, not crumble—the fortress hadn't crumbled. They had shut the gates, and he was no longer allowed inside; a stranger—a *danger.*

It had all been torn away from him in a moment, as though his entire life had been a façade, as though nothing was real, nothing had ever been real.

Despite his efforts, tears spilled over. The world had shifted overnight, and he had fallen into an endless nightmare—alone.

The Watchman pushed him toward the door, impervious to his anguish, unaware of the walls collapsing around him and the cracks splitting the ground beneath his feet, of the scream building in his chest, the pressure demanding release.

For one white-hazed moment, Danton's head filled with wild schemes. He'd shove the Watchman away, slip through his grasp—run, as Kataryn advised.

To where? To *whom*?

The second Watchman flanked him, and his plans turned reckless, angry. He'd grab the sword and they'd be forced to kill him. His death would spawn a bloodbane, and they'd all die. It served them right.

Horrified at how quickly his thoughts had turned to vengeance, he let his rage slough away. In the vacuum that followed was only his collapsing world.

The Watchman pushed him out the door, and he stumbled, his body shaking so hard it made walking difficult.

There, on the little dirt road outside their home, was a tiny cage set on a wagon bed.

"Please," he begged the second, younger Watchman, who had yet to speak—clawing for some shred of decency in the man. "You have to believe me. I-I didn't do anything. This isn't my fault."

The younger Watchman didn't reply, and the bearded Watchman shoved him into the cage, the man's motions getting rougher as every second passed, his initial politeness clearly a pretense. Danton lurched forward, hit the bars on the other side, barely held himself up. The cage was small, so small he'd have to curl up to lay down, so small he couldn't stand without crouching.

Iron bars shut behind him with a clang, and he whirled to clutch at them, white-knuckled. To look out over the faces in front of him. His mother stood near his father, his arm around her, her face buried in his shoulder.

Kataryn stood to the side, her hands clasped in front of her, eyes to the ground.

Freena wouldn't look at him. That was when he saw Loena.

She met his eyes. Lifted her chin. "That's what you get," his sister hissed, disgust marring her features. "Demonspawn."

No one contradicted her, and their silence seeped into his heart like poison. *Demonspawn. Is that what I am now?*

Something was dripping onto his arms, and amidst the ringing, the swaying of the world, the darkness that had gathered, it took him a moment to register it as his own tears.

Lakyn was nowhere to be found. Kija was nowhere to be found. If they knew what was happening, they didn't care.

Even neighbors had come out, a mixture of fear, disbelief, and revulsion on their faces. People he had known his whole life. He was now a scandal, a byword, an aberration.

He backed away, pressed himself against the other side of the cage. Reality closed in around him, suffocating him more than any cage could. It was a prison, locking him away from everything and everyone he'd ever known.

The Watchman smacked the horses, and the wagon lurched forward.

Danton stumbled once more but caught himself. He stayed there, plastered to the bars until the faces of his family and the only life he'd ever known faded away into the distance.

He was alone. Completely and utterly alone, and no one cared. He slid down the bars, buried his face in his knees and sobbed.

The wheels of the wagon rumbled against the country road as it crawled through the endless flat of Arlana. Danton huddled in his portable prison, his arms wrapped tightly around his knees. He had no room to stretch in this cramped cage.

His skin burned and his head pounded from exposure to the summer sun. His back cramped whenever he tried to move. He felt every jolt as the wheels dipped into ruts, every bump as they grated on rocks. Cotton filled his mouth, and his lips cracked and bled silver blood—his own body continually reminding him how he had ended up in this situation.

Reminded him? More like taunted him.

At night, he curled into a ball and shivered, no blanket and nothing to cushion him from the splintery wooden wagon bed. Between his aching muscles and racing mind, sleep was more of a haze.

Not that he expected any comforts. There was nothing for him at the end of this road. His guards only had to keep him alive long enough to get there; the idea of compassion for someone facing a death sentence never seemed to cross their minds.

He reached down and picked at the bread crusts one of the guards had thrown into the cage when they'd stopped for lunch. It was stale, but he put it in his mouth anyway, barely able to work up enough saliva to break it down. The skin of water they'd provided wasn't much better; it tasted foul, and one of the guards had spat in it before offering it to him, while the other looked on and laughed.

He'd thought about refusing to eat or drink at all. He might die of dehydration before they reached their destination, wherever that was. Maybe the bloodbane that spawned at his death would kill them, too. That would be poetic justice.

But he couldn't bring himself to that point. There was nothing for him at the end of this road, yet he ate their scraps, drank their fetid water, some dying ember of hope still pushing him to survive.

"Hey, demonspawn." The bearded guard poked him, and not gently, with the butt of his spear.

Danton didn't respond. He'd only just managed to fall asleep after another long, uncomfortable night. Instead, he curled into a tighter ball, shielding his eyes from the rising sun.

The guard poked him again, this time hard enough to bruise.

He sat up, though it cost him dearly, every muscle shrieking from cramped disuse. "Get off!" he shouted, grabbing the bars of the cage and shaking them.

They didn't even give him the satisfaction of rattling.

The guard laughed until he coughed, spittle flying into his beard. "Oh, ho, the little demon has teeth after all."

Danton gritted said teeth as tears welled in his eyes. "Just leave me alone."

Leave me to die in peace. Betrayed and alone, confused and angry, he vacillated between rage and an all-consuming grief that ate at his hope, more pernicious than the growing hunger.

The guard continued to laugh. "Or what? You'll use your demon powers on us?" He turned to his partner, perhaps hoping the other guard would share in his cruel amusement, but the other guard eyed Danton nervously.

"Perhaps you shouldn't poke a sleeping bear," the younger guard said.

Bearded waved his hand. "Eh, if he could hurt us, he would have already. You know how these new ones are. They're newborn babes, can't do anything but cry." He sneered at Danton. "Do we need to go back and drag your mama along, demonspawn, so you can suck at her tit and silence your mewling?"

The mention of his mother did him in. Danton turned away from the guards and tried unsuccessfully to master himself. Instead, he buried his face in his knees, unwilling to give them the pleasure of seeing him cry again.

He wished he knew what powers he supposedly had. He'd tried, once, in one of those ever-dwindling moments of hope, to reproduce the light from his hand, but had failed. He didn't know how it worked, and he had no one to teach him.

Not that it mattered. That light had been utterly harmless, anyway. Now, if he could light them on *fire*, that might be useful.

I'd do it, too, he thought savagely, and he'd never wished harm on anyone before.

He hadn't. Not really. Couldn't the heretic gods see that?

Or were his wild thoughts of vengeance on his family, his growing hatred for these guards, a sign of what had always lurked beneath? Perhaps he *did* deserve this. Perhaps there had always been evil within, waiting for the right moment to burst forth.

Maybe this wasn't a mistake. Maybe the priests were right. Maybe this was for the best.

He brushed angrily at the tears on his cheeks.

These moments of self-doubt were another poison to mix into the cocktail of grief and rage and hopelessness that roiled in him. It was best not to think at all.

But that, too, was denied him.

Danton stared dully out the bars of his cage at the gathered group of children. They jostled each other for position, speaking in hushed tones and giggling.

It was the same in every village they passed through. The whispers. The looks of fear, of hatred. The insults.

Even from children.

Finally, a girl from the group darted forward and hurled a small rock into the cage.

Danton didn't move. Just let it hit him on the arm. It stung, but what did it matter?

The girl darted back to the group, which waited with a collectively held breath, as though he might strike them down for her audacity.

When he did nothing, they grew bolder, chasing the wagon as it trundled down the street. "What's wrong, demonspawn?" one boy called. "Can't you save yourself?"

A few hung back, uncertain, but that was the best he got. Uncertainty, like Kataryn.

Adults pulled their children away with stern words, not out of compassion for him, but fear.

Not a few of those same adults spat on him as they passed or muttered under their breath. Others fled into their homes, slamming doors.

One small child stood in his garden while his mother weeded. He was sucking his thumb, and as they passed, he pulled it out of his mouth and waved—as though Danton were part of some parade.

Instinct drove him to smile at the child. He lifted his hand to return the wave, and the boy beamed up at him. That grin was a breath of fresh air sweeping through the toxic fumes he had been breathing since he'd been taken.

Then the mother noticed what was happening and scooped him up, casting a dirty look at Danton, as though his very attention might contaminate them, and whispered to the child. He thought he caught something about bloodbane.

The clean air dissipated as quickly as it had come. He wanted to rail at them—he didn't understand why this had happened. It was unfair. He hadn't asked for this. And he certainly didn't know how to summon a bloodbane, for Temoth's sake.

They left the village behind and he looked at his hand, clenching his fist, stomach churning. His thoughts returned once more to his supposed powers. What if he *could* do it again? Would it do any good? Maybe he could figure out what else he could do, if anything, before they reached their destination, break free, escape…

And then what? Where would he go?

There was nowhere for him.

Universally reviled and feared and hunted by the Conclave, he would never be anything but a fugitive living in constant fear of discovery.

Even "freedom" was a prison for someone—

His throat tightened.

—like him.

Danton sat with his back pressed against the bars, head tilted back, staring at the clear night sky. At least the bars on his cage extended above him as well, rather than a solid roof, so he had a chance to see the sky before he met his fate.

He knew. He'd tried not to think about it, but he knew.

Sedation. He had to be stilled for the sake of the world—not killed, or his death would spawn yet another bloodbane—and then humanely cared for as a vegetable until he died in some safe location far away from civilization.

Given the way the guards had treated him after taking him, he doubted anyone was going to be "caring" for him, whatever the Conclave pretended. He suspected the guards' cruelty knew no bounds; he had no doubt that he'd been shielded from even worse treatment because they were afraid to open his cage. No, it was far safer, and more amusing, for them to torment him from a distance in all the little ways that eroded his dignity, his very humanity.

Assuming he still counted as human.

Whatever sliver of hope had been left to him was slipping out of his grasp. His grief had gnawed a hole in him, but it wasn't empty. No, despair had swelled to fill the space where once hope had lived and it pulsed outward, tearing at the edges of that hole, making it bigger.

So, he stared at the sky instead, a vast emptiness that could swallow his own void, make it seem small, even if only for a few minutes.

It stretched into the endless distance in either direction over an empty plain. Stars glimmered and a crescent moon hung above his head. It was almost peaceful. If it weren't for the bars obscuring his view, he might pretend he was out in the field with his siblings, racing to be the first to find the constellations as his mother named them.

The sky tilted. The stars mocked him. It was a tainted memory, sullied by everything he'd lost. His sweet moment of tranquility disintegrated, ash between his fingers.

He'd once thought, like everyone else, that Banebringers were demonspawn, worshippers of the heretic gods. That they did something to deserve this. They used their powers to sow discontent and evil across the continent and needed to be caught and Sedated for the sake of everyone.

The only time he'd questioned the priests' teachings was when that old couple from his childhood had disappeared. They'd always been kind to him, giving him hot cider after he'd gathered cow chips for fuel in the winter or a quick lesson in whittling. They hadn't *seemed* evil.

He'd been ten the year they disappeared; he'd easily put it out of his mind as an anomaly that had some explanation he didn't understand.

But he knew *himself*. He'd never even known someone who secretly worshipped the heretic gods, let alone numbered himself among them. He'd never done anything evil. He had no desire to unleash havoc on the land. He didn't even know *how*, though perhaps he might now out of sheer rage, if he could.

He turned his head to look at the cruel watchmen who'd overseen his journey to *wherever.* They were both awake, eating, laughing around a campfire. They'd tossed scraps from their meal his way, as usual, but he hadn't touched them. They'd thought it was amusing to tread them into horse manure first.

Anger coiled once more, a sleeping serpent that roused itself now and again. It felt good, only because it pushed away the despair for a while. Their cruelty, their malice? It was enough to drive anyone to madness. Or was it?

Fear trickled down his spine. The fear that he was losing himself, even as bitterness churned in his stomach. Maybe *this* was why Banebringers were evil. Maybe it had nothing to do with the heretic gods. Maybe the rest of the world drove them to it. And maybe he was sliding down that slope, too.

At some point, Danton must have drifted off, because he woke with a start.

He uncoiled himself and sat up, confused. It was still the middle of the night. The stars had shifted, but dawn was hours away. Yet *both* guards were awake, limned in the light of the campfire, arguing.

That must have been what had woken him.

He didn't even have to strain to hear what they were saying. "…bloodbane about. Saw the notice at the last village. A wolf, I think."

"Bloodwolves don't live around here," the older, bearded guard said. "Can't be that. A hawk—"

A large shadow flitted across the sky, and both guards ducked.

Danton looked up, completely unconcerned. He'd ceased caring about the possibility of bloodbane attacks. He was as good as dead anyway.

But it was merely a cloud skimming the moon.

The guards relaxed. "It's nothing," Bearded said. "Go back to sleep. I'll watch if you're too scared."

"Can't sleep now," the younger guard said, his eyes still darting about the campsite. "I *know* I heard something."

Danton peered through the bars of his cage into the darkness. *Was* there a bloodbane out there? Maybe it'd eat him and finish this. Hopefully, it was one small enough to get into the cage. A couple of bloodrats, perhaps, to gnaw him to death. That would be ironic. Could have started there and saved himself this misery. Or let Loena get eaten.

He shuddered, pushing away such dark thoughts.

The tall grass on either side of the dirt road rustled.

"There!" the younger guard shouted, pointing to one side of the road. "I heard it!"

Danton heard it too, but he didn't see anything.

"You didn't hear nothing," Bearded snapped. "Just the wind." He thumped his spear on the dirt and turned his back on the section of grass, as if to prove the point. "Burning skies, man, it's a good thing we're almost there——"

A sharp *twang* cut through the air, and an arrow flew out of the darkness and struck Bearded in the back of the calf.

He yelped and fell to the ground, cursing, and his spear rolled from his hand.

The younger guard drew his sword, twisting this way and that to find the unseen assailant.

Danton watched with numb curiosity, and perhaps some disappointment. Bloodbane couldn't use arrows. He didn't know much anymore, but *that* he was certain of.

Another *twang*, followed by another arrow, flying from the same location into the younger guard's calf.

Bandits? So long as they killed him too, rather than leaving him here to starve to death in a cage in the Arlanan summer sun.

Though, if the bandits were trying to *kill* them, they were failing miserably at the job.

Bearded had stumbled to his feet, dragging one leg, and another arrow buried itself in the other leg. He went down.

The younger guard tried to crawl the opposite direction, into the grass, and for a moment it looked as though he'd succeed in escaping—though where he imagined he'd go, Danton couldn't guess. They'd left behind cultivated land hours ago. Truthfully, the guard had been right to worry about bloodbane. Most of them lurked away from civilization and would greedily set upon a lone, injured human if it bumbled into their territory.

But the grass bent flat, followed by the sound of scrambling along the ground, toward the guard. Then the guard yelped.

Danton rubbed his eyes. The younger guard's body was now *dragging itself* back toward the campfire.

That was it. Danton had snapped, fallen off whatever cliff he'd been hanging on to. He was hallucinating. Right?

The guard thrashed and screamed, kicked out and...*connected* with something?

There was a grunt and a curse from nowhere. Then, the younger guard passed out.

Unbidden, Danton rose to a crouch, his hands clutching the bars of the cage, his eyes wide.

The body dropped to the ground.

The bearded guard, still conscious despite the arrows in his legs, tried to scrabble away, but he was too injured to go far. He grunted, and rope appeared out of thin air, wrapping itself around the guard's hands.

Danton was frozen, gaping. He was losing his mind. It was finally happening. Next thing he knew, he'd be summoning bloodbane. Maybe that was what it took, that was the key to unlocking his power. One merely had to go mad first.

The younger guard was dragged over to the first, and then the rope tied the two guards together. The unconscious guard's dead weight pulled the other guard to the side, and they toppled over.

There was a heavy sigh that issued from neither guard. Then, a man appeared, his back to Danton.

Danton thought his eyes might be stuck open permanently. He slid to his knees and clutched the bars.

The man had brown, unkempt hair, and was wearing plain brown trousers and a tan, billowy shirt. Across his back was a bow, and at his waist hung a quiver.

The man prodded at the pair with his foot. The bearded guard, still conscious, stared up at him with wide, glazed-over eyes.

"Well," the man said, "this is gonna hurt, but I don't want you bleeding out." He pulled a bag off his shoulder, rummaged around, and produced some rolls of clean cloth and a palm-sized jar. He proceeded to treat the guards' wounds—the wounds he himself had inflicted, starting with the unconscious man—removing each arrow, applying some sort of salve from his jar to the bandage, and then wrapping the wounds tightly.

When he turned to the conscious guard, the man offered the guard a piece of leather to bite down on.

The guard responded by spitting in his face. Awkward position he was in, he missed.

"Have it your way," the man replied, then jerked one of the arrows out.

The guard screamed and promptly joined his partner in oblivion while the newcomer finished up.

He stood, rinsed his hands with a waterskin he found next to the campfire, and dried them on a guard's shirt.

Then at last, he turned to face Danton. "Not bad, huh?" he asked, a lopsided grin on his face. He picked at a cut on his chin —a tiny thing—but the blood that had seeped was silver.

Danton's head spun. "You're a Banebringer!"

The man inspected the fleck of silver in his hand, then tucked it into a pouch hanging on his belt. "Well. Unless I'm mistaken, which would be unfortunate, given all this trouble I went to"—he swept his hand around the campsite—"you are too."

Danton's parched throat worked, then the questions spilled out. "Who are you? Where did you come from? What did you do? How did you do it? And why in the abyss didn't you just *kill* those bastards? And why heal their wounds after?"

The man held up his hand. "One question at a time. First, let's get you out of there." He searched the guards' bodies, and after a moment, produced a key. He held it up, pleased with himself, and walked over to the cage.

Danton scooted back, pressing himself against the far end, though he didn't know why. The man didn't seem intent on hurting him, and even if he did, who cared?

But he was a Banebringer. An actual Banebringer. Not like himself—some fledgling *whatever he was*. This man was a Banebringer who had powers and knew how to use them.

He didn't…*seem* insane…

The cage door swung open, and the man stepped aside. "Your freedom awaits, Dal," he said, grinning again.

The door yawned, and the world outside seemed enormous. He shrank back against the bars, trembling. His aches and pains and the pit inside came rushing back, temporarily stayed by his attention on what was happening outside.

But he was free. He was no longer destined for Sedation, for the death of nothingness.

The man ran a hand back and forth through his hair. "You… coming out?"

Just leave the cage. He could do that much. He closed his eyes briefly, took a deep breath, and carefully picked his way out of the cage. *Everything* hurt, and the moment his feet touched the ground, he collapsed.

It wasn't so much that he couldn't support himself, though that might also have been true. It was that he suddenly didn't want to. Tears blurred his vision. Freedom? What freedom? Everything was gone...everything...

He curled in on himself, sobs wracking his shoulders as everything came back. The terror of that night, the confusion of the next morning, the fear, the betrayal, the frightening anger, the mental and physical torment of the past few days.

He didn't care that the man was watching him, didn't care that they needed to get away from here, didn't care...just didn't care. About anything at all.

When he couldn't cry anymore because his body hurt too much, the dirt next to him puffed up, and the stranger's feet appeared in his vision. "I get it," the man said softly. "I really do."

"Just let me die here," Danton rasped.

The man crouched in front of him. "Yeah. Yeah. I get that too."

Danton slowly pushed himself to his knees, wiping at his eyes with his sleeve, and studied his rescuer.

The man wasn't Setanan, not completely. His skin had the bronze shading of a Fereharian. What was he doing *here*, in the breadbasket of Setana?

The man's grin was gone now. His brown eyes watched Danton seriously, thoughtfully—and in them was the compassion Danton had so desperately wanted from someone, anyone, along this miserable journey.

In the eyes of a stranger. Someone who didn't even know him. A *Banebringer*.

"Come on," the man said. "Let's get you fed, cleaned up, and on the way to somewhere safe."

"I want to go home," Danton said, the words coming out unbidden. Tears sprang to his eyes, and he blinked them away.

That was impossible. He knew it, and he was pretty sure the man knew it too.

The man paused, studying him. "How old are you?"

"Sixteen," Danton said.

The man sucked in a quick breath through his teeth. "Burning skies," he muttered, then stood up and offered Danton a hand. "Well, I won't suggest a woman to drown your sorrows in, then," he said, looking back at him with a hint of that lopsided smile again. "A bit young for that."

Danton's brow furrowed.

The man's smile faded. "What's your name, kid?"

"Danton," Danton said.

"Nice to meet you, Danton. I'm Vaughn." His hand was still extended.

Danton stared at his hand. "Why did you help them?" he asked. "You could have just—you could have just killed them." The coiled serpent in his gut agreed, but he tamped it down. He nodded toward the bow on Vaughn's back. "I saw how accurate you were with that thing."

Vaughn's hand dropped, and he glanced at the unconscious guards. "Well," he said. "Guess I don't want to become what they say we are."

So...that wasn't inevitable?

The lopsided grin slid across his face again. "Or, if that's too philosophical for you, we can say I like to think about how their minds will melt when they wake up and realize a Banebringer saved their lives." He made a wiggly gesture near his head. "Take your pick."

What a strange man.

"Look, we can talk more on the way. I'll answer all your questions and more." He hesitated. "I can't and won't make you come with me, but if you want to, we should go." He extended his hand again.

Danton hesitated. His eyes flicked to Vaughn, then to his hand.

He looked back at the cage, the door still open, then at the unconscious guards. The past few days had been a blur of terror and grief and pain, and the future was certain to hold more of the same. A large part of him would rather crawl back in that cage and die.

But the slightly greater part…

At least he wouldn't be alone.

He reached out, grasped Vaughn's hand, and allowed Vaughn to pull him to his feet.

"Great," Vaughn said. "Let's go."

Carol A. Park

When I thought about a short story that would embody the idea of grief and hope, I didn't have to turn far.

Thicker Than Water is set in the world of my *Heretic Gods* series, where there is hardly a character that hasn't experienced some sort of traumatic loss. Danton's experience is representative of the titular *Banebringers* in that series, who are cast out and hunted for something not under their control. He wrestles with the grief that results from the unexpected loss of identity and therefore the loss of the community—family, friends, a way of life— that was part of that identity. But what is lost can be found—even if it isn't the same as it was before.

Carol A. Park is a fantasy author who lives in western Maryland with her husband and two active elementary-aged boys. When not writing or doing other author-y tasks, you can find Carol working at her day job (Support Lead at a patent law firm), chasing her children, dreaming about playing video games again, or reading. Her novels are generally characterized by nuanced magic systems, character-driven stories, and mature romance.

Find out more about Carol A. Park at
www.carolapark.com

DEATH IN THE UNCANNY VALLEY

M.L. WANG

Stormfly
Lv. 3

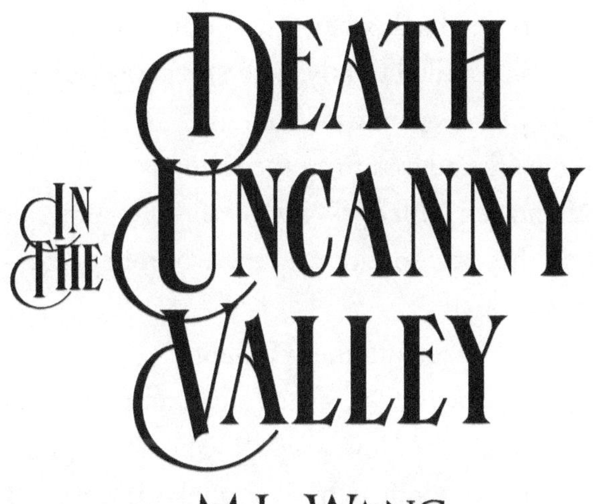

DEATH IN THE UNCANNY VALLEY

M.L. WANG

Cassanterra sagged against her staff, her breath coming in painful gasps. A field of firewyrms lay slaughtered around her, some half-consumed by the earth, some impaled on jutting shafts of rock, their blood oozing orange into the jewel-bright green of the meadow.

"An astounding feat, Milady!" a voice exclaimed as a gaggle of local peasants emerged from behind the ridge where they had been cowering. "You dispatched those monstrosities with such ease and speed!"

"Well, it would have been easier and speedier if I had my partner with me." Cassanterra frowned at the gawking farmers.

"Now, if you'll excuse me,"—she straightened, shaking orange blood from her armor—"I have to get to the Fourth Spire."

"Ah, yes, the Starspire." The peasants murmured among themselves in reverent tones. "I'm told those who reach the top leave with powers beyond belief."

"I know." Cassanterra fixed her gaze on the horizon, where the tower cut a pearly slit in the sky. Still so far away. She had just slung her staff to her back when the ground shook, making her pause. "Sorry." She smiled tightly as the civilians yelped in alarm. "Sometimes my powers get away from me."

"Cassie!" a voice thundered from the clear sky.

"That's your power, Milady?" one of the peasants said, unable to comprehend this new sound from the world beyond.

"Cassie! This has to stop!"

"What was that?" asked another peasant.

"Nothing. Just the wind," Cassanterra muttered, and turned her back on the crowd. "Now, *shut up!*" she shouted back at the sky, her own voice magnified by her quake powers. "I need to concentrate!" Hands before her, fingers outstretched, she willed Heaven and Earth to still.

"Cassie…" The voice in the sky ached. *"I'm really trying here."*

"I mean it, Dad!" Cassanterra stamped the ground, opening a chasm that nearly swallowed one of the stumbling peasants. "Shut up and leave me alone!"

"You're scaring me. Please!"

"I said LEAVE ME ALONE!" Cassanterra's bellow filled the world, drowning out even the rumbling sky. The intruding voice pulled back, defeated, and the world finally stilled. As the ground stopped shaking, the peasants were left staring in amazement. Some had fallen to their knees.

"There." Cassanterra Earthshaker let out a breath. "If I scream loud enough, I can always make it stop."

"You called this entity 'Dad'?" one of the peasants said. "Can it be…? Are you a child of the Immortals?"

"Yes." Cassanterra fixed her eyes on the Starspire. "Yes, I am."

"Hail the demigod!" the crowd cried, falling to their knees. "Hail!"

Cassanterra just rolled her eyes and pressed on.

A crystal teardrop floated before Sam's nose.

The tear hadn't come easily and, as he watched it turn amorphously in the absence of gravity, it didn't seem to belong to him. He definitely should have cried more. Louder. Longer. Maybe he had shed so many tears over the years that he'd dried up? All those nights he had sobbed into his pillow, knowing this would come… and now that it was here, he felt spent and distant. Like this was all happening to someone else on a tiny planet, turning like that salt tear in the meaningless vacuum a million miles away.

"Sam?" His classmate poked her head into the chamber, and he quickly batted the tear away. "It's our turn in the gym. You coming?"

"Not today."

"Are you sure?" Ahn asked, gripping the circular door frame to keep from floating off. "It's a long way to Mars. You don't want to atrophy this early in the game."

"I know." Letting his muscles deteriorate during the first month in space could easily mean he would have to turn around and head back to Earth on the first available shuttle from Mars. And Sam's adventure couldn't end like that. *Mom* wouldn't have wanted it to end like that.

After a nervous silence, Ahn ventured, "How are you feeling today, anyway?"

"Weird," Sam confessed.

"If it's not out of line to say… you've seemed a little weird this whole time."

"What whole time?"

"Since we left Earth. You were so intense and full of energy during training. Now that we've actually launched, you're… I don't know. Different."

Ahn was right again. Sam hadn't felt right, even before the call about Mom. He just couldn't understand why. He'd trained for this trip for two years, thrumming with excitement through every grueling exercise. The Mars program was supposed to transform his life into something better, bigger, and entirely his own. The distance was supposed to free him from all the problems that had bound him before he left Earth. But somehow, he felt just as stuck as he had on the ground.

"Come on," Ahn said. "I'm sure you'll feel better after sweating a little."

"Yeah," Sam sighed and reached to his chest to unfasten the harness that held him at his workstation. "I'll be right—"

Something buzzed, and they both looked at the tablet secured to Sam's desk.

"Oh," Ahn said as she read the caller: *Dad*. "Um—never mind, then. I'll, uh… catch you later."

"No—" Sam started, suddenly wanting more than anything to escape to the gym, but Ahn had already pushed off the doorway. The circular doors whooshed shut behind her, leaving Sam alone with that dreaded *buzzzz*!

Teeth gritted, Sam picked up the tablet and answered the video call. "Hey."

"Sam…" Dad's hair seemed to have grayed in the two days since their last painful interaction. "How are you holding up, son?"

"What do you need?" Sam asked shortly.

"What? Why would you ask that?"

"Because you only ever call when you need something."

"That's not..." Dad trailed off, seeming to realize how hollow *'that's not true'* would ring. "That doesn't mean I don't care how you're doing."

Sam scoffed and cast his eyes up at the white lighting panel for a moment to get his temper under control. A deep breath before he turned back to his father's face on the screen. "I'm as well as I can be. That's all you need to know." *All you deserve to know.* "Now, why are you actually calling? More confusion about Mom's will?"

"It's not me, Sam. It's Cassie."

That got Sam's attention. "What? Is she okay?"

"No—I mean—she's not hurt or anything. It's just that... I haven't been able to reach her."

"You *lost* her!?" Sam said, ready to fly into the rage of his life. Three days of custody and Dad had managed to lose his fourteen-year-old daughter?

"No, no, she's here. She's just..." Dad sighed and turned the screen so Sam could see. Cassie was crunched up on the couch with her knees drawn up to her chest, a silver VR helmet obstructing her face.

"She's... playing a game?" Sam said.

"Yeah. Something called *Elemental Heroes: Starfall?*"

"Okay..." It was the game Sam and Cassie had played during their long days in the hospital waiting room. They had spent whole summers wandering the hills and forests of *Starfall*, fighting monsters for stardrops and building up their arsenal. Not that it had done them much good. If Sam remembered right, they had never gotten past the Starspire on Level Four.

"So, she's playing an old game to get away for a while." Sam would probably be doing the same if he had been forced to move in with this idiot right after losing Mom. "So what?"

"She won't come out." Dad's voice was strained. "She's been like this since the funeral."

"Wait, the funeral was *three days ago*. She hasn't stopped playing for *seventy-two hours?*"

"Not really. I mean, she's taken the helmet off to snack and use the bathroom a couple times, but she won't speak to me. Please, Sam. I don't know what else to do. Maybe if you talk to her."

"Yeah," Sam said, skipping, *'How the hell did you let this happen?'* "Take me to her. Let her know I'm here."

Picking up his tablet, Dad walked Sam over to the couch where Cassie huddled in an old hoodie that had belonged to Mom.

"Sweetheart." He put a hand on her shoulder. "Sam's here to see you."

Cassie made an inarticulate sound and squirmed away from the touch, head pressed into the back of the couch as if to burrow further into the helmet.

"Cassie," Dad tried again, shaking her slightly.

In response, Cassie *screamed.*

Even through the screen, forty million miles away, Sam cringed. The sound was too raw to come out of his sweet baby sister.

"You see?" Dad turned back to Sam. "I don't know what to do. Sam, please… What do I do?"

Without realizing it, Sam had reached out and touched the edge of the screen, wanting to hold his sister—as if there weren't a universe between them. He shook his head. "I don't know." He had never known Cassie to act that way while playing any game. It had his hands shaking slightly on the tablet. "Has she said anything to you about *why* she needs to be in the game? That game specifically?"

"Just that she had to get to some tower or something?"

"The Fourth Spire?"

"That's the one."

"How could she have even played to that level?" Sam wondered aloud. "It takes two people to get past Level Three."

"Well, the nurses mentioned Marian was wearing a VR helmet when she passed away. I think she and Cassie were playing this game together."

"Seriously?" Sam let out a laugh in spite of everything. "*Mom* was playing *Starfall?*"

"Yeah, why?"

"Mom doesn't play that game. It's not her style."

It was a corny game not really meant for moms or, frankly, for anyone over the age of fourteen. Mom had played a lot of VR games with Sam and Cassie when they were growing up. But *Starfall* was explicitly the one Sam and Cassie had played while Mom was in surgery, resting afterward, or simply too sick for the excitement. It had been the perfect escape from the hospital. Difficult enough that fighting the monsters consumed all their focus, shiny enough that it didn't remind them for a moment of the real world. And it belonged to just the two of them. Why would Mom have been playing it?

"Before she passed—the last time I spoke to her—Marian mentioned that she had started playing some of your old favorites with Cassie."

"Why?"

Dad sighed. "Why do you think, Sam? Your sister misses you so much. You *did* just leave her and Marian on Earth."

"That's not my fault!" Sam protested. "What was I supposed to do? Just sit around waiting for…" He couldn't say *'waiting for the inevitable'*. It sounded too callous. "This is what Mom wanted, you know. She *told* me to jump on this chance the second I was approved for a scholarship."

"I know that's what your mom wanted for you, but… Sam, that's no excuse to leave your family at a time like this, when you knew it was so close to the end."

"You don't get to say that to me!"

"Hey now. Watch your tone—"

"What exactly do you call what you did, Dad? One month, you find out Mom has a terminal diagnosis, and the next, you're looking for an apartment?" Sam had been eight years old when Mom first got sick, and Dad decided that being a husband and father wasn't for him after all.

"There were a lot of reasons—"

"I don't give a shit about your reasons!" The wound was so old now; talking about it shouldn't still make Sam's voice crack with emotion. "You don't get to talk to me about ditching family!"

Quiet on the other end. Dad had turned from the screen, unable to face the son he had all but abandoned ten years ago. Sam's hands were in fists, ready for a fight, ready for the next stupid, self-centered excuse his father threw at him. But the return fire didn't come.

"You're right."

"I'm *what?*" Incredulous, Sam just managed to bite down on a venomous, '*Who are you and what have you done with my father?*'

"I have no right," said this strange, defeated man with Dad's face. "I wasn't there when you and your mom really needed me. I was young, and scared, and I wasn't the father I should have been. But part of being a man is learning from your past—"

"Don't start," Sam cut him off. "Not with me, do you understand? You have *nothing* to teach me about being a man."

"I know!" Dad finally lost his temper, as he always did when things got real. "I know, okay? I'm not asking you to forgive me. I'm asking you to help me..." He seemed to choke on the next words. "Help me be better."

It was an olive branch. The kind Sam would have killed for when he was younger. But it had been too many years and Sam's anger had grown too deep. "In what universe is it my responsibility to help you be a better parent?"

"In the universe where you have a little sister who loves you, and misses you, and thinks the world of you. She needs a family, Sam. And it might suck, but I'm all she's got right now."

"She's got me!"

"Does she?" Dad raised his eyebrows. "When was the last time you spoke to her? Did you even call her after Marian died?"

"Of course, I called!"

"Outside of the funeral?"

Sam's fingernails dug into his palms, but there was nothing he could throw back because they both knew the answer. When it really mattered, Sam had been just like his dad.

"That's why I need your help now, Sam. Think whatever you want about me, but help me be here for Cassie. Because she doesn't deserve this."

Sam sighed, his throat squeezing painfully. "Fine," he growled because if he kept arguing, he was going to scream—or cry. And Dad didn't get those tears. They didn't belong to him. "I'll help." *Only to prove that I'm a better man than you.* "For Cassie. But I'm not going to do any good talking to her over this call."

"What do you mean?"

Sam resisted the urge to roll his eyes. "You really don't know your daughter, do you?"

"Excuse m—"

"I'll be back in one minute." Securing the tablet, Sam unfastened his harness and pushed from the wall. "While I'm gone, go into Cassie's stuff and find her spare VR helmet."

Floating his way down the corridor, Sam found Ahn in the gym, working out on the gravity-simulating elliptical.

"Ahn," he said. "Sorry to interrupt. I need your help… and your VR helmets."

The elliptical slowed as her brow furrowed. "My VR helmets?"

"Yes. Please?"

"I thought you didn't play those games."

"I don't anymore." Not since leaving the world he had been so desperate to escape. "This is an emergency. Come, float with me. I'll explain."

Every Marsbound student got to bring only one pound of personal items with them. Ahn had taken up most of that weight with her two precious VR headsets. Antiques, like the one Sam had used as a kid.

"Be gentle with it, okay?" she said as she handed one helmet to Sam. "You know how to use it?"

"Yeah," Sam said. "Don't worry."

Once he had slipped the helmet on, Ahn activated it with a thumb to the scanner. The visor whooshed over his eyes and the interior bands formed to the shape of his head. It took a bit of searching across the display visor to dig up *Starfall*; it was such an old game.

"*Elemental Heroes*?" Ahn snorted, her voice distant beyond the helmet. "Really?"

"Shut up."

"Username?" the headset prompted.

Sam sighed before answering, "Stormfly Windmaster."

"Password?"

Another sigh. "1234567."

"Thumbprint?"

Sam pressed his thumb to the side of the helmet, allowing him into the account he had made as a kid—and the past rushed up around him. The hokey tumble of lute strings, the orchestral swell, as the world of *Starfall* enfolded him like the arms of an old friend.

"Are you in, Sammy?" Dad's muffled voice asked from the tablet.

"Yeah," Sam said as a bank of rainbow-tinged clouds raced to meet him, "it's launching." Stormfly's armor was falling into place around him, silver wings unfolding from his back to catch the wind. "In a second, I'll switch to immersive audio, and I won't be able to hear you. Did you find the extra VR helmet?"

"Yeah, but I've got no idea what to do with—"

"Ahn's going to walk you through it," Sam said, assuming Dad would be as hopeless with a VR helmet as he was with any tech beyond a socket wrench. "When you've got it working, she'll find a way to get you to our location—so to speak."

"Okay…" Dad said. "I don't know about this, Sam." He had never really been willing to put a toe outside his comfort zone.

"Well, this is the way to reach Cassie," Sam said. "If you actually want to help, I'll see you inside." But he knew better than to think he would see his father before he removed the helmet. Dad only knew how to run from things that scared him.

All but confirming his suspicion, Dad said, "Alright, well… Good luck in there, Sam."

Not Sam, he looked down at himself with a shudder as *Starfall's* audio washed the real world from existence. *Stormfly.*

He had last modified this character design when he was eleven and it showed. Every opportunity for something spiky or shaped like a dragon had worked its way into his armor. If not for game physics, a guy wouldn't be able to move in this get-up. The fact that it still fit like a second skin was a little embarrassing.

Stormfly's boots hit the clover-studded grass in the middle of Level Three—presumably where Sam had last logged out. He hadn't consciously retained a mental map of the level all these years, but when he looked up the emerald slope before him, he knew that when he reached the top, a horde of firewyrms would come sizzling up to meet him.

Extending his metallic wings, he flapped them once to make sure they still worked the way he remembered. The single wing-beat pulled him several feet off the ground, and unexpected emotion overwhelmed him. It had been here—caught in the make-believe sensation of flight—that Sam had first wished he could be weightless all the time. If he just found wings powerful enough, maybe they could carry him away from anything.

Three more wingbeats, a rolling tickle of motion in his stomach, and Sam—*Stormfly*—had surged up over the ridge. A field of firewyrms opened below him. Hissing, they lifted their red reptilian heads and turned their yellow eyes on him. The frills around their jowls quivered and flared as fireballs glowed in their gullets.

Stormfly could ascend above the wyrms' spitting range and up into the infinite clouds of *Starfall*. Part of Sam wanted to keep rocketing skyward, just to relive the hope Stormfly had once given him. That a man really could be as light as the wind if he just found the right pair of wings. But he knew now that even leaving the planet didn't give him that lightness, and the way to Cassie was through the monsters. So, Sam folded his wings and plunged earthward into the fire.

Sam may not have played *Starfall* in a long time, but he *had* gotten better at gaming in general. And, hot off his space training, his reflexes were the best they had ever been. There were a few stumbles as he readjusted to the magical gameplay: he momentarily forgot how to jump and got scalded, and at one point he drew a lamp instead of his windsword. But, even with the hiccups, he still tore through the firewyrms in what had to be record time.

Beyond the wyrms' meadow was a town of NPCs beset by a stone bull. Beyond that was a river of acid-spitting serpents. Stormfly made quick work of each obstacle, accelerating as he reacclimated to the feel and physics of *Starfall*, blazing ever closer to the Fourth Spire.

Logically, he knew where he would find Cassanterra. He just wasn't prepared for the upswell of emotion as his wings brought him over the trees and he finally caught sight of her. The Earthshaker looked as she always had: green cape blowing in the breeze, armor almost as ridiculous as Sam's, but with gold tones instead of silver.

Cassanterra turned to face Stormfly, and that was the first time it was obvious to Sam that his sister had changed. The person behind that familiar gold armor was different. Older. If there was one thing *Starfall* did really well for a game of its era, it was the way it mapped a player's expressions onto an avatar's features. Cassanterra's face was the same as it had always been, but there was a guarded quality to her smile that hadn't been there when they were younger. This was the face of someone who had thought that maybe no one would come.

"You're here," she said. "You actually showed up."

"Of course I showed up."

Another flap brought Stormfly to the ledge beside Cassanterra, where his boots touched down on sun-warmed stone. Far below, mirror-smooth water reflected the canyon walls at the foot of the mountain, the spire above, and the rainbow nebula of clouds over that. Trying to swim across the lake or navigate the narrow walkway along the shore would wake the virtually unbeatable hydrle that slumbered beneath the water. An earth elemental like Cassanterra couldn't cross the lake without an air elemental like Stormfly to give her a lift—or at least someone to back her up against the beast.

The hydrle might be the most fearsome monster on this level, but until the water was disturbed, the lake was a place of peace. Stormfly and Cassanterra had spent as much time here as any place in the game, regrouping before facing the canyon of monsters that would inevitably send them back to the beginning of Level Three. This had always been their place to scheme, to think, to talk.

"Honestly, I thought you'd be away on your other quest forever," Cassanterra said.

"And leave you to climb to the Fourth Star yourself?" Bless technology, effecting a casual air was so easy through Stormfly. "Not a chance!"

"Well, it took you long enough to show up," Cassanterra said. "I hope your other quest was *very important*."

The rules were that they never talked about the real world while they were in the game. Not directly. Denial was the only thing that had made those summers in the hospital bearable. Here, Sam, and Cassie, and all their problems didn't exist. There was only Stormfly Windmaster and Cassanterra Earthshaker, legendary heroes whose biggest worry was how they could upgrade their armor to look cooler.

"To tell the truth, the other quest hasn't gone quite the way I imagined," Stormfly said.

"What do you mean?"

"I thought it would feel good to be on a mission so far above the clouds. I'd never have to touch the ground or bother with any of the monsters there. But it didn't feel good, Cassanterra. Right from the beginning, it felt… empty up there."

"You're not acting like yourself, Stormfly." There was a vaguely accusatory note in Cassanterra's voice.

"I know." Damn it. He *was* falling out of character. Stormfly rarely talked about feelings—least of all Sam's. "It's just… it's good to be here with you, Cassanterra. With my feet on the ground."

"If it's so good, then why have you been away all this time?" Cassanterra demanded, and the deep calm of her voice filter didn't quite mask the anger. "Why did you leave in the first place?"

"I had to," Stormfly said, and Sam realized that he had never really talked to Cassie about this. Not properly. Maybe because Sam knew that, if he had, the guilt would have been too sharp. "It's like…" God, how to keep this in character? In universe?

"Remember that week we spent trying to get into that cave under the Second Spire? Behind the bramblebees' nest?"

"Yes." Cassanterra's perfect brow crunched with Cassie's confusion.

"We thought there must be something there that would help us fight our way up the Spire. We were so sure. This quest was a little like going into that cave. I just had to see."

"But there were just a bunch of stardrops in that cave," Cassanterra said impatiently. "Nothing that helped us up the Spire."

"Yeah." Stormfly looked at his feet. "Some quests are like that."

"Well, I know exactly where I'm going with this quest," Cassanterra said, "no matter what anyone says. I know where Mara is. We just need to get there."

"Where who is?"

"Mara Tidesong," Cassanterra said. "My teammate."

"Oh." Mara would be Mom's character, then.

"We've been adventuring together since you left. She helped me get through the Dread Canyon to the Spire."

"Whoa, no kidding!" Sam said, sheer awe momentarily washing all his concerns away. Mom had always been better at gaming than either of her kids, but after two summers of trying, Sam and Cassie had never actually reached the Fourth Spire.

Cassanterra didn't bother hiding a smug smile. "Pretty cool, right?"

"Cool? It's incredible!" Sam said.

"Mara went ahead to claim the Fourth Star while I held off the monsters."

"Right." As far as Sam knew, that was the only way to secure a star on this level. One player had to hold off the scorpisaurs while the other beat the clock up the Spire.

"I really thought I would be able to hold them." Darkness flickered over Cassanterra's expression. "But I got distracted, and a greater scorpisaur got me..." Knocking her back to the beginning of the level, where she had been stuck all this time, unable to get back to Mara. It just wasn't a journey for one player.

"And you didn't see her again?" Stormfly's gravelly voice filter didn't allow for whatever emotion had its claws on Sam's throat. It didn't allow for tears. Thank goodness.

"I'm sure she's still there," Cassanterra said confidently— though her character voice always sounded confident—"if we can get up the tower. She'll be there."

"Yeah…" Sam didn't know what else to say. He didn't actually know what happened to an avatar when its player ceased to exist mid-game. But he understood now that Cassie couldn't leave the game until she found out.

"Looks like we've got some monsters to kill," he said. "We'd better get to work planning."

The moment the pair started strategizing, it was like nothing had changed in the last eight years. The excitement was the same. The sense of moving toward something important was just the way Sam remembered. It didn't seem to matter that their goal was more fraught than a simple star of bright pixels. The deeper they dug into the swirling, sparkling *how*, the less the *what* mattered. That was the undying magic of *Starfall*.

No elemental could kill the hydrle in its home element. The best any player could do was get past the creature, which would then drag its cumbersome body from the lake to pursue its prey up the mountain. In theory, the water-based hydrle could be killed on dry land, though Stormfly and Cassanterra had never managed it. For years, their strategy had been to outrun the giant. This was difficult, given the hordes of scorpisaurs and cyclobats that guarded the way up the mountain. Stormfly and Cassanterra had never managed to get through all of them before the plodding hydrle caught up and finished them off. But if Cassanterra could get through the Dread Canyon and up the mountain with Mara, she could do it with Stormfly.

When they had their plan, Stormfly took Cassanterra in his arms, drew in a deep breath, and plunged from the ledge. Swooping low over the lake had seemed counterintuitive when they had first started playing *Starfall*. But controlling *when* the hydrle noticed them was safer than letting the monster spot them and attack on its own time.

As Stormfly spread his wings, slowing their descent, ice-blue eyes opened in the water below. Stormfly flapped hard just as the hydrle's first head burst through the lake's surface. The two elementals veered left through the crystal spray, missing the monster's jaws and the spout of poison it sent jetting into the sky. At that point, the hydrle had only three heads. Stormfly wove between them, knowing where they would break the surface, and set Cassanterra down on the opposite shore.

"Nice!" Cassanterra said as the hydrle's great shell trembled with rage, setting bubbles shuddering across the lake's surface. Not waiting for the monster to slink ashore, the pair raced onward.

It had taken Stormfly and Cassanterra two months to figure out how to defeat the largest scorpisaurs of the Dread Canyon. The dance they had eventually perfected was as sharp in Sam's mind as any of his Mars training. Stormfly circled just out of range of the monster's pincers and barb, effectively drawing its six eyes so that Cassanterra could open the earth in two trenches, trapping all six of its legs. The moment the monster was caught, the two elementals closed in with flawless timing. Stormfly dodged the arc of the scorpisaur's tail and spun in the air, severing the stinger. Both pincers struck inward at Cassanterra, only to meet the force of her shockwave shield. As the creature's claws ricocheted wide, exposing vulnerable joints, Stormfly wheeled in again and severed the right pincer. At the same time, Cassanterra lifted her quake staff and slammed it down on the joint of the left pincer, sending exoskeletal shards in all directions.

"That was fun," Cassanterra beamed as two more scorpisaurs scuttled into view beneath a chittering cloud of cyclobats, "but there's something I didn't tell you when we were planning."

"Yeah?"

A very Cassie grin split the Earthshaker's face. "I can actually take a scorpisaur on my own now."

"No way!"

"Just cover me."

Taking Cassanterra at her word, Stormfly exploded upward to meet the bats with a wind pulse from each hand. The blasts hit the swarm of bats, destroying half of them and scattering the rest. As the screeching creatures regrouped, Stormfly drew the windswords he had spent months saving for and spun. In the vortex of steel and bladed feathers, the remaining bats came to pieces. As their fragmented bodies rained into the ravine below, Stormfly looked down to find that the canyon walls had collapsed before Cassanterra's outstretched hands. A scorpisaur's barb stuck from beneath the rubble, twitching.

"Holy shit!"

"Hey!" Cassanterra looked up at Stormfly admonishingly. "Language!"

"Sorry." Stormfly descended to alight on the rocks beside a twitching scorpisaur leg. "It's just… I didn't know you'd gotten so good."

"Well, a lot's changed while you've been gone."

As more scorpisaurs clicked and skittered from above, slow footfalls shook the lower mountain beneath their feet. The hydrle was nearly on them.

"You go on ahead," Cassanterra said.

"Are you sure?"

"Yeah, I've got these creepy crawlies."

"But you…" Stormfly blinked Sam's confusion. "Don't you want to be with me?" If Mom was really at the top of the

Spire… "You should be with me. Isn't the whole reason you wanted me here so you could—"

"*This* is what I wanted." Cassanterra gestured to Stormfly and monsters closing from both sides. And with a stab, Sam remembered Dad's words: *your sister misses you so much.* Was this really all Cassie had wanted? One hour with her big brother in this place they used to share?

"Cassanterra, I—"

"I told you to go! I can handle this!"

"Okay," Stormfly said with cautious but growing optimism. Cassie really had gotten better since he'd last seen her play. "I'll see you at the top, then."

Cassanterra drew her staff with a determination that Cassie had never possessed. At least not the Cassie Sam had known. There was an adult hardness to the way she squared her shoulders and turned to face the hydrle. "See you at the top."

A forcefield shimmered around the Spire, making it impossible for flighted air elementals to enter from any point except the canyon. Zigzagging between scorpisaur pincers, Stormfly baseball-slid under that forcefield, rolled to his feet, and launched upward. The Starspire's glowing pearl exterior raced by for a moment before opening onto a great balcony, where he touched down.

And there, in the center of the main chamber, was Mara.

She was the type of avatar Mom would have designed—conspicuously cohesive for such an aesthetically ridiculous game, with light turquoise armor and a cascade of navy-blue hair. The water elemental—*Mara*—still breathed and blinked, swaying faintly with the impression of life, even though the woman who had made her real was gone. She had a hand stretched out to touch the prize star with a distinctly *Mom* expression. It wasn't the smile of someone pleased with her own accomplishments; it was the smile Mom wore when she knew she had done something to make her kid happy.

She had been wearing that expression—beaming—when Sam read his Mars Institute acceptance message and looked up at her in shock.

"You sent it! You sent my application! But I thought—"

"It was time," Mom said as Sam, weak-kneed, sank onto the side of her bed. "You have a life to live, kiddo."

"But are you sure you actually want me to go?" he asked. "Especially now… when the doctors say we're so close to the end."

"The end could be any time, sweetheart. That's been true for years now. It's not a reason to hold your life in limbo when you have so much you want to do."

"Mars could always wait." Just saying the words physically hurt. Sam pushed them out anyway. "I-I could go to school somewhere else. Somewhere closer to home."

But Mom was shaking her head. "This is a journey you need to take while you're still this antsy, vibrant, growing thing. If you don't get up there, I worry you won't learn what it means to have your feet on good, solid ground."

"I don't understand."

"Ah, that's okay." She rubbed his upper arms before squeezing his shoulders with her painfully thin hands. "You won't until you go. That's why you *have* to go."

"I don't want to leave you," Sam said. Not because he meant it at the time, but because it felt like the right thing to say. "I feel bad."

"You shouldn't, my darling. As long as you're pursuing your goals, building the life you want, I'm happy."

"But…" Sam didn't understand how she could really mean that. "You never got to have this." Mom had trained to be a space engineer once. She had put it on hold for her kids—*for just a little while*, not realizing that *little while* was all she would have. "You never got to have your life."

"Oh, Sam. Just because I don't get to have an experience for myself doesn't mean it loses its shine. As long as you're out there, flying free, you'll be my wings."

"God, Mom." Sam cringed. "That's corny."

"Corny but true." Mom scrunched her nose and pinched Sam's cheeks. He had never understood how, even in the worst of her sickness, she could still pinch his cheeks hard enough to hurt.

Mara Tidesong's hands were strong, her face full, and her eyes bright. She was Mom, as she had been in Sam's early childhood, before the sickness had worn away at her. Stormfly touched those wiry blue fingers, and they felt wonderfully real.

Specializing in water, Mara wouldn't have the power of flight or blunt force. A water elemental's strength was her flexibility. How had she gotten Cassanterra over the lake? How had she dealt with the cyclobats so high in the air? How had she ascended the Spire? Sam had never played a water elemental in this game. He didn't know how it worked. But somehow, in a few weeks, Mara had done for Cassie what Sam never could. Maybe that was nothing to do with being a water elemental. Maybe that was just being Mom.

"I'm so sorry." Sam didn't realize he was speaking aloud until the words were out. He had spent so much of his childhood thinking of the hole his mom would leave when she died. He had never thought that he would be the first to leave an absence, that Mom might have to fill in for him. "I didn't want to do that to you." His voice broke. "After you did everything you could for me, I ended up being just like Dad. I wanted to be better than that, Mom. When it mattered, I wanted to be more like you…"

Mara was still wearing that Mom smile, overflowing with love. *It was time. You have a life to live, kiddo.*

"I know that's what you said," Sam said to the echo of Mom's face and the memory of her voice. "I know you said that as long as I was living my life the way I wanted, you'd be happy. But I'm sorry… I didn't think about whether Cassie would be okay or the extra strain that would put on you."

Holding Mara's hands in his, Sam lowered his head until his brow touched hers.

"I don't feel the way I thought I would in the Mars program, Mom. Here, playing this stupid game with Cassie… this is the best I've felt since leaving for Mars. And I guess that's good. That's a relief." Sam almost laughed with the realization. "It means I'm closer to you than I thought. I hope, maybe, I'm even a little bit like you."

Sam let out a laugh. Because there, clutched tight to his mom, was the first time he realized that a *Starfall* avatar could cry—big crystal teardrops that shattered like glass at his feet and seemed so much more substantial than the tears he had mustered out in space. This wasn't a game feature Sam had ever needed. But things were different now.

"I'm not flying away anymore, Mom. I promise."

There, in that shimmering place outside of time, Stormfly poured out all the tears Sam hadn't been capable of.

"Mara…" a voice said, and Sam turned to find Cassanterra at the doorway. The earth elemental was all torn to hell, parts of her armor dissolved by hydrle venom, but she had done it. Somehow, she had beaten all monsters of the Canyon—or at least stalled them long enough to make the slow climb up the tower stairs. "You're here."

As Stormfly drew back, Mara's eyes drifted with the game's default programming, blinking and tracking the new presence in the chamber. She smiled right at the Earthshaker drawing toward her. Acid-marred boots came to a stop on the pristine floor. For a long time, Cassanterra just stared at Mara, a little girl looking at the only person in the world who hadn't chosen to leave her, and Sam abruptly felt ashamed to stand here with them. He took another step back.

"If you need to talk to her, I could give you two a minute—"

"No," Cassanterra said, touching Mara's hand. "I told you, this is what I wanted. For us to be together." She turned to look at him and extended her free hand. "One last time."

Sam understood then that Mom wasn't the only person Cassie was mourning. And of the two, Mom certainly wasn't the one who owed her an apology.

"Cassanterra…" He dropped the voice filter. "Cassie. I'm sorry for not being with you through this. I didn't mean to…" He fumbled, realizing Cassie didn't need any excuses from him. "I love you."

Cassanterra looked at him sharply, the raw Cassie in her eyes piercing his armor and avatar. "Then you shouldn't have left."

"I had to go."

"But you didn't have to go the *way* you did," she protested, "without calling, without ever even talking to me about it." Somehow, though her avatar didn't accommodate it, Sam knew her lip was trembling. "You didn't have to do that."

"I know," Sam said quietly. "I was trying to figure out what I really wanted."

"So, what *do* you want?" Cassie demanded. "To get away from your sick mom and loser little sister?"

"No!" Not after the weightless loneliness of space. "I want to make the kind of life Mom wanted for me, that's rich, and full, and means something to me. But I…" Sam finally understood what that really meant. "I realized that the life I want has to have you in it."

"How is that supposed to work with you on Mars?"

"Well, we're both here now, aren't we? We can still do this together. And I can call."

"It's not the same as having you in the room."

"But it could still be fun. It seems like you and Mom had a great time playing this game together. Even though it wasn't the same as when you and I were little."

"Yeah…"

"Things have changed—and they're going to keep changing as we get older—but you seem to deal with that okay." Sam smiled. "Definitely better than I do. I mean, look at what you did to those scorpisaurs back there!"

Cassie couldn't help the pleased smile spreading across her avatar's face. "And you didn't even *see* what I did to the hydrle!"

New footsteps drew Sam's attention, and he turned. Four avatars he didn't recognize had landed on the balcony—though two of them were oddly familiar.

"Hey there, Sam." The speaker was a towering fire elemental Sam just recognized as Ahn—though the androgynous character looked nothing like his classmate. The giveaway was in her posture. Ahn had a playfully poised way of standing, with her back straight and her head tilted just slightly to one side. "This is my high school friend, Jan," Ahn jerked a gauntleted thumb at the air elemental to her right, "and her brother, Ben." She nodded to a second, taller air elemental to her left. "They agreed to help me with your delivery." The fourth avatar was smaller than the others and not as steady on his feet. He stumbled when Ahn put a hand on his shoulder and pushed him forward.

"*Dad?*" Cassie said in disbelief.

Being too young to remember the divorce, Cassie hadn't grown up with Sam's bitterness for Dad. She still had a chance to build a different kind of relationship with her father. A better kind. *Just because I don't get to have an experience for myself doesn't mean it loses its shine*, Mom had said. And there was the shine. In Cassie's disbelieving eyes, glowing that her father had braved virtual reality to be here with her.

Ahn had brought Dad in as a generic fire elemental in plain black armor. The rush-job avatar had defaulted to Dad's hairstyle and facial features, creating an uncanny valley version of Sam's father that was as unsettling as it was ridiculous. He was blinking his molten-lava eyes, dumbfounded as a baby in his new virtual surroundings. And, though *Starfall* avatars didn't turn green with motion sickness, Dad was plainly on the edge of vomiting. Apparently, the motion simulation technology that made flight so exhilarating for Sam was a bit much for Dad's roller-coaster-averse stomach.

"Jan, Ben, thank you so much!" Sam said earnestly. "We really appreciate this."

"Ah, this is a breeze for them." Ahn waved her hand dismissively. "Don't tell any of his cool college friends, but Benny was nationally ranked in this game when he was a kid."

"Really?" Cassie's eyes lit up in amazement.

"Anyway, this seems private," Ahn said with a glance at each of her companions. "So, what do you say we hop out? Maybe finish off that hydrle before it wiggles its way out from under all those rocks?"

"Sounds like a good time," Jan said as Benny waved goodbye.

"Nice to meet you guys! Good luck with your, um… whatever this is."

The air elementals each took one of Ahn's arms, spread their wings, and the three of them disappeared over the edge of the balcony.

"Well, Dad," Sam said with a smile. "How are you liking *Starfall*?"

"Sam…" Dad slowly pointed at Stormfly, then at Cassanterra. "And… Cassie?"

"That's right." Sam covered his amusement.

"And…?" Dad's eyes drifted to Mara.

"Yeah." Sam's smile faded slightly.

"Jesus," Dad whispered. "This is so weird!"

"I told you we'd find her here," Cassie said to Dad.

"So, that's Marian?" Dad asked, looking at Mara. "As she was when she…?"

Sam nodded.

"Oh, Marian…" Dad reached out as if to touch her but pulled his hand back. "W-will she…" He paused to swallow. "Is she just going to be stuck here forever?"

"No," Sam said. "I assume she'll disappear when someone claims the prize star and ends the level."

"When does that happen?"

Sam shrugged. "Whenever we're ready." He looked to his sister. This was her game. It was her call. "Cassie?"

Taking a deep breath, Cassie nodded. "But I want to hug you first. I want one hug with all of us, together."

"Of course!" Sam put his arms around his mom and sister. Mara responded according to the game's programming, squeezing them back. It was the sort of hug she hadn't been able to give since she got sick. Warm, and weighty, and totally secure.

"Come on, Dad," Sam said after a moment. "Bring it in."

Slowly, unsure of his in-game body, Dad stepped forward and put his arms around the huddle, one hand on Cassie's back, one on Sam's. There were so many years of hurt between the four of them; hugging like this in real life would be as emotionally unbearable as it was physically impossible. But the sparkling veil of *Starfall* made this sort of thing easier. It might not take the pain away, but it refracted it, making it easier to look in the face. Easier to embrace.

Here, Stormfly was able to whisper what Sam never could: "Thanks for coming, Dad."

Cassie rested her head on Mara's chest, eyes squeezed shut. Very softly, she said, "Everyone's here."

"And we love you," Dad said with gentleness Sam had never heard before.

Maybe it was too late for Sam to forgive his father, but it wasn't too late for Dad and Cassie to build something new with each other. And Sam realized that he earnestly wanted that for his sister—earnestly enough to put away his own resentment and help Dad change, if that was what it took. Because if Cassie couldn't have Mom, this was the least she deserved. This was the least they both could give her. His hand found his dad's virtual shoulder and squeezed.

It was only when Cassie's grip eased that Sam and Dad stepped back. Mom's avatar was gone, but she had left something behind. She must have been close enough to touching the star that the game registered it as part of her. When the hug broke, the star had diffused between the three remaining players, changing them.

Sam noticed the change in Cassie first. "Whoa!"

"What?"

"Cassie… look behind you."

She twisted around and started. A pair of wings unfurled from between her shoulder blades, gold to match her armor. A ring of air-elemental silver encircled the green earth-elemental gem on her chest.

"But earth elementals can't fly in this game!" she exclaimed.

"Not at level three," Sam said. "Remember, we never got to this spire." It wasn't until Sam reached out to touch one of Cassie's wings that he saw the stone bracers around each of his arms. Quake gauntlets! A green ring had snaked around the silver orb on Stormfly's chest. Meanwhile, Dad had a ring of blue around his fire gem and ice crystals in the back of each of his hands that would allow him to control water.

"So, this is what the Fourth Star does?" Sam marveled. "Do you think that if we get to the higher levels, we'll be able to control three elements apiece?"

"Well, it's not like a player's going to get there on their own," Cassie scoffed.

"I know that. You got time this Thursday?"

"What?"

"Just asking because that's the day I only have one class."

A grin split Cassanterra's face, bright and mischievous and all Cassie. "Yeah, I've got time."

"And bonus: we have a fire and water elemental on our team now…" Sam tilted his head toward Dad. "Even if he *does* need some work."

Flexing his virtual fingers, Dad had somehow managed to set his hands ablaze. "Oh no!" He flapped his arms frantically as though to shake the flames off, which only made them flare brighter. "Help!"

"Dad!" Cassie giggled. "Just clap."

Dad started clapping, which set the fire spurting in irregular bursts.

"Just twice, Dad!" Cassie said, still laughing. "It's twice to turn it on, twice to turn it off."

"Okay, well I can't—I can't—" Dad was still flailing, the instinctive panic response to fire clearly overriding his ability to hear instructions.

"Try the ice crystals," Sam cut in, recalling something he'd seen water elementals do in the past. "Touch one of your ice crystals."

Hyperventilating, Dad haltingly smacked one of the crystals. And sure enough, his ice powers activated, casting swirls of frost over both hands to snuff the fire. "Oh, thank god!" He blew out a breath.

"Now that you're not on fire." Sam held out his hand to his dad. "Ready to fly out of here?"

"I can't fly."

"It's okay. Cassie's new to flying too. But I've got you. I've got you both."

The family joined hands, and two pairs of wings spread against the white of the Spire walls.

"As long as you're out there, flying free," Mom had said, *"you'll be my wings."*

The weight of the quake gauntlets around Sam's wrists should have made the ascent a struggle. The inexperienced flyer and non-flyer clutching his hands should have dragged him down. Oddly, Sam rocketed from the spire with an exhilaration unlike anything he had ever felt. Not weightlessness, but *power*. After all, what was flight without a little gravity?

M.L. WANG

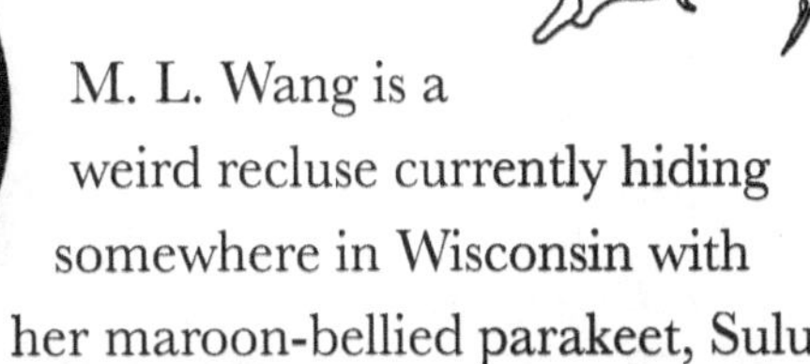

M. L. Wang is a
weird recluse currently hiding
somewhere in Wisconsin with
her maroon-bellied parakeet, Sulu.
She enjoys gruesome nature documentaries
and long walks in circles around her room. Her other works
include the *Theonite* books and *The Sword of Kaigen*.

Find out more about M.L. Wang at
mlwangbooks.com

SUMMER SOULS

CLAYTON SNYDER

For Alan—You were always there

SUMMER SOULS

CLAYTON SNYDER

Souls could only be caught by moonlight, and even then, only in summer. Something about winter kept them hidden; frost was like faerie iron to the delicate lattice of their light. But in high summer, when the moon shone on the thick grasses like a beaming mother, you could stand in the warm fields with emerald blades tickling your shins and watch them rise from the earth like fireflies.

We stood in the grass, my sister Kiva and I, glass jars in our hands, waiting for the moon to rise. We ran among stalks of burred summer wheat, soulstuff filling our jars until they glowed like the sun. We'd lie on the soft earth, whispering stories to one another by starlight. Above, the constellations guided our fancies. Polestars to the wayward sailors of our imaginations.

This one was a pirate. That one, a merchant. The other, a murderer, but he did it for love, and oh, how his soul shines! And then, before dawn, we'd let the souls go, watch them drift into the sky with the others, mothers, sons, fathers, and friends. Here, a pair so close they had to be lovers, or maybe enemies. There, a single wisp, but bright as a star. A child, surely.

Ten years we had together. Ten years is an eternity to a child. Not so long to the earth, or to the adults who grow from those children. To a soul, ten years is the inhalation of a breath.

Mother had passed the year before, summer's heat compounding the misery like weight added to sorrow's yoke. I wondered, sometimes, if it had been Kiva's death that took her. Like a bird latched to her soul, I watched that grief hang on. Each morning it would try to fly away, only to sink its talons deeper each night. Finally, one morning on the cusp of summer, the sadness took her. I don't recall all it entailed. A cough? Wasting? Did she simply decide to stop living?

In death, the details are unimportant. If only because the details don't change a thing. Still, I remember the feel of her hand in mine. The skin like parchment, fingers like bundled twigs. And Kiva? Perhaps I was too young. Too burdened by my own grief. I recall only that she was here, and then she was gone.

But time waits for nothing under the sun, not even grief, and so it was in the third year of Kiva's passing, a man wearing a frayed suit and hauling a strange machine with a wagon arrived. His knock was like a woodpecker on an oak, quick and sure. *Tap tap tap.*

Mother's loss left me alone in our old home with only memory and the lessons she'd tried to impart. I opened the door, and for a moment, stood half-in and half-out, aware of the violence a man alone with a woman was tempted to. I kept a knife on a small table nearby, and my free hand crept toward it.

"Pardon, miss," he grinned.

He was tall and lanky, a pale scarecrow of a man.

"What d'ya want?" I asked.

He gestured behind him, at the thing on its wagon. It was the size of a beehive, all silver and brass and glass. A wooden cabinet stood beside it.

"I'm on my way to the fair. I'm offering you a one-of-a-kind chance," he said.

Mother always said one-of-a-kind chances were rarely that. If you lived long enough, there were few things that didn't come around at least once more. Still, that machine gleamed in the setting sun, and something drew me to it. Maybe it was the memory of Kiva's sense of wonder. The way she spun her tales, of men and women and children, souls all a-dance in the gloaming. How she only had one chance at anything. What might she have been?

I gripped the knife, holding it in front of me, the steel glinting in the half-light. I hoped there was enough shadow to hide my shiver. This man might be more huckster than predator, but I wanted to be sure. He raised his hands when he saw me holding the blade and stepped back slowly.

"Easy."

I lifted my chin. "Show me."

"Sure, sure."

He backed his way to the machine and took a moment to open the cabinet. He drew a softly glowing jar from its shelves. Wistful memories of my sister shouldered me in the guts and the jar blurred for a moment. I blinked away tears. The man didn't notice. He moved to a tube of brass protruding from the side, the end narrow and sharp like a mosquito's needle. With a quick motion, he pierced the lid of the jar with the tip. The soul floated to the hole and slid into the black mouth of the pipe.

The machine lurched to life, humming with a resonance that reminded me of starlings in a grove. A glass globe on the side opposite the brass pipe lit with a gentle glow.

"What is this?" I asked. "Sorcery?"

"Just watch," the man said.

The glow in the globe intensified, a soft sun writ on crystal. Then it resolved. A ship at sea, painted in sepia tones. A man, his hair and beard plaited, his eyes black and hard, a cutlass in his hand. The swell of the waves, a mirror of the swell of the clouds above. The scene changed, men, bleeding and dying, wild eyes above grinning teeth. Blood tinted in that same faded brown as the ship. And more. Gulls above a hundred ports. Masts bobbing in the sun. The rage of the sea. And then, waves, waves, lassitude.

The vision faded. I stepped back, blinked.

"What… what was that?" I asked.

"A single life. Haven't you ever wondered who these souls are?" He gestured toward the field, warm lights rising from the loam.

I had. Once. And I knew at least two of them. I kept that to myself.

"The fair?"

"Yes," he said.

I knew I could not afford it. What money Mother left me, I parceled carefully. I squirreled away what I earned by taking on odd jobs. I bought an old goat to save on milk, and even that would only pay for itself over a long stretch. The fair would set me back months. He must've seen my face fall.

"Listen," he said. "I saw something in you just now."

I remembered he was a man again, and how close he stood. He smelled of metal and oil. I stepped back, raised the knife. His hands went up.

"I saw something alight in you when you saw this, is all. I'll come back next year. And the next. As long as people will pay, I'll be back. And I'll tell you what. I'll take this track." He gestured to the ruts that led through the village. "Every year."

"Yeah?" I asked. "What's the catch?"

"A penny a year."

"That's all?" I found it hard to believe. Mother told me to never trust a man who didn't charge a fair price.

"That's all."

I had nothing to say. I'd seen something wondrous. That I knew. But to be out here, with this strange man in the dark... "Best get on now," I said.

He nodded and turned to secure his goods. While he did, I stepped back into my home. I listened at the door until the creak of wheels and the rattle of wagon boards dwindled down the road. When I was sure he had gone, I stepped outside and sat on the steps, watching the souls rise.

That night I dreamt of Kiva, olive skin in the summer sun, hair like honey. I dreamt of her laugh and her smile, the way we ran through the trees, the fitful light beneath the canopy. Eventually, that flicker and fade from dreams woke me. I walked to the kitchen and pulled a dingy jar from a shelf beside its twin. I held it for a moment, wiped away the dust until the tips of my fingers were brown, then took it to the field. I stood with supple grass tickling my shins, bare beneath the hem of my shift, then sprinted into the field with a low *whoop* and caught a soul or two. I peered at the glowing embers in their glass prison and waited for that old exhilaration, the sudden wellspring of joy that came from being clever and quick and free beneath the canopy of night. It did not come.

I hadn't the heart to make them wait, so I set the jar on the ground and lay beside it, folding myself into the field. There I stayed until the earth grew cold with the arrival of morning and the stars faded into the pink of dawn.

He came again the next year. Summer clung to the edges of autumn like a desperate lover. Souls rose in a riot of light like stars running to the sky. He tapped on my door, and I peered out. He grinned through the crack I'd opened. I didn't know if I could trust him yet, but perhaps. He'd kept his promise.

I tucked the knife into my belt and slipped the penny I'd saved from a chipped dish on the table, then stepped out to meet him. He looked at me for a long moment. His eyes flicked to the knife, then to the coin in my outstretched hand. He licked his lips.

"You've filled out some," he said.

"It was a good summer," I said. "Good harvest."

I wished he'd take the penny. It felt like a lodestone in my palm, tugging me toward that machine and its secrets. A familiar silence stretched between us, of things unspoken. Finally, he took it, his fingers grazing my palm. Frisson ran up my arm. I ignored it.

He walked to the machine, and I sat in the grass, the blades tickling my shins and thighs. As before, he pulled a jar from his cabinet and fit it to the needle. I watched the soul travel toward the glass globe suffusing with light.

A woman on horseback. The sound of tack and leather creaking. The clop of hooves on desert hardpan. A saber at her hip, a spear tied to her saddle. Her hair blew in the wind, and dust obscured the vision for a moment. When it passed, the vista opened to reveal a mesa and butte rising from the landscape like fingers searching for the sky. Behind her, a cabin, long rotted by the dry winds. A hawk called as it wheeled in the sky.

On she rode, and on and on until the vision faded. I could nearly smell the stale air in that cabin, feel the bitter taste of loss and loneliness on my tongue. I sat, staring at the dark globe, and the man came to sit beside me.

"You lost someone." It wasn't a question.

I nodded.

"I've seen it before. The ones who ache sit and stare, and they hope and dread they'll see them again," he said.

"And still you do this," I said. "Why?"

"Why do you watch?" he asked.

I looked at the sky. "You ever hope to see a shooting star? You know that moment when they burn high and bright?"

He didn't answer and I looked over at him. His head tilted up.

"Memories are like that," I said. "High and bright. But never so close you can see more than the shine."

"Yeah," he said. "Yeah, I understand."

We sat under the light of the moon until it crested the peak of night. Finally, he stood and dusted off his trousers. He covered his wagon and the things on it, then stopped one last time to look at me.

"Next year, then?" he asked.

"Next year."

The soulman came five more summers. Like clockwork, he rolled up to my door, and each summer, like clockwork, I came out with a penny. Eventually, I left my knife in the house. Had he meant me harm, I believed he would have inflicted it long past.

In five years, I'd eked out a comfortable life, though no less hard. I worked for every penny, and aside from my small bottles of wine, or a round of cheese, I spent on few frivolities. So, when he came, I brought my comestibles and sat before the machine. We shared a meal while we watched.

A liar and a thief. A lawyer. A surgeon. A herdsman. A warrior. Scenes visceral and bucolic, fantastic and mundane. I marveled at the similarities between warrior and surgeon, oftentimes the vagaries of their work separated only by the degree of applied violence. Of the way the horse drove the cattle or dragged the plow to cut the furrows for the animals to feed from. Everything intertwined, everything supporting everything else.

And I thought of the opposite ends of life. Mother, old and gray before her time. Kiva, young and vital. And there in the center, me. Alone. Five years I spent like that, finding sorrow and joy from the man with the soul machine. Five years of living on the edge of a razor, guilt and grief like slivers in my soul.

The sixth year the man came, I was nearly destitute. Crops had been bad. The goat refused to give milk, and then refused to live. I walked around, hollow in the stomach and the heart. No one needed odd jobs because no one could afford them.

So, when the soulman came, I met him again with my penny and sat before his machine. He looked at me, and I saw the light of need in his eyes that maybe hadn't been so obvious before. I felt that desire in my own soul. The need to fill the loneliness of the hours with companionship.

"You've lost weight."

"It's been a hard year."

He nodded and brought out a basket, then sat beside me. He pulled cheese and bread from it, a bottle of crisp wine. When we finished, we sat in silence. He grew bold, laid his fingers on mine, and I let him. Then he stood abruptly, in the same way someone might change the subject in a conversation they were unsure of. He walked over and pulled the jar from his cabinet, the soul inside like fire on water. He started the device, the glass glowing the warm yellow of a summer sunset.

Kiva stood before me, writ exquisite in that globe. Small and perfect and kind and glowing with life. I watched as we ran from tree to tree, giggling while we played hide and seek. Watched as she bit into an apple, the juice running down her chin; watched as she laughed at a butterfly tickling her nose. Finally, the vision slid from grass to a blue sky, clouds like schooners, sails full in the wind.

When it faded, the soulman did not leave. Not because he expected to stay, but because I insisted. His name was Thom, and his body was as pale as his smile. We finished sometime in the small hours.

"What was her name?" he asked.

"Kiva." A long silence. The chirp of crickets in the summer heat. I wondered, even now, if she heard them. "Where do the souls go?" I asked.

He lifted a hand, waved it in a dozy haze. "The machine uses them up."

A knot formed in my chest. "You mean it uses the memory up."

He shook his head, coarse hair rasping against the pillow. "It uses them for fuel. Burns them right out. Shooting stars, right? Souls are just memories we can't let go of. It's our fault they stay behind."

"You believe that?"

He shrugged, the rasp of his shoulders on the sheet loud in the quiet room. "Who was she, anyway?" This last, sleepy, half-mumbled.

I didn't answer. Shame burned my chest at not asking what happened to the souls before. Then rage that he should imply my sorrow chained my sister to this world. As if her plight and her end were my fault. I stifled my emotion, forced my hands not to shake, tears not to spill. I made myself calm the way Mother told me I had to be if a man ever hurt me. Because, as she always said, they will.

When he finally drifted off, I found the knife and pulled Kiva's jar from its shelf. The moon was high, so I threw back the curtain. Pale light flooded the room, and I knelt beside him. He nearly glowed in the beam.

"Thom," I whispered.

He didn't stir. I placed the jar over his chest. Rise, fall. I pressed the knife against his throat, watched his pulse bob the edge up and down.

I thought of the memories and brief joys he'd brought me and hesitated. Of the meals we'd shared and the nights, when he'd sit so close, I felt his heat. I thought of the things I'd been taught growing up.

Mother said often of life: *Our lives are like the stars, and the stars make the sky. Some burn bright, others dim, but they are all the same stuff. When they cease, they return like a wave into the sea.*

Still, he slept. Breaths of a man oblivious to the path of destruction he wrought. Ignorance? Entitlement? I didn't think it mattered. I let the rage I'd denied come, and it flooded back, rushed into my hands, making them shake. Filled my mouth with the taste of pennies. Sorrow chased its heels like a starving dog, overtook it. I coughed a sob and dropped the knife, swept the jar from his chest. It tumbled to the floor and cracked.

The blade clattered to the floor, and I let it lie where it fell, bright steel glinting in the moonlight. Numb with sorrow, shaking with rage, I stumbled from the room and fled to the field. There I lay, lost in the grass, and watched the souls rise to the stars, like embers from a fire. Sorrow carved a hollow in my gut and tears streaked my cheeks

In my core, where sadness and joy constantly warred for the truth, I found no answers. Instead, I recalled something else my mother had told me: *Grief is only meant to be held for a moment. Beyond that, it turns from water to oil. It clings and threatens to set us ablaze at the slightest hint of a spark.* She'd let it consume her. I'd spent most of my life afraid of fire.

I tilted my face to the sky. Souls danced in the pale light of the moon, an endless procession of the dead. In time, Thom made his way from the house, bleary-eyed and confused. He lay next to me, his hand finding mine. We didn't speak, and I clenched his fingers, maybe enough to hurt. He didn't complain.

I didn't know what I was doing, but I knew I had to start somewhere. I had to move on, or this ache would cut me in two.

A knife of never letting go. And though I hadn't yet forgiven him, maybe never would, I found a small measure of peace there among the dead. And for once, I wasn't afraid.

CLAYTON SNYDER

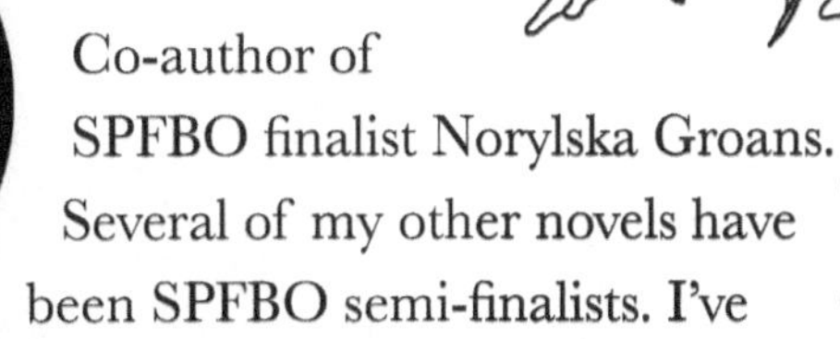

Co-author of
SPFBO finalist Norylska Groans.
Several of my other novels have
been SPFBO semi-finalists. I've
also authored numerous short stories, my
most recent, Injustice, at Three Crows Magazine, which has
been compared to Gene Wolfe's work.

I currently split my time between work and writing. I
have worked as a systems admin, chainsaw operator, and
once did an ill-advised stint as a bodyguard because I am
'really tall.'

Find out more about Clayton Snyder at
claytonwsnyder.com

RELIQUARY OF THE DAMNED

RACHEL EMMA SHAW

*For Anna, who would have shared her memoir with
the world if she could*

*I wish I knew the right thing to say
when I had the chance to say it*

We miss you

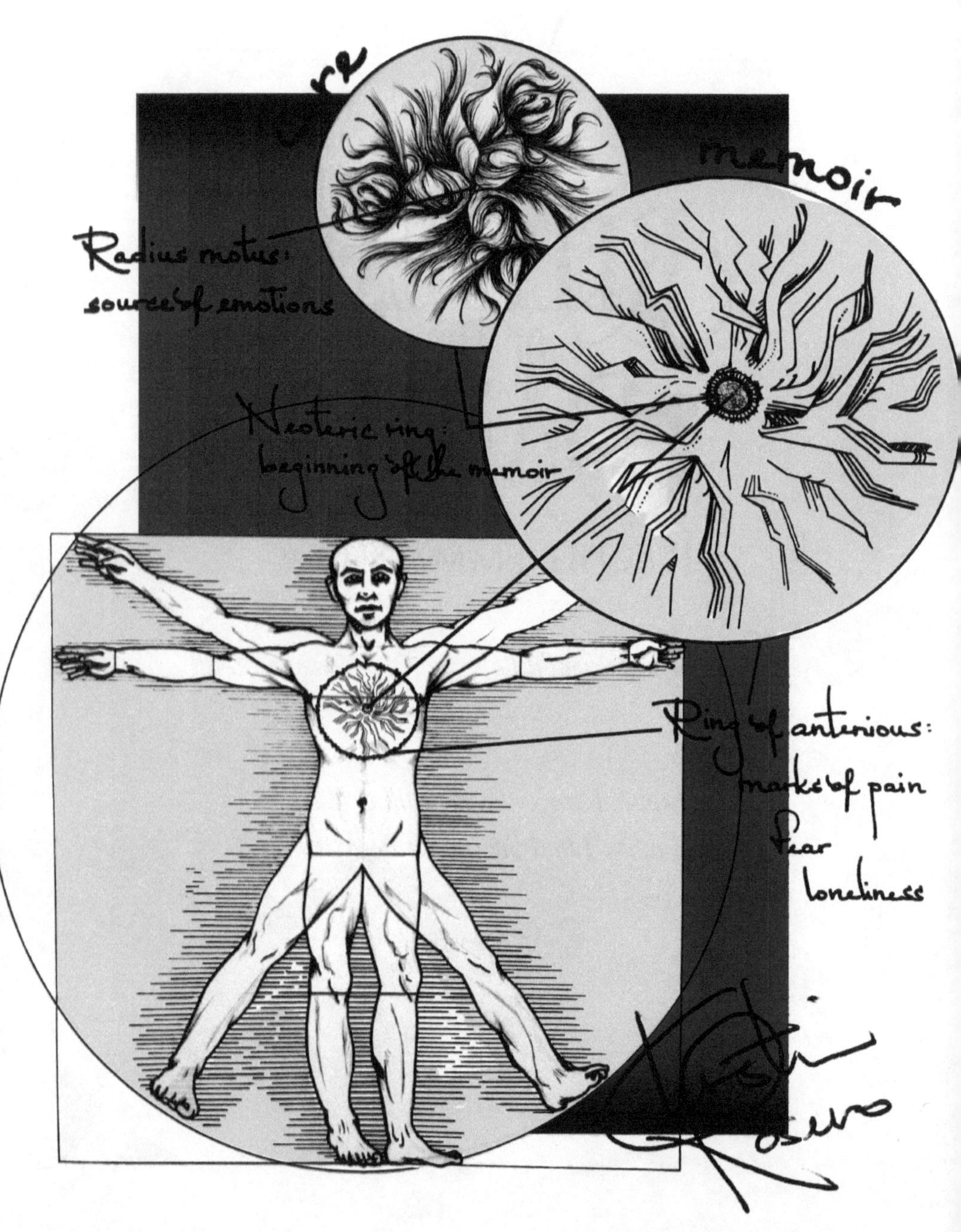
memoir
Radius motus:
source of emotions
Neoteric ring:
beginning of the memoir
Ring of anterious:
marks of pain
fear
loneliness

RELIQUARY OF THE DAMNED

RACHEL EMMA SHAW

Boarded-up windows and doors lined the refuse-strewn alleyway as Eolin crept along it, doing her best to ignore the rats shrieking about her as they fought for scraps. She squinted at the worn numbers above each doorway she passed, searching for the Reliquary of the Damned as a group of clearly drunk men jested with each other up ahead.

The Reliquary called to her, ringing like a broken bell in the night, its summons drowning out all of her doubts. Anyone with any sense would have stayed home. The dregs weren't a safe part of the city, but Eolin was beyond caring. What good sense she had once possessed was now no more than dust ground down by neglect. Abandoned by apathy. Why not try visiting the dregs when nothing else helped?

She had heard the stories. Everybody had. Everyone knew about the Reliquary's open-door policy when it came to the marked. How its patrons were encouraged to have their memoirs on display for all to see. The thought of people doing so sounded so ludicrous that Eolin couldn't believe it to be true, but what if it was? Could those who visited really feel no shame for the scars etched into their chests? Eolin couldn't imagine it, but that only increased her need to see the truth for herself. If she was going to find her people anywhere, then the Reliquary of the Damned seemed as good a place as any to start. Certainly more so than the clearskins she waited on in exchange for bed and board.

Would there be others like her inside? People too damaged to fit in elsewhere? Relief and anguish warred inside her at the thought. One because of the connection she longed for. The other because she hated the thought of anyone else having been through anything like what she had.

"Just let us in already!" one of the drunks further down the alley called as he shoved against a larger man stood before him, blocking a doorway.

"Ain't happening," the larger man replied, his voice a deep rumble that Eolin almost didn't make out as she shifted a little further into the shadows, watching the troublemakers, a thrumming of unease pulsing in her core.

"You really think you can stop us?" one of the trio asked as he lurched forward, his long, brown hair falling about his face with the flounce and self-importance only a clearskin could truly pull off. Eolin hated sizing people up so readily, but knew well enough how pointless it would be to give twits like the three men up ahead any benefit of the doubt.

"Besides the fact that you're already too drunk to be let in, we all know why you're here," the bouncer said as the two others held back the more determined of the three, whispering something in his ear that Eolin couldn't hear.

"Look, why don't you do us all a favour and get gone?" the bouncer continued, sighing as if this was a regular occurrence. "I'm not letting you in."

The trio relented, but Eolin didn't like the excitement in their voices as they passed her, glancing back over their shoulders at the bouncer. Waiting for them to pass, she shrank further against the wall to avoid drawing their attention, in no mood for dealing with a clearskin.

"You can come out now."

The bouncer's low rumble echoed off the walls, making the alley seem emptier than it had a moment before. Eolin spun around, surprised to find him looking her way, since she assumed he hadn't seen her. Wishing she picked a darker shadow to hide in, she debated turning back around and heading home for the night. The Reliquary was clearly a lure for the city's bad elements.

"Or stay there," the bouncer said with a chuckle when Eolin didn't move. "But you're safer in here than you are out there."

Was that a promise?

Was she really going to do this? If he demanded she remove her privacyguard before he let her in, then she would be out of the alley faster than he could call her a coward. But could she really let this chance to find others like her go?

Amusement danced in the bouncer's eyes as Eolin stepped out of the shadows, making her way cautiously over and stopping before him as he looked her up and down.

"You're new."

"You're not," Eolin retorted, causing the man to chuckle.

He knocked on the door at his back, and a metallic clang rolled down the alley. A moment later, the door screeched open, unleashing a soft-amber glow and the chatter of voices from within.

Peeking through the gap in the door, Eolin shuddered, unsure if the source of the shudder was the cold night air or her core.

Glancing at the bouncer, she silently asked for him to repeat his reassurances, but he just cocked an eyebrow.

"If you don't want to go in—"

"No, I do. I do. I just…"

Coward. If her core was visible, then the bouncer would have seen her fear. He would have seen how it was pulsing out of control, almost to the point of forming relics of her fear. Did he let quiverers inside the Reliquary? Perhaps they were stopped inside once they had removed their privacyguards and everyone could see the evidence of their anxieties on their chest.

The bouncer reached for the door as Eolin hesitated, caught between longing to enter and fear of what awaited her inside. As he began to shut the door, the music and voices within faded, swallowing Eolin again in the alley's darkness.

Fear of living a life where she would never know the truth chased Eolin under the bouncer's arm and she darted inside. The door clapped shut behind her, cutting off the bouncer's laughter as he sealed her inside the Reliquary of the Damned.

Flames concealed by tempered orbs lit the balcony Eolin stepped onto, the low hum of voices and song reaching up to her from below. The music wrapped around her body, drawing her towards the railing and the sight of everyone already gathered in the Reliquary, pulling her out of the darkness she felt like she had lived her entire life in.

"Want me to check your coat and guard?"

The voice came from the shadows and Eolin spun to see who had spoken, surprised she had missed the blue-haired girl sitting in the alcove. The girl had her legs propped on a table as she leaned back, her eyes closed. A colourful array of outer garments Eolin assumed to belong to the guests hung behind her, but what caught Eolin's gaze was the absence of a privacyguard to conceal the girl's memoir and core from view.

The coat-check's neckline hung low, revealing the skin across her chest, along with every relic she possessed. Each of the mottled scars peppering her memoir told the story of her life up to that moment, and the sight took Eolin aback. It was one thing to be told about how those who frequented the Reliquary felt no shame when it came to displaying their marks, but it was another entirely to see it.

The relics in the woman's memoir swirled out from her core, creating a pattern of should-be secrets that Eolin couldn't tear her eyes from. She knew she had no right to see the girl's relics, but there they were, visible to any and all.

The voyeurism of seeing something so private caused a blush to creep up Eolin's cheeks, and she forced herself to look away, but was unable to escape the memory of the relics she had already recognised on the coat-check's memoir. The intense black of grief. The faded mottling of regret. Pity welled in Eolin at the sight, and she wished she knew the right words to say to the almost stranger.

How could she know so much about this woman she had only just met? Unease pulsed like sludge in Eolin's core, and she hated the knowledge she had acquired just by looking. Had she really thought herself capable of being so exposed? Of letting others pry into everything she had worked so hard to keep hidden all these years? Foolish, foolish girl.

"I… I can't," Eolin said as she backed away towards the door. "I'm sorry. I shouldn't have come here."

"You can keep your guard on if you'd like," the blue-haired girl said as Eolin reached for the door handle, stilling as the coat-check waved at the fabric pinned across Eolin's chest. "We don't mind. Nobody down there'll make you take it off before you're ready."

Leaning back, the coat-check closed her eyes again, resettling on her seat as she left the question and its answer to Eolin. Stay or go? There would be regrets either way. The question was, which could she live with?

Air crackled about Eolin as she approached the balcony's railing, the milling crowd below coming into view a little more with each step. She devoured the sight of the people littering the lower level, watching how some swayed to the music, while others leaned over the bar, trying to catch the attention of the servers. Small circular tables peppered the room, each occupied by groups engaged in animated conversations.

Eolin lost count of the number of memoirs on display, staring in wonder at the men with their bare chests or their low-necked waistcoats that did nothing to hide either their memoir or their core. The women meanwhile wore dresses cut so low at the front they fell almost to the midriff, the women's breasts cleverly concealed even while they revealed something Eolin considered excessively more intimate.

As she stared at them, the strange notion that the memoirs on display were all so similar and yet so unique struck her. Some held marks of anguish and rejection, others of insecurity and humiliation, but the same patterns could be seen in all of them, and there were certainly no members of the great unmarked in the room. The realisation brought a strange calmness to Eolin, helping her work up the courage to make her way towards the steps to join them. In a way, judging from the state of their memoirs, she already had.

Doing her best to keep her gaze averted, Eolin took one hesitant step down the spiralled staircase after another, unsure of the etiquette in a place such as the Reliquary. When she reached the lower floor, she made her way over to an empty stool at the bar, finding a much-needed anonymity in the press of the people gathered there, laughing and clinking their glasses. She tried to catch the attention of a woman behind the bar, only to sit back in defeat, her gaze wandering over the reflections in the mirror behind the bottles. She looked out of place, the dark grey fabric of her privacyguard somehow making her seem lifeless compared to the animated people about her. She forced her reflection to smile, but the blond woman staring back at her only looked even more out of place.

Beside her, a man's core beat with frustration as he leaned over the bar, trying to flag a server down, but his was the exception. Most of the cores of those about her didn't pulse with emotion, instead they sat empty in the centre of the memoir, absent of any negative emotions the core displayed.

The realisation that followed caught Eolin off guard. How had she never noticed the core could be just as revealing by what it didn't show as what it did?

Across the room, apprehension filled a woman's core as a man approached the table she sat at with a friend, and the strange dynamics that must exist inside the Reliquary slowly became apparent to Eolin. How much more honest people would have to be with the truth revealed to all in their core like that? She hadn't much thought about the implications of the core being on display before arriving, too consumed by the thought of the memoir being on show and all that would entail, but while the relics littering the memoir drew the eye, telling tales of traumas past, the core was no less revealing. How could you lie with any success if your core gave away your anxiety? Was it polite not to get offended if someone's core flickered with their dislike of you, even if their smile said otherwise? The thought of it all filled Eolin's core with anxiety, but as she looked about at the cores reflected at her in the mirror, she couldn't see that anxiety shared anywhere else. Instead, her gaze locked on a pair of dark-brown eyes staring back at her in the mirror.

Shame stained Eolin's cheeks as she looked away from the woman, embarrassed to have been caught prying.

"What can I get you?"

Turning at the voice, Eolin met the friendly smile from the woman behind the bar as she stood waiting for a response, her core blank where it sat in the middle of her exposed memoir. Relics of loneliness and depression circled out from the core above the woman's heart, reading like a story filled with emotional battles that had been fought year after year.

Realising she was staring again, Eolin dragged her gaze up, meeting the woman's eyes as an apology spilt from her lips.

"You're allowed to look," the woman said, laughter filling in her voice. "That's sort of the point of being here, isn't it? So, what do you want?"

"Get her the house special," another woman said from beside Eolin, nodding to the man on the next stool over. The man vacated the stool and the woman who had spoken took his place.

Eolin froze at the sight of the dark-brown eyes that had been watching her in the mirror, a heat burning her cheeks as the dull tolling of embarrassment beat in her core.

"I didn't mean to stare. I'm sorry, I—"

The woman chuckled, finishing her drink with a quick motion before placing the empty glass on the bar, nodding for the bartender to refill it as she said, "You're new."

"Why do people keep saying that?"

"You've got the look. Most who end up here do, but they lose it after they've been back a few times."

"If they come back," Eolin observed, taking great pains to keep her gaze from drifting any lower than the woman's chin.

"I think you will," the woman said, her full lips curving at the corners.

"You got all that, and my core isn't even on show," Eolin said as the bartender returned, placing two glasses before them as Eolin fished for her coin purse. "Who knows what you'd see if I took my guard off."

"No need for that," the woman beside her said, pulling out an elegantly carved, long-stem pipe from her pocket and tapping a sprinkling of dried leaves into it. "The Reliquary's mine. I like to offer all newcomers a drink on the house. Seems to help put them at ease. I'm Taya, by the way."

"Eolin."

"You're from the north country, right?"

"You've seen a lot of us come here."

"Enough," Taya said as she kindled the leaves and took a quick draw on her pipe.

Eolin's gaze flickered down to Taya's memoir before she could stop herself. She dragged her eyes back up, only to find Taya watching her with an interest that made Eolin's cheeks burn in shame.

"Spend enough time here and your memoir will look the same," Taya said, gesturing with the pipe to where Eolin's memoir and core lay hidden beneath her privacyguard.

Realising what Taya meant, Eolin paused, glancing about the room, taking in the memoirs about her with a new interest. Empathy echoes littered the room. The relic existed in the memoirs about her in far greater number than Eolin had ever imagined.

More sepia than the black of the other relics, the empathy relics reflected the emotion that had caused them, mirroring the marks that must have originally formed on whichever poor soul had the bad luck of being the source of that particular pain.

"The healers get them worse," Taya said, taking a swig of her drink. "They spend their lives trying to fix what there's sometimes no fix for. Ironic, isn't it? Nobody ever asks who will heal the healers."

"Is that why you created this place?"

Taya raised an eyebrow as smoke billowed from her mouth. Embarrassed by having asked so personal a question of a stranger, Eolin looked away, blaming her over familiarity on all the memoirs about her. Sipping her drink, she reeled as the heady liquor tumbled down her throat, heating her insides as it fell.

"Sharing can be a great healer for the soul," Taya said, glancing pointedly at Eolin's privacyguard. "Especially when the one you're sharing with is a stranger."

Taya's meaning hung in the air, making Eolin blush. She decided to take another sip rather than face the challenge posed. Not yet, at least.

"The first time's always worst," Taya continued, exhaling a coil of smoke. "But if you're not game, perhaps there's another way the Reliquary can help you?"

Using the end of her pipe, Taya gestured around the room, pointing at the memoirs of those closest. "Take a look. See any relics you recognise?"

Not needing to look, since she already knew the answer, Eolin nodded. Grief, shame, loneliness and more.

"What about here?" Taya asked, gesturing at her own memoir. The act was so intimate that Eolin had to fight back another blush.

"Some," she said, wetting her dry lips as she stared at the relics they shared.

"It's alright," Taya said, smiling as she took Eolin's hand, hovering it over her chest.

The familiarity and joint strangeness of the motion made Eolin's breath come in shallow pants, her thoughts lost to the warmth of the skin so close beneath her fingertips.

"Show me," Taya said as Eolin met her gaze.

Moving their hands hesitatingly, Eolin hovered their fingers over Taya's relics of isolation and loneliness. There were others too, but those were all she could bring herself to share for now. Pulling her hand back, she stopped as Taya's grip tightened. Meeting Taya's gaze, she found it searching hers, silently asking for permission. For what, Eolin didn't know, but she gave it all the same.

Lowering their hands, Taya grazed the pads of Eolin's fingers on the rough skin of her relics. Taya's emotions rushed into Eolin and the crowd about her faded as a deep well of loneliness tore through her flesh, burning into her until it seared away every other emotion. The isolation was overpowering, like she would never know the touch of another again.

"Empathy. Like I said, this place will do that to you," Taya said, nodding to the tear trickling down Eolin's face as a crash tore through the bar, silencing the conversations about the room and throwing the musicians off-key.

Glancing towards the source of the commotion, Eolin frowned at the balcony and the figures shifting about like shadows. It was too dark to make them out, but their cheering at having made it inside could be heard easily enough.

Muttering under her breath, Taya put her pipe out and rose from her stool, signalling to someone at the back. A moment later, a large man emerged from the crowd, heading for the staircase the drunken men were already making their way down. Eolin recognised the men from earlier as one leapt over the banister, jumping the last few steps, chased down by the bouncer from outside.

"Apologies about this," Taya said to Eolin before moving towards the drunkards, who were already in the process of stripping to their bare chests and descending on those stood closest to the stairs.

One of the men turned, and Eolin caught sight of his unmarked chest. There wasn't so much as a single relic on him. Even his core lacked the shame and embarrassment Eolin would have felt had she been intruding like he was.

The memoirs of his companions were just as empty of relics, and jealousy stabbed through Eolin. Why should they be free of scars when others had to carry their burdens? She hated how the rich could afford the benefit of private healers. Those men were the epitome of privilege, their lives pampered and sheltered from all of life's injuries.

"Alright, that's enough now," Taya called, trying to steer the men back towards the staircase, only for them to jeer at her, the one who had been arguing with the bouncer outside slipping away into the crowd.

Eolin watched as he commented on the memoirs of those he passed, laughing at some, flinching from others. He seemed to take great amusement at the sight of relics he probably couldn't even read. People who could afford to have their wounds healed rarely bothered to learn the language of the damned.

Eolin was still glaring at the man when he spotted her, his eyes narrowing on the sight of her privacyguard before he lurched her way.

"What's this? Why so shy?" he called, slapping his hand to his memoir as he strode her way on unsteady legs. "Take it off! Why come here if you're not going to take it off?"

Reaching her, he grabbed her privacyguard, pulling on it as she tried to fight him off. Her hands shook as she shoved at him ineffectually, her core thrumming with fear as she fought against his grip, desperately clutching the fabric that was keeping her secrets concealed.

"Get off me!"

"Leave her be," Taya snapped, appearing beside the man and snatching his arm away, but he kept his grip on Eolin's privacyguard. The brooch on Eolin's right shoulder gave, and the fabric dropped, exposing the thick mess of relics concealed beneath.

Shame burned Eolin's cheeks, and she watched the emotion flare to life in her core as she scrambled to catch the fabric, her humiliation growing. She could feel the eyes of all those around her as they stared at her secrets.

Her pulse pounded as she fought the urge to run, her skin crawling from how exposed she was. A tear rolled down her cheek, but she managed to keep her gaze locked on the man's, staring into his laughing eyes so she wouldn't be tempted to look and see what emotions danced in the cores of those about her. Empathy? Disgust? Fear?

Unable to stop herself, she glanced at Taya's core, relieved to find fury pounding there as Taya rounded on the man, her eyes blazing with rage.

She wasn't disgusted by what she saw? The sight of Taya's rage sparked Eolin's own, and she rose, following the man through the room as he moved on, unaffected by the damage he had inflicted.

"No," she said. "You don't get to stop there. You want to intrude on the pain of others, then why go halfway?"

"What are you—"

Eolin grabbed his hand and dragged it to her chest. She pressed it to her relics, holding him there as he tried to pull back. He was the first person to touch her scars and the feel of his skin on her flesh was more intrusive than she could have imagined, but she pushed past that, watching his face contort, his hand shaking as she held it to her chest. The echoes of her emotions flickered in his eyes. Somehow, they looked even worse when inside another.

She looked down at his core, recognising the emotions she had already lived through as they beat there in sepia. Empathy. Good.

Moisture and an unspoken apology gleamed in his eyes as she let him go, standing back as Taya and the bouncer grabbed him, shoving him towards the stairs and the friends who had already been escorted outside.

Turning, Eolin sat back on her stool, her hands shaking as she lay them atop the counter, waiting for the music and chatter to resume. Realising that her privacyguard was still down, she reached for it, only to pause.

She was still staring at her memoir in the reflection of the mirror when Taya joined her.

"Sorry about that. We try to keep them out, but they can be determined little shi—"

"It's alright," Eolin said, reaching for the still-attached side of her guard and unpinning the brooch. She let the thick gauze fall, staring at her memoir's reflection in the mirror. The humiliation and vengeful rage in her core were already fading, soon to be gone forever, too insignificant in the grand scheme of everything she had gone through to leave a relic behind.

"See," Taya said with a smile. "I told you it helped to share."

"I think you're right," Eolin said, watching the emotions fading from her core, leaving it blank.

"Now then," Taya said, tapping at her pipe and lighting it up again. "How do you feel about sharing some of those stories you've got to tell?"

RACHEL EMMA SHAW

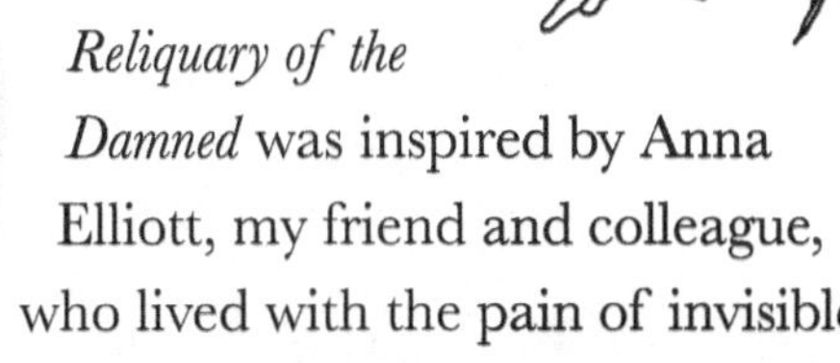

Reliquary of the Damned was inspired by Anna Elliott, my friend and colleague, who lived with the pain of invisible disabilities throughout her far too-short life. Anna shared her passion for making the invisible visible with me. Her goal of removing the blindfolds we tie around our eyes is what sparked this story. Now she's gone, I hope this tale helps her efforts live on.

If you enjoyed exploring the world this short story was set in, then keep your eyes peeled for *Written in the Flesh*, the full length novel set in the same world, and that goes even further into exploring a society where the scars of our minds leave marks on our skin. *Written in the Flesh* will be the fifth novel published by Rachel Emma Shaw. As an author, her works explore psychology through the lens of fantasy. Her first published novels followed an ill-fated memory thief with a tendency to corrupt the identities of those left in her wake. Rachel's second duology was darker still. Set in a city where death and decay rule the constant night, *Sacaran Nights* explores what it is to leave a legacy, especially for the poor souls trapped by the hopes of the dead.

Find out more about Rachel Emma Shaw at
rachelemmashaw.wordpress.com/books

THE QUIET

MADOLYN ROGERS

In memory of my aunt Janice, whose spirit burned bright

The Quiet

Madolyn Rogers

The cries of the wounded faded. Solana paused, scanning the battlefield in the predawn murk. Nothing moved, save a few village warriors, poking through the thick grass searching for the fallen. During the night, screams had guided Solana from body to body. But now, there were fewer moans, and they were far weaker. Many had likely died of their injuries before she could reach them. The thought brought only resignation, the dry taste of dust in her mouth.

She sighed, raising her arms over her head, stretching her aching back. Strands of her long, dark hair came loose, tumbling into her face. Impatiently she pulled the mass back again, twisting it into a loose knot. Lowering her hands, she caught a glimpse of her palms. The red-brown of dried blood stained her dark flesh like clay. She rubbed her hands on her trousers, grimacing.

She heard the clomp of hooves and turned to see a horse and rider approaching from the east. Behind them, dirty bronze light smudged the sky, heralding dawn. Solana squinted at it. Colors had seemed brighter to her before… before three years ago. Absently, she fingered the vial hanging from her neck. Once she had loved the dawn. She tried to remember how beautiful it was, its pinks and golds spilling across the sky, but it was like a long-forgotten painting, the image slipping from her mind's eye. Now sunrise was a murky, pallid jumble drained of vivid color, like everything else.

The horse came to a halt, and the rider slid off stiffly. She staggered a step, with a muffled curse. She was old, her long braided hair graying. The red sash around her waist matched Solana's own.

Solana took stock of the direction the rider came from. "You're from Nalja?"

The old woman nodded, picking her way toward Solana around the rocks and hummocks. "Aye, right enough. I rode all night." She glanced about the field, mouth pursed. The twisted body of a barbarian tribesman lay not far off, and just past it, one of their own. "I see I'm here near too late to do any good. I'm Gayna."

"Solana." She extended a fist to touch the older woman's. Gayna's seamed, dark face was as craggy and beautiful as the cliffs to the west. She reminded Solana of her grandmother, gone these many years. Solana tried to remember the old woman's laugh, her gentle touch, but they eluded her. It was long since everyone she loved had died and left her in a world of dust. "I'm pleased to have you. There's more work yet."

"You managed by yourself all night?" Gayna's dark eyes were keen on her.

"I had to. I'm the only healer in my village." Solana pushed back her memories of the lightless hours: the ragged yells, the clash of metal, the endless search for the wounded amid the pounding melee. It hadn't seemed real then, and now it felt almost like a dream. "The Vedshri attacked in the dead of night. They were after the herds."

Gayna shook her head, mouth twisting, and spat. "Devourer take those pale-skinned devils." Her anger was cold, a wall of ice.

Its chill couldn't touch Solana. She hadn't felt anger in a long time, even toward the Vedshri. "I haven't seen any sign they're devils. The tribesmen fight fiercely, it's true, but they are human like us."

"Human, yes, but not like us. There are sorcerers among them." The words fell soft into the dawn light, bringing their own breath of cold.

"Is there really such a thing? I've never seen one."

"Oh, they're real all right, but rare. They say even the Vedshri fear them." Gayna turned to trudge across the field. Faint moans of pain rose from beyond a tall stone, and she angled that way. "Devourer, what a mess. So many dead. At least we beat them. Thank Sythorla for that."

The words slid off Solana. She could feel neither grief nor triumph at the night's work. A grimy weariness dragged at her, the futility of it all.

They rounded the rock and found the wounded man—one of the Vedshri, curled around himself, whimpering into the dirt. He cringed away from them, fear in his eyes.

Gayna's lip curled. "Leave him. He's not worth our effort."

Something twinged in Solana's heart, a stirring of emotion long forgotten. He might be a Vedshri, but she couldn't walk away. "Why? They bleed like us, die like us. And we are healers."

Gayna measured her. She drew a breath as though to retort, and then let it go. "As you like, then."

They knelt and rolled him onto his back. The tribesman clutched one hand to his left shoulder. Bright blood oozed through the rent leather and stained his fingers. Like all the Vedshri, his eyes and hair were as dark as Solana's, but his skin was as pale as clotted cream. That fair skin made him appear exposed, vulnerable as an unearthed grub. Solana leaned close, and the strange smell of him wafted over her, pungent herbs and musky sweat layered over the stink of blood and voided bowels.

Together, they cut away his leather vest and peeled back his flowing garments, uncovering the long gash of the wound in his shoulder. He gasped and babbled in his own tongue, his tone pleading. The sword had cut deep, gristle and sinew showing. Blood soaked his clothing and the ground beneath him. Solana studied the sweat coating his pale brow, the dryness of his lips. He would not last much longer. Unbidden, she thought of her husband. Had Bornaz died like this, bleeding out, surrounded by enemies? The vision brought nothing but a muted ache, a hollowness where pain had been.

Gayna dug mudroot from her pack, placing the twisted brown roots against his torn flesh. He stared at her, eyes distended. Biting her lip, Gayna squeezed nightmilk from a fleshy stalk, the white drops vanishing into the bloody mess of his shoulder. He babbled something, the foreign words sharp, edged with anger, as though he thought the herbs might harm him.

Gayna dropped the plant from trembling fingers. She met Solana's eyes. "I don't think I can heal him, after all. Not after all his kind have done to us, all the deaths I've seen. I can't bring myself to do it. I'm sorry."

"It's all right. I'll do it." Solana rested her fingers against his wound and closed her eyes. She felt for the power hidden in the roots, what they called the quia, the earth magic. Its energy moved in her mind. She could sense it with an inner sight, see the movement of those strands, their distinct nature. The bright ripples of nightmilk joined the slow, dark surge of the mudroot, like sparkles upon deep water. She called on the mingled quia of the plants, pulling it into her flesh. It came slowly, reluctantly, as though she tugged on a great weight. She could summon only a trickle of it. The quia ran warm through her veins, comforting but faint.

She directed the stream of quia through her fingers, into the man's wounds. It pulsed through his rent flesh. She urged the quia to spend its power, to knit his muscle, sinew, and vein. The quia resisted, like a stream running wild, trying to flow in every direction but the one she wanted. She focused her mind, her breath coming hard. Slowly she mastered the power, forcing it to obey, to sink into the torn edges of his flesh and pull them together. She felt the mending begin, flesh knitting, bleeding slowing. Relief weakened her. Faint, yes, but enough.

It had not always been so hard to heal. Once she had wielded the quia readily, its power potent and easy to direct. Now it was like handling a weapon with numb arms.

Gayna grunted. "That's done it. He'll live."

Solana released her hold on the quia and wiped sweat from her forehead. This night had taken its toll. She had spent her modest power on the wounded time after time, bringing herself close to exhaustion. Some she could save, and some she couldn't. At the moment, all of it seemed pointless. She swallowed bile. "Is the Vedshri's sorcery really so different from what we do?"

"Very different. Their power doesn't come from the earth like ours, but from another world. The varya, they call it. It's unnatural." Gayna shook her head, eyes distant. "Their sorcerers can call raw power to their hands and shape it to their will. The things they can do with it would curdle your blood."

"You've seen one?"

"I saw one once, long ago. I hope never to see another."

The tribesman made a muffled sound. Solana glanced at him. He was crying, tears squeezing from tightly closed eyes, chest heaving. Surprise froze her. For the first time, she wondered what her village would do with him. Had she saved him only for imprisonment? For execution?

His fate troubled her, but distantly, like some old story. She could feel no sadness, not for him, not for Bornaz, not for herself. She'd lost the ability to feel such things three years ago. She had nothing left to give. Nonetheless, she stroked his damp hair back from his forehead, shushing him like a child. This, at least, she could do.

Gayna watched her. "You have a gentle way, even with these devils. Are you married, Solana? You have children?"

Dawn's light contracted like a tunnel. Solana blinked back the darkness. "My husband died three years ago, in a skirmish with the Vedshri." Bornaz's killer could have been this man, for all she knew. The thought should have stirred something—anger, disgust—but she felt only a great weariness. She stood abruptly, wanting nothing more to do with him.

Gayna rose too, her eyes concerned. "No children?"

Unconsciously, Solana touched her belly, the great hollowness within her. "I was pregnant when he died. I lost the baby a month later. It was violet fever. Nearly took me too."

Gayna drew a breath. "I'm sorry, love." She looked away, looked back. "You're young still, though." The old woman reached out to brush a strand of Solana's hair back from her face. "And a beauty."

People always said that, as though it mattered. As though it meant Solana could have whatever she wanted. They never seemed to look past the surface to see the darkness within. Solana shook her head, wordless.

"You could marry again. Have more children."

The words fell hard on her heart. Solana forced her lips to move. "The fever burned me out. I can't bear another."

Gayna caught her breath. "You sure?"

"The seer at Hadoc told me, but I already knew." She had sensed it. She was an empty vessel, incapable of giving life. That knowledge had once brought agony. But now the hard truth of her barren womb brought no more than the taste of dust to her mouth.

"Syth's blood, that's hard." Gayna's dark eyes held pain. The depth of it, her ocean of feeling, belied the shallow pond Solana's heart had become. It hit Solana, how much she'd lost, how empty she'd become. The contrast would have shamed her, but she couldn't even feel that.

She shrugged, turning away, unable to face the other woman. "Let's keep going."

They found the next wounded man near the river. One of their own, the blacksmith Tollo. He was a great bear of a man, his arms thick as logs. He had three small children and would laugh like a bellows when they jumped on him. His wife was pregnant with their latest. Now he writhed in the grass, hands clutching his stomach. He had been slashed through the gut, his insides spilling out. Gayna gagged on the stink. Solana breathed through her mouth, letting the stench roll over her.

Gayna examined his belly with trembling fingers. Regret shadowed her eyes. "There's nothing we can do for him. He's too far gone."

Tollo moaned like a wounded animal, his hand flailing to catch Solana's. His fingers tightened around hers, wet with sweat and gore, clammy with death. She sensed the darkness pulling at him, the earth calling him. Yet still, a spark of life clung. She could feel the fierceness of his fight, his will to live. She wanted to nurture the flame. But it was as though it burned on the other side of a wall, unable to reach her.

Three years ago, she could have saved Tollo. She knew it in her bones, despite Gayna's words. Then, the quia had run through Solana's veins like heady wine, thick and wild. She had wielded it like a master. She could have summoned enough to heal his ruptured belly, to feed his desperate spark. Now that power was gone, beyond her clumsy reach.

Her chest squeezed. She wormed her fingers from his grasp. Tollo would fade as Bornaz had faded, as she was fading. There was nothing to be done about it. Nothing. Futility rang in her head, the echo piercing her silence.

Gayna scowled at her and seized Tollo's hand between her wrinkled palms. She held it, muttering words of comfort as his life choked out. His breath burbled and then went shallow. His last gasp faded and his face went still, empty.

Solana watched, a dull ache in her chest. She longed for that emptiness. To end the struggle, as Tollo had. To let go. She stood, her head light.

Gayna surged to her feet, her brows drawn. "Devourer, girl, you're cold as ice. What's wrong with you?"

Solana looked away, unable to meet the fire in her eyes. She fumbled for words. "I couldn't take the pain. After my baby died. I couldn't breathe." The words were inadequate, no more than pale shadows of the reality. It had felt like her lungs were full of shattered glass, piercing her with every breath. "So, I went to the seer at Hadoc. I had her take it from me."

"Take it from you?" Confusion swept away the anger in Gayna's face.

"My pain." Solana fished out the vial that always lay safely under her tunic. She held it up to the light. It was filled with a roiling liquid, its darkness shot with violent colors: crimson and plum and virulent green. The vial held all the brilliant color lost from her world. "I carry it here now, where it can't touch me. The seer pulled it out of me. I thought it might hurt, but it didn't. Nothing has ever hurt since."

Gayna opened her mouth and closed it again. She wet her lips. When she spoke, her voice was hushed. "What is it like, to live without pain?"

"Quiet," Solana said. She had no other word for the muffling numbness of it. She moved through a world as remote as though under glass, passing through her own life like a ghost. Untouched. "I didn't expect the world to become such a quiet place. Colors dull, music distant, touch… meaningless. I can barely feel the quia. But I like the quiet."

"I understand." Gayna laid a hand on her shoulder and squeezed. "My son died when he was a young man. Days were, I thought I'd like to follow him."

Solana had no answer, no words of comfort or love. She dropped her eyes. "Come on. We'd best see if there's anyone we can help."

They trod through the deep grass toward the riverbank. One of the village warriors, a young woman, prowled nearby, sweeping through the brush with her sword.

"You find anyone?" Solana called.

Even as the woman shook her head, the brush nearby rustled. One of the Vedshri bolted from the bushes with a strangled cry. He darted away from the warrior, toward Solana. His sword in his hand, coming for her. Gayna cried out and stepped away. But Solana stood still, transfixed by the blade. It promised quiet, dark and thick, a quiet nothing could penetrate. She welcomed it.

The village warrior bounded after the Vedshri and struck him down with a single blow of her sword. A fountain of blood spurted high, drops of it landing warm on Solana's face. Disappointment settled into her bones.

Gayna grabbed her arm. "Were you daft, standing there?"

Solana shook her head and attempted a shaky laugh. "The quiet makes me slow, sometimes. One of the drawbacks, I suppose."

In the weeks that followed, Solana dreamed of that blade. The quiet it promised would be deeper than any she'd ever known, an oblivion that would blot out even the memory of pain. She longed for it, woke in the night aching for it. She tried to put those thoughts away, to bury them deep, but still, they rose in the silent hours. Thoughts of that quiet consumed her, stealing her sleep, shredding what little peace she'd found since Bornaz's death.

During the day, she went about her work as always, saying nothing. She tidied her hut, tended her garden, ate her simple dinners alone. She healed sick livestock and villagers, watching them recover, laugh, hug. They moved on, their life flowing by, while hers stagnated.

A month later, she delivered Tollo's baby, a tiny girl with a mighty yell. Solana wrapped up the squalling infant in a blanket and handed her to her exhausted mother. As she let go of the baby, her arms felt emptier. Or perhaps it was her heart. The baby latched onto her mother's breast, and Tollo's wife clutched the girl close, tears spilling from her eyes. Other village women crowded around, hugging her, crying, laughing. Life renewed, even after Tollo's death.

A renewal Solana could never have. There would be no baby for her, no family, no future. She watched the women celebrate, steps away from her and yet distant as in another world. None of it touched her. She could feel nothing, not even regret.

That night after her lonely supper she opened a drawer she never touched. It held her few mementos of Bornaz. She ran her fingers across them—his pipe, the fancy belt buckle he loved, the braided bracelet he wore. They were only things, cold and hard, meaningless. They couldn't bring him back.

She hesitated, her hand hovering over the necklace he'd given her at their betrothal. He'd bought it in Hadoc, an extravagance he could barely afford, every one of its gleaming gray stones the same size and perfectly polished. Solana hadn't worn it since he died. She fished it from the drawer and slid her fingers across the beads. Those smooth cool stones slipped through her grasp like the days of her life, each one identical.

She saw her future stretched before her, a string of days without end, without meaning. As cold as the stones between her fingers. As unending as their chain. There would never be anything new. The weight of that future settled over her, crushing the breath from her. She couldn't bear the weight of so much nothingness. She wanted only the quiet the seer had promised. Not like the one she had, an imperfect, aching thing. She wanted a deeper, darker quiet.

The next day, she went to find it. She slipped from her village before dawn and walked west, toward the craggy cliffs. She traveled all day, her feet sore, her throat dry, and reached the foothills in the late afternoon. The cliffs rose beyond, sheer and beautiful. Solana's throat ached at the sight. It stirred a memory of something she couldn't put a name to—possibility, maybe. Hope.

She scrambled up slopes of tumbled stone, cutting her hands, and pushed through brambles that tore her trousers. Her face was scratched, her throat burning with thirst. None of it mattered. Solana was seizing her future, cutting the chain of endless days. Though she moved toward oblivion, the impending change gave her strength. At last, she was making a choice, taking her fate into her own hands. She would seek a high cliff with a sheer drop and find her quiet at the bottom. Perhaps she would even find herself, at the moment of ending it all. Perhaps Bornaz and her lost baby would be waiting on the other side.

She crested another slope and stumbled across a path. It seemed a gift; this would lead her up into the cliffs, as high as she needed to go. Likely, it was a Vedshri path, since this was their territory. In the past, she would have been afraid. Now, nothing mattered but what she sought.

So, she was not surprised when, an hour later, she rounded a turn and ran into a Vedshri. She stopped, her breath catching.

The tribesman held a knife. It captivated her with its deadly promise. The ghost of a smile touched her lips. This was better, after all. It would be fitting to die on a Vedshri blade, like Bornaz.

Then she saw what the tribesman held in his other hand. His fingers clenched tight around the arm of a girl. She was Vedshri too, with streaming dark hair and wild eyes. She might be five years old. She wore a loose smock the color of blood. Her chin had a stubborn set, her eyes bright with intelligence. Save her pale skin, she could have been Solana as a girl. Solana had been willful once, full of fire.

The man stared at Solana, as shocked as she. They stood like that, unmoving, for long moments. The knife trembled in his hand.

"She have to die," he said, his accent thick. His tone was pleading, as though asking her to understand. "The village elders say. She wicked."

"Wicked?" Solana's voice was barely a whisper. The horror of the scene curled thick around her. The girl had the same sharp chin as he, the same long nose. She was his daughter. Solana felt certain of it, and sickness settled in her stomach. His daughter, at knifepoint. She protested, finding her voice, forcing more strength into it. "How can a child be wicked?"

The man's throat worked, as though struggling to find the word. When at last he spat it out, it lay heavy on the air. "Unnatural."

Solana shook her head. "No. You can't do this."

Pain flickered in his eyes. The girl struggled in his grasp, crying out. His knuckles whitened around her arm. "*Abragna, Raylin,*" he hissed in his language. The knife shook harder in his other hand. His fingers spasmed, and the blade slipped free, hitting the dirt. He shoved the girl toward Solana, letting go. The child fell to the ground with a cry.

His face contorted, eyes squeezing shut. Brimming tears splashed out to glisten on his cheeks. "Your people do it! Not me." He turned and ran up the path, stumbling, nearly falling.

The girl jumped up and took a few staggering steps after him. "*Dede!*" she shrieked.

But he never looked back, only ran faster, until his dwindling shape disappeared among the rocks.

The girl let out a wordless scream. Solana had screamed like that, the day they brought Bornaz's body back to her. As though the world had broken under her feet and would never be mended. She felt the agony of that scream, distant and muffled though it came. It echoed in her heart, and her knees went weak.

The child looked back at Solana. Those wild, dark eyes were drowning in pain, a torment beyond tears. Solana recognized it, the desolation of a world lost. "It's all right," she said, though she knew it wasn't. The girl would never be all right again. She was as broken as Solana.

Broken, but fierce and raw, her pain unmuted. Her whole body shook. The air around her grew heavy, like the air before a storm. She raised thin hands, and light crackled across them. A pale violet light, like nothing Solana had ever seen.

The child stared at her hands and shrieked, her voice full of fear. Around her, rocks shook. A pebble bounced into the air, then another. Then dozens. A larger stone broke free, arcing up and hovering above her. The girl's dark hair drifted, weightless in the charged air, strands brushing against the quivering stones. Her eyes were wide, terrified.

"You're a sorceress," Solana whispered, as numb as though locked in the strangeness of a dream. She stared at the girl in her red dress—a child like any other to the eye, save for the unearthly light sparking from her hands, the crackling power around her. The varya, an energy summoned from another world. Now Solana understood why her tribe feared her enough to kill her.

More stones lifted. The child lashed her head from side to side, crying out. Light surged across her hands, growing stronger. Bigger rocks rose, more chunks of granite breaking free to soar above her. She stood amidst a forest of floating stone. She wiggled her hands frantically, as though to shake off the light coating them, and the stones began to circle, sliding sideways in the air.

The girl had no control over it, Solana realized, the thought piercing through the dreamlike strangeness. Perhaps she didn't even know what she was doing. Her panic fed the power, and the sight of her power further fueled her terror. She was helpless before her own sorcery. Solana took a step toward her, wanting to comfort her, to heal her. She ignored the rocks, ignored the danger, speaking only to the pain in her eyes. "I won't hurt you. Maybe I can help you."

The girl babbled something, her voice shrill with warning. The rocks spun faster. The breeze of their passing, only feet away, lifted Solana's hair. The whirlwind of stone made a low roar, and a shiver crept down Solana's spine. So, she would die not by a Vedshri knife, but by Vedshri sorcery. For the first time, the thought brought regret. If she died, she couldn't help the child.

The girl gazed about her with mad eyes, mouth open, and batted her hands together as if to stifle their light. Pale lightning jumped between her palms and caught fire, flaring over her hands. She screamed in agony as her flesh scorched. The vortex of stone crescendoed, rocks crashing together. Some crumbled, smashed, a rolling avalanche in the air. The mass of rumbling stone spun higher, and she stood below them, her eyes shocked, her hands smoking.

Then the stones crashed. With a thunderous boom, they fell, plummeting onto the girl. She disappeared in a cloud of powdered dust.

Solana cried out. She ran toward the child, but the dust blinded her. She stumbled and choked, rubbing her eyes. When the cloud cleared, the girl was gone. Nothing but rock remained.

Solana's cry turned to a mewl of protest. For the first time in years, something like fear ran through her veins. She knelt by the mound of stone, grabbing for rocks, tossing them aside. She dug frantically, gasping. Her hands bled, scraped raw. She ignored the damage, heaving larger stones. A weak moan rewarded her efforts. Solana yanked off a large, flat rock and brushed away a scree of pebbles. There lay the girl, her legs still pinned beneath the stone.

She was unhurt. Of all the things Solana had just seen, that was the strangest. Dust covered the girl's dark hair. Her eyes were red, her nose running. Her hands were blistered, burned as though by fire. But not a scratch on her, not a bone broken. Her power had protected her.

Solana's mind reeled, her breath coming short. She had never imagined such power as this wisp of a girl could wield. But for all that, the child looked terrified. She writhed, drawing as far from Solana as she could. Tears ran down her cheeks.

"Shush, shush." Solana stroked the girl's hair back from her face with trembling fingers. On a hunch, remembering her father's words, she essayed, "Raylin?"

Her eyes widened. She stared at Solana, her breathing shallow.

"I won't hurt you, Raylin." Solana spoke soothingly, knowing the girl could understand nothing but her tone. She pulled off more stones, trying to free her legs. It was no use. One of the largest boulders lay across Raylin's skinny calves. It was too heavy for Solana to lift, or even roll. She pushed against it till her muscles burned.

Raylin sobbed, struggling. Solana laid her hands on the girl's frail chest to still her. "You can free yourself, Raylin. Use your powers as you did before."

Panic filled the girl's eyes. Perhaps she couldn't do it. Her burst of power might have burned out, depleted the child for who knew how long. Solana caught one of her thin wrists and turned it over to study the burns on her palm. She'd lost control of the varya; it had run wild and turned on her. Maybe it could even kill her if she summoned too much of it. Raylin was only a child. Even if she understood Solana's words, she might not be able to do what she asked.

Solana laid a hand on the great stone. She sensed the quia within, darker and heavier than the energy of plants. It was too heavy for her to draw into herself. She had no way to free the girl. Raylin would stay trapped beneath this boulder until hunger and thirst took her. The girl would die.

Everyone died: Bornaz, Tollo, the nameless baby that had once nestled in Solana's womb. They all turned to dust, like the dust on Raylin's hair, in Solana's mouth. The dust of death.

She leaned against the boulder, head pressed against its cold stone. Rebellion rose in her. Not this time. No more death, no more loss. She pulled back, eyeing the boulder. She could move it if she had her full power.

She didn't let herself think of the cost. She tugged on the chain around her neck, and the vial came free in her hand. She held it up to the daylight. The sun shimmered against its dark contents. The vial gleamed heavy with the promise of pain.

There was no other way. She uncapped the vial, scrunched her eyes closed, and tipped it back. The roiling liquid-not-liquid ran down her throat, seared her chest, settled like coals in her belly. She opened her eyes, gasping, as the world came rushing back.

Colors assaulted her, so bright they hurt. The fire of the sunset beyond the mountain to the west, spreading its glory across the sky. The verdant green of a tree just up the path, the vibrant blue of a bird in its leaves. Sounds came piercing, the girl's wail like daggers. The scratches on Solana's face and hands burned her, a bright red irritation. Her sore feet throbbed, a deep violet ache. Shards of glass filled her chest, a blinding white pain.

Solana curled around herself, hands clasped to her head, rocking as she tried to breathe. Every lungful of air came twined with agony. She moaned, and her cries mingled with the girl's. Her grief and the girl's—they were one and the same.

Solana looked up, drawing a saw-edged breath. The only way forward was to embrace the pain. She laid a hand on the stone, feeling its dark energy, and drew it into herself, let the torrent of it course through her veins. The quia burgeoned, a rush she had almost forgotten. She held it inside, shaped it, and sent it back to the stone. She nudged the rock with its own dark power, and it obeyed. The boulder stirred and rolled off the girl.

Raylin drew a breath, sitting straighter. Her thin legs were unbroken, shielded from the crash of the avalanche by her power, but the long minutes beneath the stone had left them bruised and scratched. Solana reached out a hand, wanting to heal her. The girl cried out, shrank away, scrambled up, and ran.

Solana stumbled to her feet and chased her, breathing hard. She was tired, and the girl was quick. She lurched up the path after Raylin, fear clawing at her throat. If she didn't catch the girl, Raylin would run back to her tribe, and find death there. Solana turned an ankle on a stone, caught herself, and kept going. Waves of agony surged from her twisted ankle. It didn't matter. After all this, she couldn't fail Raylin.

She caught her a few yards up the path, wrapping her in her arms. The girl twisted in her grip, turning to beat on her chest. Screams tore from her throat. Solana held her, heedless of the beating. It hurt less than the splinters in her heart. "Shush, shush," she whispered, stroking her dusty hair.

Raylin collapsed into her arms, sobbing. Solana held her tight. She sank to the ground and let the girl cry, while the sun set, and the stars appeared. Pain suffused Solana with every breath. Every loss scraped across her as raw as the day it happened. Memories flooded her: Bornaz's touch, the light in his eyes, the kick of her baby inside her. All gone.

Solana cried too, the pent-up grief of years. Her tears fell into the girl's hair, while noisy sobs wracked Raylin's tiny body. At last, the girl fell still. Her breathing quieted into sleep.

Solana rubbed her eyes and looked up at the sky, blazing with stars. Her twisted ankle throbbed; her battered hands ached. Even the air prickled against her skin, burned in her nostrils. A thousand smells came with the breeze: rich scents of new growth, of decay, the musk of animals passing by, the unmistakable scent of water. Cool air nipped her ears and chilled her body. She had forgotten how raw and fierce the world could be. She had no shelter now. Nothing to blunt its intensity.

But past it all, the iron band of Raylin's thin arms steadied her. The child clung to her, even in sleep. Solana knew she would never let her go.

It was madness. How could she raise a Vedshri child, a sorceress? How could she corral her wild power? The villagers would fear and despise her. Maybe Solana would have to take her to Hadoc; maybe the seer could teach Raylin to control the varya. Maybe, in the city, they could find a place for themselves. Solana stared down the future, seeing the rocky path she must tread. She would never know quiet again.

Tears slipped down her cheeks. When they eased, the shards in her chest seemed dulled. For the moment, she was more weary than wracked. She became aware of the girl's warmth against her chest, the sweet scent of the herbs in her hair. Raylin's breath came steady, easy now. Crickets chirped in the grass nearby. The stars sparkled above. A kind of peace stole across Solana, despite the pain. She held both inside her, the warmth and the pain, letting them mingle. She settled into the stillness of the night. Maybe there could still be moments of quiet in her life.

A new kind of quiet.

Madolyn Rogers

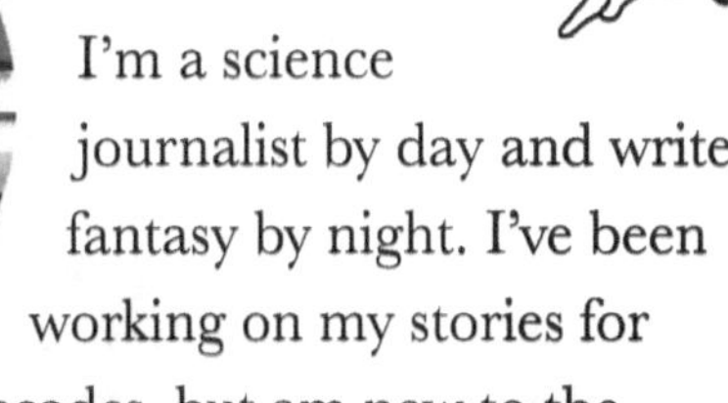

I'm a science journalist by day and write fantasy by night. I've been working on my stories for decades, but am new to the self-publishing community.

I put out my first book, *The Copper Assassin*, in 2020, and the sequel, *Jackal of the Mind*, in 2022. "The Quiet" is set in the same world as those stories, but takes place hundreds of years earlier and on another continent. This story was inspired by my own experience with crippling depression as a young woman.

Through fantasy, I wanted to explore the strange duality of depression—that as miserable as it is, it can also be a refuge, its numbness a shield against unbearable pain. The protagonist has her pain magically removed, but the process steals her joy as well. Her world becomes a quiet place, its colors and sensations muted. The story delves into what it's like to live that way and the trade-offs involved, informed by my own life journey.

Find out more about Madolyn Rogers at
www.madolynrogersauthor.com

THE PAPERWEIGHT WATCH

KRYSTLE MATAR

For Nana
I miss you

Ishmael

THE PAPERWEIGHT WATCH

KRYSTLE MATAR

Try not to sulk too long, Ishmael.

That's what my mother told me before she died. They weren't her last words, but they're what stuck in my mind. Of all the things she told me as we were climbing up the Qasan—stories of her childhood on the mountain range, of the beautiful, slow romance between her and my father, of the conflict and violence that drove so many Qasani people off the mountains where our ancestors lived for generations—it's *those* words I remember most clearly.

She knows me so well. No. Knew me. She's gone now, and I'm alone.

I buried her in the green verdant valley where she was born, like she wanted. I've had weeks to grieve her since then, but I constantly catch myself thinking about her as if she's still alive. I thought I had exhausted that well of grief on the fast, desperate journey back down the mountains and the miserable trip across the ocean in an intercontinental vessel. I spent too much time in my cabin drinking and sulking.

Returning home only gives me transient, half-hearted relief. Yaelsmuir isn't exactly a happy city, but at least I know the rhythm and the shape of it. I know how to stay out of trouble and where to go looking for it when I need the distraction. The Dominion is so much different from the Qasan. Maybe the Qasan of my mother's memory was as peaceful and wonderful as she said, but maybe not. The Qasan is a dangerous, violent place now. Stretches of empty loneliness punctuated by violence and blood when you're unfortunate enough to encounter soldiers. My parents—and so many others—left for a reason.

It's strange to think the last time I stepped off a barge and onto the docks of Cattle Bone Bay, I was coming home to my family. I'm glad the journey is over, but... When I made this journey last, I had just completed my supervised training to be everything the Dominion military wanted me to be for the diplomatic division. This time I've arrived, for the first time ever, to my life after I've buried both of my parents. Is it home at all without them here?

It's raining when I arrive. Of course. Rain and sleet cover the docks and the cobblestones with ice. Normally I'd step into Cattle Bone Bay for something to eat, but it's too cold, and I can't convince myself I'm hungry. I *should* be hungry. I've lost a lot of weight on this journey. The walking and the sweating and the long climb up the mountain range pushed me to the very limits of my endurance, and to make it worse, the grief takes up physical space in my gut, supplanting the hunger I usually feel. I eat when I know I *must*, and that's it.

I cross the bridge to the Boardwalk Market instead of lingering in Cattle Bone Bay. I was born on the Bay side of the river, where apartments are too small, and there's never quite enough coal in the winter, and everyone is tough as old leather because it's the only way to survive. I'm too tired to stay like I usually do. I just want to go home—but I have to force myself to remember that my parents won't be waiting for me this time.

Ama, I'm so glad you're home, my mother would say when I walked through the door. But she won't say it this time, because she isn't there anymore. I left her behind in her shallow grave that I dug with my own hands. *Have something to eat. Doesn't the Army feed you? What kind of Army lets their best diplomats get so skinny?* She would be devastated to see how thin I am this time.

And my father would wander over, asking random questions because he understands that my career means I have to keep secrets, but he wants to know how I am. *How was the weather? What did you eat? Was the journey very long?* He'd ask about Colonel Deri, my trainer and handler, because he's impressed that I'm working with someone whose family is such an influential part of Dominion history. And I'll tell him the stories that everyone knows about the Deri family privateers smuggling Qasani refugees across the ocean when families first started fleeing the conflict and while so many other nations were turning our people away. And we'll fill the time with small talk because he wants me to know I can talk to him, however vaguely, if I need to. He'll respect my secrets.

Or… he *respected* them.

After my father was murdered, my mother decided she didn't want to fight the illness that was killing her. There wasn't any point, she said. Her every day was made of pain as the disease consumed her. Her soul was tormented from losing her husband suddenly and violently. It was a terrible burden to live in a world where someone as peaceful and loving and gentle as him could be murdered in his office. She didn't want to live in Yaelsmuir anymore, so she asked me to take her back to the Qasan so she could die in the mountain valley where she was born.

I couldn't even blame her. In those ugly days after I found my father's body, I wanted to crawl into a bottle of brandy and never come back out. I think she saved my life by needing me. Because she wanted to go back to the Qasan, I didn't have the time to lie drunk in a Yaelsmuir gutter, drowning in self-pity and impotent rage.

I try to comfort myself with what *is* still here. The Boardwalk Market is just the way I remember it. Ice clings to the wooden sign that hangs above my father's shop. Or my shop, now. The sign only says *Saeati's*, and the engraving of our name is clotted with ice. The windows glow with light and movement on the other side of the thick glass, but I can almost hear them; I know all the sounds of my family's business. Our employees know each other, and they speak as they work, a beautiful blend of bilingualism between Qasani and the Dominion common tongue. Each of them has a unique rhythm, each person's tools make their own song of progress. And the watches we have, ticking, ticking, ticking. I love the steady predictability of a ticking watch. It sounds like home.

I hate the cold. I hate the winter and the ice and the snow. I hate that I'm standing outside in the miserable weather, but I can't quite bring myself to face these people. Somehow the comfort of them is daunting—I can't step into it just yet. I'm not ready.

I promised my mother I wouldn't sulk too long, but I need a bit more time. To gather enough composure so I can face these people who kept my father's dream alive while I was gone. I climb to the apartment above instead. Everything is empty and still. My mother doesn't meet me at the door, and my father isn't puttering around the kitchen, helping himself to snacks. It smells stale. Everything is how I left it, covered in sheets to keep the dust off our things, because I didn't know how long I would be gone. Or even if I would come back. Some part of me expected to die on the journey, as if the grief would split the world open and swallow me whole. But nothing so dramatic happened, so here I am.

Try not to sulk too long, Ishmael.

I stand in the silent stillness of my parents' apartment. It's all mine now, I suppose, the home we lived in and the shop below. The furniture hiding under the drop cloths, the roof that leaks sometimes, especially during the spring thaw. The tools, the stock, the inventory—so many *things*, cogs and jewels and springs, tweezers and pliers and screws, gold paint and watch faces and tiny metal hands—so much precious metal—so many little glass domes. My thoughts are stuck in an endless list of the *things* that are mine now—my parents' clothes, even the bed they shared. And all the people that keep Saeati's alive, the employees who make the expensive watches and custom pieces here in this building, the ones who make the cheaper watches in the factory space we have on the other side of the river. If I strain my ears, I can hear the shop below my feet, the murmur of voices, maybe even the collective sound of dozens of watches ticking at once. Maybe that's just my imagination, trying to breathe life into this place. We've lived here since my father moved us from Cattle Bone Bay. He was so excited to be on the rich side of the river, to have a proper storefront where we could build and sell our best pieces. I was thirteen then—how old am I now? Ten years... I've been here ten years. Or, they have—I've been away so much with Deri and other diplomats in training, so the apartment has been home in theory more than in practice. And now it's all mine because they're just gone.

Ama, don't stand in the door, my mother would say if she saw me gawping this long. Her voice had gone raspy the last few years, which made her sound more exasperated than before. *This is your home, not a museum. You don't need me to give you a tour.*

It's so quiet in here without them. It *feels* like a museum now. A shrine to their lives, empty and unoccupied. I feel like an intruder.

My father's wall clock draws me in first. It's the easiest thing I can do to make things feel like they should—there's always working clocks in this place. I wipe the dust off the beautiful oak body, finding the key so I can wind tension into the movement. I set the hands to the right time and get the pendulum swinging—the familiar ticking fills the apartment. A much heavier ticking than the little pieces we specialize in, with far more presence. It will chime every half hour. It's something predictable, a little piece of normalcy. Somehow, it only makes the place feel emptier because it's my father's clock, and the fact that it's ticking again only serves to reinforce the fact that he's not here. We didn't make it—my father preferred the tiny movements that go in pocket watches and delicate pieces, and so Saeati's specialized in those things. But this clock was abandoned with us, and my father spent years trying to repair it. I tried to help him when I was around instead of roaming around the city, looking for trouble. He didn't swear often, but he cursed at this clock near a thousand times. It defied us for years, refusing to work no matter which pieces we replaced. We pulled the whole thing apart, trying to figure out what the problem was, saying it was a shame to throw such a beautiful clock away even if it made him want to pull his hair out. He fixed it himself after I left for the Officer's Academy. I came home as a member of the Dominion diplomatic division, and the clock was mounted on the wall, ticking away. The first of many things I missed in favour of my career.

I tried, so many times, to tell myself that this was the natural order of things. I was not beholden to my parents, or tied to them. It was normal for me to step away and find my own path in the world.

And yet I still feel guilty about it. Like I created too much distance, held too many secrets. Maybe it's the Dominion way to separate your life from your parents, but Qasani families stay together. They sprawl in their mountain valleys, and they build tight-knit communities. Generations live in the same homes, and they can trace their lineage back to the hands that laid the foundation stones. Or… they could, back when. When they still lived there. Before war between other nations chased them off the mountain.

So maybe this wanting to stay close to them is in my blood. Maybe it lives in my marrow, even though I'm Dominion-born, even though they lost track of *their* family when they fled the mountain.

There's an empty, tinny ache in my gut as I realize I've come to terms with all of this too late. I went to the Qasan and learnt who my parents used to be, but I left my mother's bones on the mountain like she wanted, and my father isn't here waiting for me. I can't tell them what I've come to understand about the difference between how they grew up and how I did. I can't ask them to tell me more. They're gone.

Why didn't they tell me more when they were alive? They didn't talk about the Qasan much, not until my mother announced she wanted to go back. Why didn't I ask them when they were still here?

The ticking of the wall clock is only marginally comforting, and I find myself wandering aimlessly through my parent's apartment, trying to decide which pieces of furniture to uncover. Furniture that I've never sat in because it was my mother's spot, or my father's. They were nothing if not predictable in their routines. I can see my father in the big wingback chair he kept near the fireplace, his spectacles in his lap, newsprint on the floor beside him, chin on his chest. Snoring softly. And my mother bustling around him. Hovering near him, flitting away, an inexhaustible bank of energy—and she wondered where I got it from. And she'd keep finding some excuse to go back to the area immediately beside his chair until she woke him 'by accident' so she could apologize and pretend to be devastated that she disturbed him. He'd invite her to settle in the chair beside him, and they would talk about the news from the paper he'd failed to read.

I leave those chairs covered. I won't sit in them. The memory of them takes up too much space.

The mantle, though. The massive wooden slab holding a little personal shrine to the Qasani gods. I wipe the dust off the candles and the incense plates and the little brass dishes filled with incense cones. One separate scent for each of the six gods. Musk for Ishka, the mother of the soul. Lavender and clary sage for Haiet, the mother of blood. Cypress and fir for Khafia, the mother of bone. Vetiver root for Ordunn, father of the earth. A citrus blend for Shammat, father of the sun. Cinnamon and rose for Zabyras, father of rain.

Prayer holds such an important place in the Qasani routine, and each scent holds a memory. At harvest feasts, we burn incense and give tribute to the father gods. Sun, rain, and the earth. Births and funerals are the providence of Ishka. Weddings are a tribute to blood and bone, for a Qasani wedding is a promise of devotion, a twining together at the beating heart.

I didn't have any incense when I buried my mother in the valley. It makes it harder to accept she's gone—I didn't get to process it with the proper rituals, with the community around me, with the long roots of our culture. There's comfort in knowing that Qasani bodies have gone into the ground the same way for generations, and Qasani souls have been heralded back to Ishka time and time again. But my mother didn't get those things—there was no Im-Aqi there and no women to cry over her body, and I can't help but wonder if Ishka received her soul or if she's stuck wandering in that lonely, empty place forever.

Breathe—don't think about any of that. It's done, and I'm back in the Dominion, and it's time to try to go back to living. Or something like it.

I wipe the dust off the trinkets that my parents collected over the years. Things from the Qasan, things from Yaelsmuir. One by one, I clean each trinket. And I add something new—a tintype portrait of my daughter. It's in rough shape. It got scratched and dinged as I carried it with me up the mountain. The iron is starting to rust, the varnish flaking away in places. Hopefully, her mother will send me a new one soon. Maybe I'll dig out the older ones I have, spanning from when she was a few months old. Line them all up on the mantle, behind my parents' things. She was a secret from so many people for so long. I told my father about her, one of the few people who heard the news from me not long after she was born, but by then, it was already clear that I wouldn't be involved in her life. So my father asked me not to tell my mother. *It would break her heart, Uba. She would want to know your daughter. It's best just to leave it, I think. We'll talk about it one day.*

I told my mother that she was a grandmother as we climbed the mountain—and my father was right; it was so incredibly painful. We both cried together, she and I, but then we could talk about my daughter, who calls another man her father, who doesn't know yet that she has Qasani lineage. And there was comfort in sharing, in grieving together, in explaining how all my hopes and dreams got away from me so completely. This was one of the few times my father was wrong, I think. The story of my daughter had been one secret too many. There were so many things I *couldn't* say to my parents because the division required me to keep quiet about what I was learning to do, but this one thing, my daughter, I should have shared. At least we could have been in pain together instead of me feeling isolated.

All I have are these photographs her mother sends me. Maybe one day my daughter will know me. But now, at least, I can line the photographs up on the mantel, among the memories of my family and the things we use to pray. She can exist just a little bit more.

Breathe—don't cry.

Into the kitchen, but maybe it was a mistake. The kitchen is the emptiest part of the apartment. I told Mr. Saan and the rest of the employees to take everything before I left with my mother, so it didn't rot and go to waste while I was gone. My mother was an excellent cook—so many of my memories from when we lived in Cattle Bone Bay are of the delicious food she made, teaching me our culture with the recipes she remembered from her childhood on the Qasan. There's more space in this kitchen than there was in our little Bay apartment, but she spent less time cooking. My father paid me a wage for helping in the shop, so I usually bought my own food from the beautiful places on the boardwalk, or the familiar places in the Bay. She shifted into having a bigger role in the business. She had such a good head for numbers that she took over the books. I can see her at the dining room table with a fountain pen and a ledger book, conferring with Mr. Saan over inventory and shipping and net profits and company growth. The shop was my father's beloved project, but my mother wanted the factory so we could build Saeati watch movements to ship across the country for other jewellers to make watches.

I can also see her at the same table, stretching delicate pastry over the whole tabletop until it's thin enough to read a newspaper through. So many delicious things are baked in layers upon layers of this pastry. I don't know how to make it on my own. I've helped her with some of the steps, but the whole thing from start to finish takes too much patience, something I've never been known for. The realization that my mother will never make pastry again—never make my favourite dessert again—hits me harder than I expected. It empties my lungs, scoops out my insides.

There's nothing for me in the kitchen. The shelves are empty, and I can't make a meal out of dust and memories, even if I was hungry enough to try.

I retreat to the sitting room, but the emotions don't go anywhere. Something frantic and raw is crawling under my skin, something too much like panic. The life we used to live exists in all the places I'm used to seeing my parents. When I let my eyes slide across each room, I can see the suggestion of them in my peripheral vision, my mind filling in where they should be. My father standing by the window, watching the traffic as he sips his morning tea. And my mother, tsking at him. *You shouldn't be drinking tea on an empty stomach, Fahim. Come have breakfast.* My father sighs gently, saying, *I'm fine. I'll come when I finish my tea.*

How do I live here without them? I can't. I thought I had grieved enough on the long journey home, but now that I'm here, it's all hitting me harder than I expected. Like it's all fresh grief. Being in a familiar place is only making things worse, because I can see how wrong it all feels without them. They used to occupy this place, and the shape of them has left holes in the fabric of existence. There's no point uncovering *any* furniture because I don't think I can even use it, not without them here to fill it with life. It's better for their things to remain under drop cloths, as much ghosts as they are.

I need to keep myself busy. I need to move, need to use my mind. Read a newspaper, maybe, to catch up on what I missed while I was away, anything to distract me from thinking about how terribly off-kilter everything has become. Maybe I should have stayed in White Crown and waited there for my next deployment. Maybe entering *that* set of rituals and routines would be more distracting. Maybe seeing Colonel Deri again, his deep, calm voice, his steady confidence, would help me compartmentalize into this new version of my life.

But I didn't think to do that, and now I'm here. Gods, I need to get out of this place, need to get away from this feeling, or I'm going to seize up completely, a watch movement with too much debris in the gears—

My father's first watch catches my eye, sitting on his desk, near the window. Mostly he worked downstairs in the shop office, but sometimes he needed to get away from the noise if he was really struggling with a piece. His first watch is displayed on a stand, a little glass dome protecting it from the dust.

It's open-faced instead of having a cover to protect the glass, and there's a chronograph. The numbers are painted with gold, and the hands themselves are probably gold, too—plated or solid, I can't tell. I wonder how my father got a watch this valuable as a child. It was ticking when he got it, my mother said. He took it apart to see what was inside, and when he put it back together, he couldn't get it to tick anymore. Maybe he got too much dust in the movement, or maybe he cracked something along the way, or maybe he lost a piece. But it was this watch that set him on the path that led us all here. His first love, my mother called it. She was his second, she told me with a wistful smile. This watch captured him, mind and soul, long before my parents met each other. She knew from the beginning she would share him with clockwork. She didn't mind, because he shared his clockwork things with her, and she came to love them, too.

And it was that love of clockwork that gave him purpose and an income when they landed in Cattle Bone Bay. The watches and his ability to repair them sheltered us, fed us, sustained us. I wonder if he tried to fix this first watch after he knew what he was doing or if he'd already decided to leave it broken by then.

We talked about this watch, my mother and I, while we were waiting for death to claim her.

Maybe I'll fix it when I go home, I told her. *I'll get it running again. Probably just needs a few new parts.*

Do what you have to. But your uba loved that watch most because it was his first, and he wanted it to keep all its original pieces, even if it didn't work. It wasn't about whether or not it could keep time; it was about everything he learnt from it.

Well, I learnt everything I needed to from Uba, so I don't need his paperweight watch. I can just fix it.

I can still hear her disappointed sigh, echoing in my soul. *Fixing Uba's watch won't bring him back. But leaving it broken won't bring him back either. You're the only one who can decide what you think is best, but don't make the decision while you're still sulking. And try not to sulk too long, Ishmael.*

The weight of this watch in my hands gives me a sense of peace, like my parents still exist. They live in this place, not just in my memories, but in this business they built. We built. They live in the things we've made, watches and little clocks and toys that are famous across the Dominion.

Maybe it was a mistake to come up to the apartment first. Maybe being up here, where the only company is the memory of how things *used* to be, was an exercise in self-abuse. I've never been good at being alone. I *need* people around me. Silence is too oppressive, too smothering, too lifeless.

I slide my father's first watch into my pocket and head back out into the cold.

The rain has let off, but it's still miserable outside—cold and wet and windy. The warmth when I step inside the storefront wraps around me like a hug. There's nothing stale here, nothing still.

Nothing dusty or forgotten. For a brief moment, I watch everyone work. The front counter is unoccupied. The Boardwalk Market is a bustling, lively place when the weather is nice, but in the bitter winter wind and the deep, ugly cold, the streets are empty. My employees are at their workbenches, leaning low over projects. Custom builds, repair work, general upkeep. There's one empty bench, and I wonder who we lost, but no—we haven't lost anyone. That bench was occupied by the woman who manages the factory now. Her head for numbers is almost as sharp as my mother's, so before we left, my mother asked her to take over so the factory had the best chance of survival. I'll go see her at the factory later and thank her for keeping it together. Hopefully, it's still making a profit and running well. I suppose I should ask Mr. Saan, but I'm not ready to talk business and numbers.

My father's dearest friend, Mr. Saan, notices me. He steps away from the shelf and takes his spectacles off like he doesn't quite believe what he's seeing. I wonder how terrible I must look, how gaunt and thin. Even swathed in the many layers of wool that it takes to survive a Yaelsmuir winter, it has to be obvious how much weight I lost. I almost always lose some weight when I'm posted away because I'm too busy to eat as much as I like to, but this is worse. I rationed things carefully on the way up the mountain to make sure my mother always had enough. And then, after I buried her, I pushed myself too hard because I just wanted to get off the mountains and to the port and onto a ship so I could come home.

"Mr. Saeati," Mr. Saan says.

Everyone stops talking and looks up from what they were doing. The silence makes my bones itch. Some rise to their feet but stay at their desks, like they aren't sure how I'll react if they try to close the distance between us. I'm not sure how I'll react, either. I was supposed to be in control of my emotions by now, but I'm not. Not even close. I can feel it, bubbling through me like acid.

Coming into the shop, into the gentle warmth of this place, *is* like coming home. It was supposed to be easier to be surrounded by people and noise instead of the empty silence of upstairs. But I'm too acutely aware of my father's first watch in my pocket, and I'm aware of the places my parents *should* be but aren't, just like upstairs. When I walk back to the office, my father won't be working on watches, and my mother won't be surrounded by paperwork. Mr. Saan is in charge of the paperwork now, and the only watches built here are built by *my* employees, not by Saeati hands.

But no one moves. And I'm also painfully aware of my reputation. I love this place, these people, but the last few years, I haven't been here much, so these people don't really know me. And when I'm home, I drink maybe a bit too much. Colonel Deri warned me about it, the drinking. He told me how diplomats have to find a way to *actually* cope with what we do instead of just drinking and smoking and fucking the guilt away. But when I asked him how he copes, he told me he didn't know, so the drinking is all I have. Drinking and talking to my father, but I've lost him now. So maybe they wonder if I've started drinking yet, if I'll start throwing things. I just want to be *home* a while. Be here and sit in my father's shop—my shop now—and let life go on around me.

Something tight forms in my throat. It tastes like shame. I step around the counter, swallowing that ugly tightness, fighting for composure. There's a book filled with requests for custom orders from all over the Dominion, sent by mail or across the telegraph wire. People ask for special watches or clockwork toys, willing to pay exorbitant prices and shipping costs for something with the Saeati logo. Mr. Saan copies all the requests into the book, where they wait for someone with the skills and the creativity to take on the project. The rest of the shelves are organized with watches and clockwork things that need to be repaired. These pieces are more local, and many of the watches we're asked to look at aren't Saeati. Maybe one of these things will distract me enough that I can feel something like normal.

"You're back." Mr. Saan hovers at my shoulder, wringing his hands together, his spectacles in the pocket on the front of his suit. He dresses well, and so he should. I suppose he's the face of Saeati's now.

"Yes. I'm back. How's business been?"

"Ah—business? It was busy this summer. It's slow now, of course. But it's always slow this time of year. Not worth leaving the house in weather like this, is it?"

"No, not really."

"You were gone longer than I expected." His voice is low and gentle, like he's talking to a spooked horse, and it only makes me feel worse. "I had started to worry."

"It's a long walk up the mountain, Mr. Saan," I mutter. I know I sound petulant and rude, but I can't help it. I'm so desperately tired of falling apart at the slightest things. I've been a mess since the day I found my father, weeping on the inside, my soul crumbling. When my mother was still alive, she used to encourage me to let it go, to sob with her. She didn't like that I hate crying; she always said that it's a Dominion trait, that Qasani men aren't afraid to cry. But I don't recall seeing my father shed tears. He always just sighed at me. My mother was the sole owner of tears in our family.

"Yes, of course Mr. Saeati. A long walk, and…" He looks away, his lip trembling a little.

I want to curse him for the way he hovers and wrings his hands and can't figure out what to say. It's making it harder and harder to keep my emotions under control, because now I feel guilt and shame on top of everything, and I'm going to buckle under the weight of it all. But he's known my parents for so long, and he's the last tenuous link I have to something like family. This isn't the time to drive him away. I promised my mother I wouldn't sulk too long.

I'm trapped by him, by the lingering feeling of words that are being left unsaid.

I wonder if he wants to ask about the Qasan. Like me, he was born here, in the Dominion, though he's about the same age as my parents. Like me, he only knows the Qasan in the form of stories and other people's memories. Unlike me, both of his parents died on Dominion soil. They're buried in the little Qasani graveyard outside the city.

My father had a proper Qasani funeral—the kind that lasts for days. First, the body is laid in its shroud for three days. The women of the family stay in the room for the duration because Qasani tradition says women are the guardians of the soul until Ishka reclaims it. The women weep, and the louder the better, because the sound of their weeping will bring Ishka's messengers to the room so they can guide the soul away. A sign of a person's impact on the world is how many women will come and weep for them.

After three days, an Im-Aqi comes and tells the women, 'This life belonged not to us, but to the gods, and the wisdom of the gods is absolute.' They take the body to the burial ground, where people take turns sharing their favourite story. There's a Qasani blessing that means, 'I hope your funeral lasts a moon,' because you were so well loved that people won't stop talking.

And then the body is buried, and people feast, because there's not a single life event that the Qasani won't feast for. Not even death is excluded from this sort of celebration of sharing, because death is not an end. It is merely a moment of rest for the soul before the next life. I wonder what their next life will look like. I wonder if they'll be born close enough together that they'll find each other again. They loved each other *so* much—it seems fitting that they'd be given another life together.

My mother only had me to weep for her when she died, and I had to bury her body immediately to protect it from the ravens and the vultures. I wonder if that means Ishka can't reclaim her soul, and the thought tears little chunks out of my heart.

"I'm glad you're back," Mr. Saan says finally, and the release of the tension between us is a soothing balm on my soul. "Home, where you belong."

Breathe. Breathe even though it's hard. Don't cry.

"Any good custom pieces?" I ask. I pull the book out from under the counter and flip idly through the pages instead of giving my emotions time to run away with me. "Anything I might like?"

"Are you home for a while, then?" Mr. Saan asks. "You think you'll have time to build a custom piece?"

"I don't know. I filed my paperwork on my way through White Crown, so I'm active again. But if I start drawing something, maybe someone can take over if I have to leave before it's complete. Then you can charge extra because I designed it, at least."

"Well, there's a new request for a train that runs." Mr. Saan flips through the pages, toward the back. "It only came in a couple weeks ago from a gentleman in Cruinnich. It made me think of you immediately. It seems like something you'd enjoy."

He stops at the page. His handwriting is tight and careful, describing the potential customer's request. A father's gift to his adult daughter, because she loves trains. Not that there are many of them in the Dominion. Our cities are too far apart. In other, more densely populated countries, they run between cities. I wonder how many trains she's seen; has she been to other countries where trains are more common, or has she only seen photographs? His measurement of the wheel base is very precise, because he's started building the track already. I like that about him.

I close the book and lift it off the counter. "I'll see what I can get started."

I walk back through the shop, past all the many work benches, all the employees. Qasani, every single one of them from the Bay, like us. Some were born there like Mr. Saan and I were, some came here in the last few years. I should say something to them, something warm and friendly, something about how I appreciate them for being here when I couldn't be, running things when I had to be absent, keeping my father's name alive. If it had been up to me, this shop would have died. I should apologize for the way I've behaved in the past. I should make some kind of promise for the future we'll build together.

I can't find the right words. I don't know what the future looks like, so I don't know what to promise.

I retreat to my father's office and close the door behind me. Everything is the way I remember. And in its total familiarity, I'm also aware that there's something different. I can't pinpoint exactly what it is. The sound of my boots on the floor, maybe—is it a different pitch? Or is the lighting different? Maybe because it's so dreary outside. In my mind, this place is always sun-soaked and newly renovated, just like when I was thirteen and we moved in. My father was so proud. I still remember his excitement when he showed me our new desk. *Look, Uba,* he said, his face glowing with his joy. *A desk big enough for the two of us to sit side by side.*

When he taught me to make watches, he sat me across from him at the desk he had in our tiny, cramped apartment—and because I was mirroring his movements exactly, I learnt to build watches with my left hand. When he transferred us here to this big space that could hold this beautiful desk, I got to sit beside him. And since I built left-handed, we could sit side by side and never interfere with each other's motions. And he was always so quiet when he worked. His focus was so intense that he didn't always hear people speaking to him. Some days it felt like I could confess murder and he wouldn't hear me. His chair is tucked into the bench, like it's waiting for him to come back, just like I am.

So maybe nothing is different at all. It's just my mind, trying to find excuses to spin off into grief again. The 'difference' is that this place isn't the same as it was that very first day, when my father was showing me our work benches and our new lathe. I can see him throw open the beautiful windows—so much bigger than any windows in the Bay—to let the sunlight in, his whole body overflowing with excitement for the potential. The difference is that our shop isn't brand new anymore. It's worn and used in the best way. Filled with memories, every scuff on the floor evidence of our history here. We've put a decade of work into this business, although I didn't contribute as much as he had hoped because I chose the Dominion Army instead of staying. It only feels different because they're both dead. Because just like my mind puts the shape of my parents into all their regular places upstairs, it also puts my father here. This building was his favourite in all the world. I can see him at the lathe or at his desk or at the shelves, putting things away. He always liked his boxes just so and would stand there lining things up so they were all flush to each other, replacing labels that were worn. Sometimes I'd move his boxes on purpose, nudge them out of place or put them back in the wrong spot, just to hear him sigh at me. To watch him stand at the shelf and line everything back up the way he liked it. I'm taller than him, by almost three inches; I can reach the top shelf, but he can't—couldn't—without his step ladder. I can hear him ask me for help.

Please, Ishmael, can you just line them up properly—not like that, they'll fall if you leave them like that—would you just—

Until he was so annoyed that he huffed at me and stomped away to get his step ladder. I'd fix them properly while he was gone, just the way he liked. He'd huff again and put his ladder back.

Thank you, he'd say. *I don't know why you need to make things so difficult.*

But my mind's eye also puts him as I found him. On the floor, halfway beneath the desk, as if he'd crawled there for shelter. Tools scattered and his blood dried on the wood planks. I can smell the blood in the air as if I'm there again, as if I've stepped backward in time, and I'm living the day again. Still drunk from a long night of finding trouble in the Bay and standing frozen in this room for so long that I lose track of time—

Wishing Deri was here because he'd know what to do, he'd tell me how to fix it—

No, don't get lost in the past.

Nothing is different. I tell myself again and again. Nothing in this room is actually different. It's just that life is different, my parents are gone, and it makes everything *feel* wrong. But nothing is different.

I set the book at *my* spot and rest my father's watch beside it. I'll take a look at it first and decide if I want to try to fix it or not. And then I'll copy out the specification for the train, and I'll start sketching ideas. It will be good to create something instead of breaking things and killing people.

The paperweight watch first. I open it carefully, not sure what I'll find. The movement is cleaner than I expected. There's a lot in there, jewels and moving pieces for the chronograph to work. It's old. It was made somewhere in the Derccian Empire, so I probably can't get the right pieces here. I'll have to order them from somewhere if I want to fix it. But do I want to fix it? I don't know. Maybe I just want to know exactly what's wrong. Why doesn't it tick anymore? *Could* I get it to tick again?

I settle in my spot where my tools are waiting. They're all clean. Mr. Saan must have made sure this desk was dusted regularly. No small task, with all the tiny things in their very particular places. A few things are out of place, and I slide them back to the spots where they belong. The way I organize things reflects how I move and what I need most often. Nothing interrupts my flow as efficiently as reaching for something and it not being there.

As I begin to take the watch apart, I understand the problem—the movement had been badly repaired at some point, and now it won't be made to work without a complete rebuild. Parts have been replaced, but they didn't fit quite right, so they damaged the things around them as they moved until nearly the whole movement was destroyed. I can't fix anything in this watch, short of finding a new movement and installing it into the face so it can have the appearance of being my father's watch while being entirely new inside.

Disappointment passes through me in waves, building in strength. This feeling confirms that I *had* wanted to fix it, making it run again would be like a gift to my father's memory, but my hopes have been ground into ill-fitting pieces just like the inside of this watch. All I have left is the now familiar feeling of being a little bit too lost without him. Of being not quite enough to live up to the man he was.

The floor—the difference hits me so hard it knocks the air out of me. It *is* different, completely different. The scuffs and the stains and the old worn patterns are gone. My father frowned at the floor a few weeks before he died—*it needs to be varnished again. Do you know who does that? Why are you making faces? I thought you knew everything, Uba.*

Has Mr. Saan taken care of it? Has it been sanded down and re-varnished? It shouldn't matter so much, shouldn't make me panic like this, but the whorls and the lines are *different*, and it's all I can think about. There used to be a knot in the grain beside my edge of the desk, which I used to look at when I was frustrated. I would to let my eyes slide across the dark oval and the rings around it, watching them expand out across the plank, and that ritual let me organize my thoughts enough to keep working. It's a different fucking floor. The planks aren't as wide, aren't the same colour.

"Mr. Saan! Mr. Saan!"

He comes quickly, boots tapping on the floor along the shop—has that floor been changed, too? Did he change the whole damned floor while I was gone? Why would he change the fucking floors?

"Yes, Mr. Saeati?" He has his spectacles back on, has something in his hand—one of the big books for tracking inventory.

"Why did you change the floor?"

He blinks, shakes his head. "What…? The floor?"

"Yes!" I stomp my feet, the heels of my boots making a clatter against the wood. I wish I was strong enough to smash the wood with my feet, to rip the planks right off the subfloor and set them all on fire. "Why did you change the floor? There was nothing wrong with it. How much of it did you change? Did you change the floor in the whole shop?"

"Ah—no sir, Mr. Saeati. The new planks stop at the door to the office. I was trying to get the blood out of the wood, you see. We were all so tired of seeing it. I had someone in to try to sand it down, but he couldn't get the blood out without wearing the plank down to nothing. We were going to replace the area with bloodstains, but the patch of different sized planks looked terrible, so I had the floor in the whole room replaced."

I can't breathe. I drag my father's chair out of the way—too hard—it falls over and clatters on the new wood, and even the sound it makes on this new floor has changed, the resonance of the floorboards a different pitch than I remember. And yes—the bloodstains are gone. My father's blood, from the day he was murdered, blood that I knelt in and tried to clean before my mother saw it, blood that was dry and sticky, blood that turned the wood rusty-red in the big patches where it had penetrated the worn varnish. And me, still drunk from my long night in the Bay, fumbling and reeling, trying to grasp what had happened, trying to imagine what Colonel Deri would tell me to fix it. But nothing about that day could possibly be 'fixed.'

"You had no right." The words cut through my chest, ripping a new path, making my whole soul bleed. "You had no right to make that decision—"

"Mr. Saeati," he breathes, his voice so small it makes me feel guilty, the way he sounds afraid. "What do you mean?"

"You had no right to make a change that big without my approval." I'm trying to keep my voice calm, but I don't feel calm at all. My body is crawling with tension, muscles like burning wires beneath my skin. I need to move, I need to swing, I need to crush something in my hands—anything to get rid of this tension that feels too much like panic. There's no breathing exercise in the world that can save me from this feeling. I just need to *move*— what's in my hand? The watch, the stupid, broken, paperweight watch— "I told you to keep the shop running with orders and inventory, not renovate the fucking building. You had no right to make a change like that!"

"I wasn't renovating, Mr. Saeati," he says. There are tears gathering in his eyes, threatening to spill down his cheeks. "I was making a repair. Repairs are part of keeping the shop running, and that was the job you left me with."

"Explain to me how a stain on the floor interfered with the way business runs! Everyone could go about doing their fucking jobs without the stain affecting them at all—all you had to do was wait for me to come back, and I would have dealt with it. You had no right to make that decision while I was gone!"

He takes a breath. He's standing straight and tall in the doorway, like a guard keeping me in the office, separating me from the employees—like I'm a wild animal that needs to be contained—trapping me with my spiralling panic and the hateful new floor and my father's unrepairable watch.

"Ishmael," he says, and there's a tremor in his voice, "I know you're upset about… everything. And I'm not going to say you had an easy time of it, taking your mother back to the Qasan, but you don't know what it was like here. To come to this place every day and see that bloodstain and know that we had lost someone we *all* loved so much—" His voice hitches. His body trembles. "We had to come in here every day for jewels and walk past the bloodstains. It was making it impossible to work. I had to do something. I couldn't leave it there any longer, like a shrine to what happened."

"You can't just erase him like that! You can't just tidy up and pretend it never happened! He lived for this place—you can't just rip up floorboards and make it like he wasn't ever here. His blood belonged here! You don't understand what he did—what he gave —what the three of us went through to make this business what it is. You had no right to make that decision. That was *my* deci-sion to make! All you had to do is wait until I came back—"

I need to move. I need to let the tension out. The watch is too heavy in my hand, the stupid watch that I can't fix, that has no purpose except being broken, being a reminder of all the ways I'm failing at living up to my father's example. I hate it. I hate it for existing, and I hate it for being so thoroughly broken, and I hate my parents for dying and leaving me to carry the weight of how *good* they were when I'm so deeply and irredeemably flawed. I throw the watch with all the strength I have—I have to get it out of my hand before I implode. Mr. Saan flinches and steps back. The delicate, high sound of shattered glass scattering across the floor cuts through the white-hot rage.

Breathe, my training tells me. Colonel Deri's voice, in my ear— *breathe deep when you feel big emotions, and it helps you regain control. Our job is to be always in perfect control.*

But I can't. I can't breathe at all, and more words are searing up my throat, and I can't possibly stop them.

"All you had to do was wait until I came back, and I would have dealt with it. You had no right to make that decision without me. You can't just pretend he never existed. Even if his death was ugly, you can't just wash him away like he was never here—"

Mr. Saan's tears finally escape, making glittering tracks down his cheeks, dripping from his jaw. We're as brittle as glass, smashing against each other and shattering. "I worked beside him every day for fifteen years. He was my greatest friend. I built this place, too. For your parents, because I saw the beauty of their dream, and I wanted it as badly as they did. A business here, in this city, shaped entirely by Qasani hands, bearing a Qasani name. It's more than watches, and you know it. It's more than just the Saeati family. I stayed here after your father died because I couldn't bear the thought of this shop collapsing after all the work we put into it—I promised your mother that I wouldn't let it fall apart after she left. I promised I'd keep the Saeati legacy alive. But those bloodstains made it so I didn't want to come here anymore. I couldn't bear it—gods, there was so much blood—" His voice trembles and he has to pause to gather himself enough to keep speaking. "And if I stopped coming in, this place would have closed, and all these people would have lost their jobs." He takes a deep, shuddering breath, pulling off his spectacles so he can wipe his eyes, and I feel so small. "I know you feel like you've lost your whole world, but you're not the only one who loved them. You're not the only one who feels this pain." He puts his spectacles back on and turns away from me, looking at what I've thrown. His chin quivers and his shoulders sag, and the way he slumps makes me want to sink through the floor and into the cold bedrock beneath us. "Ah, Ishmael."

He shakes his head as he sinks to his knees to pick up my father's watch. The expensive gold case, the chronograph, the delicate gold hands. My father's first love.

All the anger drains out of me, leaving me empty and hollow and so incredibly exhausted that my legs threaten to give out. What have I done?

I go to his side and drop to my knees with him. I take the watch from his hands, and he turns to the debris on the floor. Mr. Saan starts picking up the biggest pieces with slow, careful movements, piling them in the palm of his hand. I hate that I've proven him —and everyone else, for that matter—right for walking softly around me. Right for being afraid of how I'll behave.

"I can fix it," I gasp.

The case is dented, and the glass is gone, and the hands have fallen off, and the beautiful face is splintered with a dozen cracks. Cogs and delicate pieces in the movement are shivering and clanking in ways they shouldn't—I can hear it in the discordant sound it makes, feel it in the awful shift of its weight when I move my hand.

"I can fix it."

But I can't. I can't fix anything.

I couldn't fix it before I threw it, and I certainly can't fix it now.

There's nothing for me to fix because they're just *gone*.

Every little piece of me shatters into dust, and I'm on my knees on the new wood floor. Sobbing. My father's broken watch in my hands and inhuman sounds coming from my throat. My face is hot with tears.

Mr. Saan drops the glass I broke back into the pile and wraps his arms around my shoulders to pull me closer. I try to push him away, but he's stronger than he looks. His hand presses into my back, and he pulls me closer still, until my face is buried in his layers of wool and linen. He presses his cheek against the top of my head, and I know he's sobbing, too. I can feel the way his chest spasms and hitches, feel the hot wet of his tears falling into my hair. But unlike me, his grief is quiet.

"I can't fix it." The words hurt coming out because I'm sobbing and not breathing. The truth of it sears me. I promised my mother I wouldn't sulk long, and I've come home and broken my father's watch by throwing it at my father's dearest friend. "I can't fix any of it because all I do is break things."

"Some things can't be fixed." His voice is soft and thick with emotion but as gentle as he ever is. I don't deserve him. He's so much like my father, so quiet and reserved. "Things get broken and lost and forgotten as we go through the world, things that we love, things we thought we couldn't live without. You don't need to fix everything. It's not your job. And if we're both a little broken because of the people we lost, so what? All we can do is keep going, Ishmael. The best thing we can hope for is not that we're 'fixed,' but that we find people who understand the ways in which we've been broken. People who stand beside us anyway."

We kneel on the new floor, holding the scraps and broken pieces of my father's watch, and cry. It almost feels good to be crying with company, to be crying at home, in this familiar place.

Krystle Matar

Krystle Matar
has been writing for a long
time, but things got serious
when Tashué Blackwood walked
into her life, an amber-eyed whirlwind.
His book, Legacy of the Brightwash, is a **SPFBO** Finalist.
When she isn't arguing with him or any of his friends
(like Ishmael, he argues a lot) she parents and farms.
She has a lot of children and even more animals and one
very excellent husband.

She is currently working on a lot more stories set in
the Dominion. She expects to exist in this universe
for a while.

Find out more about Krystle Matar at
www.krystlematar.com

About Our Team

Zoe Badini

I'm Zoe, a freelance illustrator from Italy. I specialize in painting character-driven illustrations, mainly in fantasy or sci-fi settings.

Find out more about Zoe Badini at www.artstation.com/zoebadini

Sarah Chorn

Sarah has been a compulsive reader her whole life. At a young age, she found her reading niche in the fantastic genre of Speculative Fiction. She blames her active imagination for the hobbies that threaten to consume her life. She is a published author and editor, a semi-pro nature photographer, world traveler, three-time cancer survivor, and mom to two kids. In her ideal world, she'd do nothing but drink lots of tea and read from a never-ending pile of books.

Sarah has been a respected book critic since 2010 (Bookworm Blues). This has served to give her an intimate knowledge of story and has kept her thumb on the pulse of the genre. She has been a developmental editor since 2017, with numerous award-winning titles under her belt. Now, she is also the staff editor of

Grimdark Magazine. Sarah has put her love of words to good use and is the author of *Seraphina's Lament* and *Of Honey and Wildfires*, and numerous other published books.

Find out more about Sarah Chorn at sarahchornedits.com

KERSTIN ESPINOSA ROSERO

Kerstin Espinosa Rosero is the author of SPFBO7 finalist *Burn Red Skies*. Her quest to be a translator has led her to live all over the world, including the US, Germany, Taiwan, and the Philippines. When she is not writing or working, she is traveling, sketching, or kickboxing. It is her goal to turn her sketches into stories.

Find out more about Kerstin Espinosa Rosero at www.ke-rosero.com

DIANA SOUSA

Diana Sousa lives in Portugal, where she splits her time between all things graphic design and illustration, writing, and all sorts of nerdy content. She's the colorist for the *Critical Role: Vox Machina Origins* on-going comic book series, as well as the *Critical Role: The Mighty Nein Origins: Caleb Widogast, Yasha Nydoorin* and *Fjord Stone* graphic novels from Dark Horse Comics. She has previously worked on Dungeons and Dragons campaign books and projects.

Find out more about Diana Sousa at dianasousa.com

Acknowledgements

This anthology has been both a dream and a process—a dream to see so many people come together to support *The Alchemy of Sorrow*, and a process as we've navigated both the joys and grief (and hope) of bringing such a project together. Truly, this anthology has allowed our authors, artists, and editors to transform our sorrow into something bright and beautiful, that brings us hope and has built so much community.

First and foremost, we want to thank our amazing Kickstarter backers, without whom this project would not have come to fruition. When we first began building this anthology, it was because of an awareness that many major outlets (both online and print) did not believe there would be enough interest in such a theme to warrant an anthology. You proved them wrong one pledge at a time, coming together to help us fund in less than two days, and hit every single stretch goal we set. More than that, your heartfelt comments, stories, and presence on the backer Discord has filled us with a deep understanding of just how important this anthology is. So many of us are grieving in so many ways, to find hope in each other's work and presence is such a gift. Thank you. (To see a full list of our backers please visit http

It is perhaps appropriate at this point to mention that these acknowledgements are being written by more than one of us—because we especially want to thank Virginia McClain. You are the visionary behind this project; thank you, V, for channeling your own grief into story, and for reaching out to each of us to offer both an opportunity to explore our own separate griefs and the chance to develop community together. This anthology has created such a haven for us, and we are grateful to you for all the love, late nights, and hope you have put into this project. You are such a hero to each of us.

We would also like to extend a massive thank you to Intisar Khanani for being Virginia's anchor in the storm that has been 2022. Intisar, you have been integral in organizing and running the Kickstarter for the anthology, as well as just generally keeping Virginia from drowning in stress. You have done so much behind-the-scenes work for this anthology and saved Virginia from so many moments of panic. You probably deserve a medal of some kind, but instead you get this inadequate paragraph of appreciation. We hope you realize how wonderful you are, a powerhouse of storytelling, and a fabulous friend as well.

We'd like to thank Sarah Chorn for your amazing editing of each and every story. We know some of these stories hit home for you in unexpectedly hard ways, and we are so grateful to you for putting your all into helping us make our stories shine while facing your own griefs. Your editing powers are exceptional, and our stories would not have reached the level they have without your commitment, expertise, and heart.

We would be remiss not to thank Krystle Matar and M.L. Wang, who both jumped in at a moment's notice to post updates for the anthology Kickstarter, or to check over documents that needed an emergency proofread, or simply to offer encouragement to Virginia and Intisar as they floundered about trying to keep things organized for backers. Krystle, we owe you an infinite supply of coffee, and M.L., we shall endeavor to keep Sulu in birb treats for as long as we can.

Sincere thanks as well to PS Livingstone and T L Greylock for jumping in at the eleventh hour with their mad proofreading skills to put the final polish on these stories. You are both legends.

Deep gratitude to our amazing artists, Zoe Badini, K.E. Rosero, and Diana Sousa. Zoe, the cover you created truly reflects the beauty and transformation of sorrow at the heart of this anthology. We could not have asked for more gorgeous art to accompany our stories into the world. Similarly, we are so grateful to K. E. Rosero for the incredible variety and beauty of the interior illustrations you have created, matching each illustration to the feel of the story it represents. Diana, we are in awe of your work in creating a map of the Land of Grief and Hope that brought elements of our stories to life while simultaneously depicting variations and challenges of journeying through grief to hope. You are all absolute artistic wizards, and it has meant so much to us to have you as part of our team and community.

We would like to extend our thanks to all those who have supported us openly or behind the scenes—to every person who helped share this project, who has offered their kindness in often unexpected and wonderful ways. Please know we appreciate you.

To the readers and reviewers we have yet to meet, thank you for being here, for sharing in our griefs, trusting us with your heart, and opening yourself to the alchemy of sorrow. We are so grateful to be on this journey with you.

www.ingramcontent.com/pod-product-compliance
Lightning Source LLC
Chambersburg PA
CBHW030708190726
48286CB00001B/233